PERSONAL RECOGNIZANCE

Vret McClintock, a young channel in training at the world-famous Rialite First Year Camp, sees a dreary life before him until the instant he overhears the voice of Ilin Sumz saying the words he's been thinking—"I certainly don't intend to stay a QN-3 for the rest of my life."

His ambition awakened by that magical sentence, he sets out to Qualify as a QN-2 before he graduates, and to meet the owner of that sexy voice! In love with her and with her illicit historical fantasies posted on a secret board run on the brand-new campus mainframe computer, Vret risks his future career to extricate Ilin from her web of secrets before they can ruin the careers of others.

The Sime~Gen Series from The Borgo Press

Other Jacqueline Lichtenberg Books from Wildside:

PERSONAL RECOGNIZANCE

SIME~GEN, BOOK NINE

JACQUELINE LICHTENBERG

THE BORGO PRESS
MMXI

PERSONAL RECOGNIZANCE

DEDICATION

MY WORK ON this new volume of Sime~Gen has to be dedicated
to all the people who have supported the Sime~Gen universe and
kept it alive in fanzines, online, and in our discussion groups.

And even beyond that large number of people, there are a few
friends and co-workers who have contributed to my ability to
cope with life on the internet.

Friends, family, and the usual list of suspects found in
previous Sime~Gen volumes are all repeated here, with one
new addition, **Patric Michael**.

So *Personal Recognizance* has to be dedicated to Patric
Michael who has during the writing of this story a) kept my
email mailboxes working, b) kept the Sime~Gen Inc. server
working, c) kept so many of our web pages working, d) managed
many image transformations for me, and taught Eric Berlin to
do many of them for me e) scolded me roundly for messing
up html but taught me better ways of doing things f) moved
heaven and earth to keep trivia out of my field of view until
I finished writing this story, and g) shared my vision of what
www.simegen.com can and should become.

CONTENTS

CHRONOLOGY OF THE SIME~GEN UNIVERSE

The Sime~Gen Universe was originated by Jacqueline Lichtenberg who was then joined by a large number of Star Trek fans. Soon, Jean Lorrah, already a professional writer, began writing fanzine stories for one of the Sime~Gen 'zines. But Jean produced a novel about the moment when the first channel discovered he didn't have to kill to live which Jacqueline sold to Doubleday.

The chronology of stories in this fictional universe expanded to cover thousands of years of human history, and fans have been filling in the gaps between professionally published novels. The full official chronology is posted at

http://www.simegen.com/CHRONO1.html

Here is the chronology of the novels by Jacqueline Lichtenberg and Jean Lorrah by the Unity Calendar date in which they are set.

-533—*First Channel*, by Jean Lorrah & Jacqueline Lichtenberg

-518—*Channel's Destiny*, by Jean Lorrah & Jacqueline Lichtenberg

-468—*The Farris Channel*, by Jacqueline Lichtenberg

-20—*Ambrov Keon*, by Jean Lorrah

-15—*House of Zeor*, by Jacqueline Lichtenberg

AUTHOR'S FOREWORD

This novel was written for those who have read at least one Sime~Gen novel, such as the first published novel in the Sime~Gen Universe, *House of Zeor* by Jacqueline Lichtenberg or Jean Lorrah's introduction to the universe, *First Channel*. The full list is at http://www.simegen.com/writers/simegen/

Most of the Sime~Gen novels and stories contain a slow and detailed introduction to the background and jargon, but those who have read many of the novels get tired of the repetition. This novel is especially for them.

If you are new to Sime~Gen or want a refresher, please read Jean Lorrah's story collection, *The Story Untold and Other Stories*, on the flip-side of this volume first.

Note that *The Story Untold* collection is set in the Year 1 After Unity while *Personal Recognizance* is set in Year 245 After Unity.

Some other novels are set during the turmoil surrounding the re-unification of the human species, Sime and Gen, into one political entity, and some of the novels trace vents during the ensuing centuries.

Please find the official chronology, spanning some 3,000 years of human future-history including some stories by fans published on simegen.com here:

http://www.simegen.com/CHRONO1.html

SIME~GEN:
where a mutation makes the evolutionary
division into male and female
pale by comparison.

CHAPTER ONE
OVERHEARD REMARK

Striding along the cactus-studded pathway across campus, Vret McClintock overheard the woman say to her Companion, "Well, I certainly don't intend to stay a QN-3 for the rest of my life. I...."

And the voice went out of range of his hearing.

He had just said those exact words to his vriamic functionals trainer. But this woman's tone of voice was low, unstressed, without defiance or pride. From her it was a simple matter of declaring her plans for her future. She was not going to stay a Third Order channel.

And the voice draped Vret's whole body in soothing velvet.

No, it's her nager that did that—her nager while she stated her intentions. And that was it, he realized, standing dumbfounded in the pounding heat of the desert sun zlinning the retreating pair. Oddly, his memory of the impact of that nager was purely tactile. He hadn't known a nager could register as tactile.

She has intentions and no reason to expect opposition. I have ambitions. I expect to be thwarted.

He stood there for another three minutes scheming ways to meet that woman.

But it was a week later before he even learned her name was Ilin Sumz, and a month until he met her in person.

CHAPTER TWO
AWKWARD QUESTIONS

"Vret, *what* are you daydreaming about?" demanded Kwotiin Lake, Vret's trainer.

"As if you didn't know," Vret flicked a nageric shrug in the direction of Kwotiin while stifling his alarm.

His vriamic functionals trainer was a First Order channel who could zlin right through any showfield Vret's Third Order system could produce. Sometimes it seemed Kwotiin could actually read his mind. Vret suppressed his nervous squirming at being questioned under the searchlight of a First's attention.

Kwotiin had been grinding away on him ferociously for the last two weeks, but Vret was learning to take it and dish it back with frills. Kwotiin relented. "My guess is you've been up all night reading those trashy historical stories on the student boards on that new computer network thing?"

"It's not trash!" snapped Vret, caught out. "It's a tried and true, solid historical study method. Some instructors encourage it."

Kwotiin was referring to the daily installments on the amateur writers' boards, historical fiction written to challenge younger students to find the mistakes in historical fact. The truth was Vret had not been reading *that* board.

"So you have been reading those stories. They're no substitute for real study, Vret."

"Actually, no, I haven't been reading that board." Again Vret concentrated on his vriamic node, blending his fields into a fog.

Of course he had no chance against the First Order channel in charge of his training, but Kwotiin would always give him points for improving his technique.

The vriamic nerve plexus connected the channel's primary and secondary selyn systems and allowed the channel to project a showfield and use it to control selyn-flow speeds. Training and exercise of the vriamic was also the key to a channel gaining control of his own Kill reflex. Kwotiin was famous on campus for the severity of his training, so Vret was proud to be admitted to his class, but he sweated.

This time, Vret's vriamic work did win a genuine smile from the Trainer. "That's very good, Vret."

Then Kwotiin broke off and paced around the tan-and-white training cubicle as if testing the selyn field insulation. "So tell me, what *is* going on with you? Over the last month or so, your attitude has changed—reversed actually."

"It has?" That was news to him, and he wasn't sure if it was good news. He waited.

"You've lost the antagonism, you're more focused on the work, and you're beginning to make serious progress in your basic skills. I wouldn't have expected it of you a month ago, but now I think you really can make QN-2 before you leave Rialite—if that's what you want."

The Rialite First Year Camp provided the best channel's training in the world. It was the only Camp always overseen by a Zeor channel, usually a Farris. Not everyone who arrived graduated from here. Vret had already been threatened with being sent elsewhere to finish his training, a fate he strove to avoid. Graduation from Rialite was a ticket to the top slots in the Tecton hierarchy.

He had been raised on stories of his twin uncles, one of whom had graduated from Rialite and risen to Assistant World Controller, and the other who had been expelled from Rialite for helping a fellow student take an illicit transfer and ended up stoking selyn batteries at a factory deep in-Territory.

Something had indeed changed for Vret, and it wasn't his

skills or his determination to Qualify Second as well as earn a Rialite Certificate. But what should he tell Kwotiin?

Vret zlinned his trainer, straining to focus through the First's showfield. He was rewarded with a relaxing of that shrouding veil of misdirection that could make a Third dizzy. Abruptly, he zlinned sincere hope within, so he confessed, "I do want to Qualify Second. But ultimately whether I get the chance is up to Sectuib Farris, no?"

"Well, ultimately—yes. If I send you to him, he will decide. Today's question is—should I send you to him? What *have* you been doing in your spare time?"

"What spare time? That history course is destroying my average and you know it." *Not that there's much of an average to destroy.*

His guilt was showing, Vret was certain. A Farris channel would zlin every nuance and probably figure it out as if he were a telepath. Some Farrises were telepaths like the Zeor heir who had nearly destroyed Rialite about a hundred years ago, and some Firsts were known to have various talents, but they were very rare and Vret couldn't see them working as teachers in a First Year Camp.

Kwotiin held the intense focus and open showfield while Vret strove for innocence, then sighed and turned away, fiddling with the test objects on the workbench, his showfield once again swirling into a perfectly controlled cloud around his true nager.

He turned, holding a rose colored stone sphere about a tentacle length in diameter then circled the transfer lounge that graced the middle of the room. "Zlin carefully," he commanded as he manipulated the sphere in his tentacles, and wrapped his field around it so Vret couldn't zlin it even though he could see it, an exercise Vret had failed a few times already.

Vret zlinned for all he was worth but couldn't discern the sphere.

"Vret, you're not really interested in spending your life working as a channel, are you?"

Vret's showfield shattered, his vriamic grip lost in shock.

Some kind of decision had been made about his future, and he couldn't zlin a hint of what it was. "I'm not very good at Healing. But I'll be better after I Qualify Second."

"Seconds spend a lot of their time managing teams of Thirds. Is that why you want to Qualify? To spend less time tentacles-on patients?"

"Seconds may spend less time dealing with patients or doing transfers directly, but they accomplish more."

"There's quantity—and there's quality...."

Kwotiin wasn't going to quit. Vret asked, "What do you want me to say, Hajene?"

"Why do you want to Qualify Second? Just the simple, literal truth will do. If you stay a Third, you'll have more spare time to devote to interests other than Healing or channeling. Over the next couple of decades the Tecton will allow more Thirds to work outside the Tecton, pursuing their own interests in other professions while channeling only part time. In that world, why would you want to be a Second when obviously other pursuits interest you so?"

Again Kwotiin's nageric focus narrowed to a penetrating beam that pierced every shell Vret held about his primary nager. Skewered, Vret confessed, "I'd guess it's because I'm afraid to stay a Third."

Why did I say that out loud? This was a revelation that had come to him only last night while reading the latest install-ment of the story Ilin Sumz was posting on the extremely illicit, totally hidden, completely secret, (everyone hoped) Bulletin Board hidden underneath the officially sanctioned and encour-aged one.

The story—immense sprawling novel—titled *Aunser Ambrov D'zehn,* made the reader part of the events surrounding Unity over 245 years ago when Third Order Channels had only just been discovered.

History recorded that Aunser had founded the Secret Pens, but that was disputed, as was every documented fact from that chaotic time.

It had cost Vret two months stipend, not to mention several dangerous favors, to discover the name of the author of his favorite novel was Ilin Sumz. And just that morning, he'd contrived an encounter in the cafeteria, nager to nager and discovered, with a stunning lack of astonishment, she was the woman he'd zlinned on the path. He couldn't stop thinking about her and couldn't stop reading her novel where the Thirds were seen, from Aunser's point of view, as nearly helpless.

"Vret," sighed Kwotiin "had it not been for the Thirds, Unity and the First Contract would never have happened. It is a very proud thing to be a Third."

Vret tried not to squirm. "There's no shame in it, but it's like being half blind, partly deaf, with patches of numb skin, and a paralyzed hand. It's just too frustrating and—all right, yes, frightening to be so—so—so handicapped. Do I really have to—to—to resign myself to this for the rest of my life?"

Kwotiin reached out and put his hand on the back of Vret's neck, laterals flicking into a quick contact, there and gone again.

If Vret had thought the First had zlinned him before, he had been wrong. He now knew he'd never been zlinned in all his life before. For less than one second, he knew what it felt like to be zlinned through and through, and all the way out again. He couldn't breathe even after the sensation was gone.

"You may not believe this, Vret, but I do think I understand. All right then, if that's what you really want, I'll see you get another chance."

Another chance? Does that mean I've already failed once? "I'll do whatever it takes." *You don't get three chances, not at Rialite anyway.*

"I'm hoping you will. It isn't going to be easy—and it won't get you out of History unless you pass that Unity Test once and for all. What is it about history that you hate so much you can't pass a simple test?"

Again the searchlight of the First's attention ripped through the flimsy shell of Vret's showfield leaving him feeling skewered and exposed. He struggled to repair the integrity of his fields while he said, "Dates—and names. I always get names mixed up."

"Well...that pretty much covers it all, doesn't it?"

Actually...no. He'd learned how much more there was to history by reading that infernal novel with the claws that dug his guts out and seeped into his Need nightmares. "I guess so." He clamped his vriamic as tightly as he could around the vast guilty secret. He tried to let the real misery at being so stupid pervade his fields.

Kwotiin laughed hugely, head back, mouth wide open to the ceiling, voice shouting in unrestrained release of tension. The ambient shivered with the purity of that moment.

Something important had just happened, but Vret was mystified as to what.

Kwotiin set the rosy sphere down in its rack on the bench and turned. "Look, Vret, you will get your Channeling License—maybe with an Out-Territory certification—even if you don't pass the history test. But overall your general career will be hampered not by your lack of passing the test, but by your lack of knowledge of the essential facts in that course. The course, boring as it is, is part of your training for a reason."

"I know. I have been trying." *And if I get caught reading that shenning novel, there goes my out-Territory license.* To get a license to go out among untrained Gens, the student had to demonstrate a serious respect for rules in general, and safety rules in particular. The Secret Boards were technically a violation of the rules, though a minor one.

"I realize that you have been trying—we all realize it. So I've found a tutor for you, a Third who is only a month ahead of you but has a thorough knowledge and understanding of history—made something of a hobby of it as a child— and is a very neat match for you, nagerically. You should communicate very well. Are you willing?"

Tutor? Someone to waste all his secret reading time on? "Sure, if you think it will do any good."

"Get History out of the way, concentrate on developing a

stronger vriamic control, work on your capacity—and I'll test you again next month."

"Test?" He could never tell if Kwotiin was drilling him or testing him.

"Today's test didn't go too well, Vret. You're not ready to try for Second yet. And besides, if you're going to pass History, you'll have no time for the Seconds' Physiology course. Seconds can zlin deeper, so they have a lot more technical material to learn about the tiny but significant differences among the sub-mutations."

The ambient in the small cubicle was suddenly clear and fresh as a spring breeze. Only then did Vret's systems suddenly relax, and he knew how much pressure he'd been under. His vriamic node ached with fatigue.

"Your new tutor will meet you in the Janroz Library, study room six, at ten tonight. Be there and bring your Cassleman and Logan." Kwotiin gathered his jacket and briefcase and was out the door before Vret could say anything.

I failed a test today. It would be nice to know if you were having a conversation or being tested with your whole life hanging in the balance.

He collapsed onto the transfer lounge, shaking as if he'd just spent fifteen minutes holding a functional.

CHAPTER THREE
THE TUTOR

By ten that night, Vret had barely stopped shaking with fatigue. The long Third Order recovery period was another reason he so desperately wanted to Qualify. He hated being too tired to think straight—and as a Third, he'd be in that condition almost all the time. As soon as he recovered, from a functional, there'd be another.

It had taken his assigned Donor more than half an hour to get him to stop sweating from what he diagnosed as a mild case of vriamic shock. "Kwotiin is harsh on his trainees, but if he thinks you can make Second, you can; no doubt about that."

Vret heaved his Cassleman and Logan and other books onto the desk in the study room. His name had been on the reservation sheet outside the door, though he, himself, had never reserved the room.

He had Collection Lab at four the next morning because he was past turnover but not yet in serious Need and they wanted him to work directly with a Gen. He hoped he'd be able to finish here and get some sleep before then. Taking donations always wore him out fast.

But...*A tutor!* Only the most uneducated kids from the back of nowhere ever got assigned a tutor. But he had said he'd do whatever it took, and he had to show Kwotiin that he meant that.

And then heaven rained peace upon his ravaged vriamic.

He whirled to find the door filled with the most incredible nager a Third Order channel could ever display. He struggled to duoconsciousness, and gaped like a first-week student zlinning a Farris for the first time. "Ilin Sumz!" The woman who had changed his life by uttering a few simple words he himself had said. *And she's going to tutor me in history!*

"You must be...why are you so surprised?" The throbbing wonder abated as she controlled her showfield. "Kwotiin said he told you I'd be glad to tutor you in history if you'll help me out with my lousy vriamic control. It's been getting worse, lately, not better."

"Um." Words vanished from his mind as if he'd never learned to speak Simelan. Then they flooded back in a rush. "He didn't mention that, but I would be most pleased to provide whatever help I can."

She smiled, and it filled the cubicle with bubbles of anticipation of delight tingling his skin everywhere. When she zlinned him, he felt her smile all the way to his bone marrow and suddenly he knew she was as interested in him as he was in her.

"Sorry." Her nageric effect toned down a bit. She went on talking in a serious, businesslike tone as she set her books down and positioned a chair, but he didn't track what she said.

I do not know that she's Bilateral, author of Aunser ambrov D'zehn, he reminded himself sternly. Participants on the secret board used nicknames for anonymity. If caught, no one person could betray everyone else, but just the person who got them onto the boards and those they, themselves, had introduced to them.

Fortunately, he didn't have to come up with any more witty comments. They fell right to work, seated side by side, his fields interpenetrating hers. She felt as tired as he did, he noted. But after that he began to track what she was saying about the socio-dynamic causes of Unity and why attempts to create something similar had failed all around the world so many times before Klyd Farris and Risa Tigue made it happen.

For the first time since he'd arrived at Rialite, history started to make sense. The words in the book actually registered, and he could remember the meaning even a half hour later. Events hadn't just happened, people didn't pop out of nowhere, they had childhoods and failed marriages and wayward children, and then made world shattering decisions based on what they'd learned from their lives.

Everything these historic figures had done had a cause somewhere back in time, and left an effect propagating through to the present, two and a half centuries later. history wasn't unlike forensic science, his favorite subject.

Sitting with Ilin Sumz, he learned how many clues could be found in how the languages changed with public attitudes. History records might say anything, but linguistic clues told the truth.

That study hour turned into an amazing night—one of many in quick succession. The mysteries of history lay bare and revealed before his inner eye.

But the highpoint of the evening came as they were parting. As he turned to walk away, he felt her attention on his back, sweeping lower, to hips, thighs, calves, and back to his shoulders. And the whole ambient glowed with pure approval. *Oh, we will be good together!*

CHAPTER FOUR
WHY THE TECTON?

Over the next two weeks, he passed three of the diabolical history quizzes Annana Menfild crafted for the Thirds. Ilin had scored a perfect thirty on each when she had taken them. But he was well satisfied with his achievement.

He'd always thought of himself as trailing the class in vriamic skills too, and had no idea how to teach such skills. But after two weeks of spending hours a day huddled over history books with him, Ilin skipped two levels in one day's testing, and caught up with her class in vriamic control. And he hadn't done anything except study with her.

Afterwards, she told him, "I just wanted to show you my best, and I guess the exercise made me stronger."

But she had an unexpected affect on him as well. While coming to see the sweep of history creating the Modern Tecton, to see the disasters miraculously averted, the terrible chances taken by ordinary men and women, the huge lies told to save lives and give merciful deaths, Vret came to understand the Tecton in a new light.

It became *his* Tecton, an enterprise he could give his life to— even die for—not merely the only career opportunity available to those born as channels.

The sudden fierce loyalty seized him during the monthly graduation ceremony. Each month, when the train brought the entering class across the desert and took away that month's graduating class, the ranking Faculty gave speeches to the departing class assembled on the platform.

The other students didn't usually stop to watch, but this time Vret wanted to see off the friend who had introduced him to the Secret Boards, so he paused on his way to his class on Gen Law. The graduates stood tall in their new Tecton uniforms, the ambient about them vibrating with a clean joy. His friend, still a Third, caught sight of him and smiled, straightening to show off his insignia.

The Farris who headed up Rialite was speaking and all attention was on him. Vret didn't hear the words from so far away, but the nageric message was so clear, so filled with confidence, that Vret felt the stalwart tradition of Rialite being passed down into these young hands.

Ilin Sumz had given him the understanding of history, the origin of that tradition, the harsh, ugly necessities that had given it birth. All at once, he felt as if he were listening to Klyd Farris giving hope to the world, and he wanted with all his heart and soul to become a part of that.

He walked away as the train chugged out of the station knowing he would give the Tecton all he had in him.

****

One fine day in late spring, they both had transfer on the same day—Vret's seventh and Ilin's eighth. To his vast disappointment, they were separated during the next three days of their post syndrome.

Unfortunately, Ilin's nageric control progress meant that she didn't absentmindedly flood the ambient with that wondrously unstressed, positive, serene ambition that had first unlocked the grip of fear from around his heart. She didn't effervesce by accident anymore either, nor broadcast sudden intil spikes or sizzle with sexual interest. And when she sank into a nageric fugue, studying a field pattern, she didn't drag everyone around her into it. At least, not unless she intended to.

When Vret asked Kwotiin about getting a post assignment

with Sumz, the trainer just laughed. "You'll be free to choose for yourself soon enough!"

But he couldn't stop thinking about her, and worse yet couldn't stop reading her novel, night by night, installment by installment. He even read all the commentaries other people were posting about it.

Sumz had taken the well known historic figure of Aunser ambrov D'zehn and magnified him into a fantasy hero by giving him the legendary ability to read minds.

Out-Territory Gens had created the legend that all Simes could read minds. Vret had found even his own abilities could seem like mind-reading to a Gen. His first couple of months here, he'd enjoyed startling the Gens who trained him by reciting their thoughts back at them.

In more recent times though, in-Territory legends had grown up around the First Order Channels, particularly the Farrises. Some of them were reputed to have used arcane abilities to make their marks in history, powers like telepathy, precognition, clairvoyance. One scoffed-at superstition said Farrises could raise the dead.

But here in Rialite where the Farrises were revered by innocent youths, exaggerated legends were used by the older students to haze the younger who had yet to study the facts of the matter.

Vret had found a kernel of truth within all of these legends, even about Farrises raising the dead by restarting a heart. But the First Order channels, The Endowed, who could do these amazing things were rare, their abilities erratic and in most cases impossible to demonstrate under controlled conditions. But Vret was certain they were very real.

Bilateral had taken that spooky Rialite legend, mixed it with fact and grafted it onto the historic figure to create a compelling fantasy character—a telepathic channel assigned to treat dying semi-juncts whose lives could be extended by a Kill.

Bilateral's Aunser dared not ask for a different assignment for fear of revealing his terrible secret—that the out-Territory Gens were right, he did read minds. He dared not stay where he was, living in the miasma of aborts, attrition and death. So he argued, begged, favor-traded, and played inter-Householding family politics to establish secret pens where those who could benefit would get two Kills a year.

His primary argument was that civilization couldn't afford to lose a whole generation of Simes at once. The semi-junct adults had to live long enough for their non-junct children to take over running the world.

Vret couldn't stop reading the discussion board arguments among the readers—and writers of other stories on the boards—about what would have happened if there had never been any Secret Pens. Some even suggested that in reality there hadn't been any Secret Pens—that there might have been one or two such pens, but nothing systematic and legally sanctioned and that Gulf Territory's system of assigning carefully matched Gens to give transfer to renSimes accounted for the survival of that final generation of juncts.

Having read Bilateral's version, Vret was sure history as it was recorded was...incomplete if not actually just plain wrong. What intrigued Vret most about Ilin Sumz was how she could be Bilateral, the author of the hottest, frankest narrative of the founding of the Secret Pens, having such field-splatter accidents all over campus, and never once betray that secret to the faculty—so many of whom were Firsts.

CHAPTER FIVE
THE SECRET KILLROOM

One evening, a new story started to appear on the Board titled *The Secret Killroom*. It took Bilateral's character, Aunser ambrov D'zehn, the secret telepath, Householding Statesman and martyr to Unity, and morphed him into a sadist and Householding blackmailer.

One plausible step after another, explaining junct psychology with textbook accuracy, the alternate-history novel seduced readers into the mind and heart of unrepentant juncts, while an imposter had taken the place of Aunser in charge of the Disjunction Center at Poliston.

In this twisted version of Aunser's story, Aunser politicked, threatened and blackmailed to get his already operating Secret Pen legalized. And he used an exaggerated telepathic ability to rewrite people's memories, and warp his victim's values until people did his bidding.

The writing was powerful, compelling, absorbing, every bit as good as Bilateral's but signed by a newcomer to the Board called, obscenely, Blissdrip.

CHAPTER SIX
HELPING THE TUTOR

Two days after he passed the final History of Unity test, Vret learned more than he ever wanted to know about Ilin Sumz's spare time activities.

Sumz came up to him on the path that curved around one of the dry washes protecting the campus from flash floods. "Vret, I have to talk to you—privately."

Vret gestured to a polished stone bench in the wash, shaded by tall and short cacti, some spiky stick things clinging to a fence, and a few scraggly trees. Little ceramic plaques adorned each plant with its species name.

At intervals, glass cases displayed genetic information on each species. "We can study some botany," he suggested, his mind more on biology. Just because they weren't post didn't mean they couldn't have good sex. Tonight maybe?

They seated themselves and pulled out some books. Even Ilin's new tight vriamic control couldn't hide her apprehension. "I've got to ask you something, and it's not something anyone should be asking. I mean it's personal."

"The answer is yes!" he blurted every nerve in his body on high alert.

"The answer to what?"

Oh, no! "Uh, well, if you want help with anything, I certainly will be glad to!" His interest had to be plain in his nager, even to a Third.

"No, not that!" Her nager shouted otherwise. "I mean, well,

not today. I mean..."

Clearly, she had been quite willing to think what Vret had been thinking. He infused his showfield with a warm smile. "Another time. What can I do for you today?"

Two deep breaths and her showfield settled into business. "Look, I really shouldn't—wouldn't at all if—well, I believe I can trust you, and we have to recruit someone, so we've chosen you. So can we get very—personal—and confidential?"

"Recruit?" His bewilderment permeated his nager.

She was zlinning him hard. Gulping, he relaxed his showfield and gave her an honest answer with his nager. He was definitely going to volunteer for anything that would mean he could spend time with her. "Confidential. Yes."

She nodded and gathered her courage. "Tremind took your bribe and told you my nickname on the boards because I told her to. And I know you're Asymmetric."

He started talking just to cover his shock. "I thought nobody was supposed to know anybody. Tremind told me she'd found out only because your roommate told her."

"Halarcy didn't tell her, I did. One day I passed you on the pathway, and your nager—well, it was just riveting. I've been zlinned by Farrises without feeling like that. So I asked around and found out your name—and that you were asking about me and reading my novel. I told Tremind to see that you found out my nickname."

"But I haven't told anyone *my* nickname." The password to sign onto the secret boards for the first time changed daily. Only someone already signed on could find out that password and invite another person to use it to sign themselves onto the secret board. Not even the mainframe administrators who were in on the secret were supposed to be able to read a person's nickname.

"Shen, Ilin!" With the hope of making Second had come the glimmering of a new ambition beyond that. "If they find out about me reading the secret boards, there goes all hope of ever becoming a Troubleshooter. You have to have an impeccable record to get into the training program and stealing mainframe space and bandwidth is bad enough without adding the Kill descriptions and other infractions of board rules in all these stories—and now there's this Blissdrip stuff that's glorifying the junct lifestyle. I can't even count the number of rules it all breaks!"

She zlinned him with astonishment, but shrugged it away and added, "If they find out about me starting this board, what do you suppose will happen to me? All you've been doing is reading! What about the rest of us? We're all in this together, even if we don't know each other."

She started the secret board? He had been writing an install-ment in her novel as four or five other writers had been posting, countering the twisted but seductive sympathy for the junct attitude Blissdrip was posting, but he wasn't about to admit that—certainly not now that she knew his nickname. *I'm not a writer. I'm just rationalizing this fascination with Blissdrip's pornographic descriptions of Killust by saying it's research to defend Ilin's novel."*

Promising himself to stop sucking Blissdrip's drippings, Vret asked, "If you found out my nickname, anyone could!"

"No, not unless they have access to our mainframe. I just correlated when you were in your room with which nicknames were signed on. There aren't that many of us, you know. Every time Asymmetric was signed on, your room was logged into the network and you were in your room, but your roommate was not."

"How could you know that?"

"Tremind lives in your dorm, doesn't she? She watched you, our mainframe people watched the logins, and eventually caught five times with a definitive correlation. The faculty could do that, too, if they knew which mainframe log to watch, who to suspect, and cared to bother.

"Vret, you have to help us find out who Blissdrip really is and stop these postings before some faculty member cares that much! *The Secret Killroom* is not only being read, it's being re-read even more often than my *D'zehn*. Since *Killroom* started, the sign-on rate for new nicknames has tripled."

Zlinning hard, Vret exclaimed, "You're jealous!"

"No, scared. Think! If we generate too much demand on the mainframe, someone on the staff will notice. If all they find in our hidden files is the kind of stuff I've been writing, there's a good chance we can convince them to keep our secret—or at least let us simply close down the board. Maybe it wouldn't go onto our records—if we work it right. But if they find *Secret Killroom* there's no hope of that. I think it crosses the line into killporn."

"You've been reading *Killroom*!"

"Shuven, I can't stop! The thing gets a grip on you. When I realized it was making me raise intil, dreaming about what the Kill had to have been like—Vret, I tried to stop reading it and I couldn't! That thing is dangerous! We've got to put a stop to it."

I'm not the only one! "I don't think it's legally classifiable as killporn, though."

"You've read killporn?!"

"No! I just read a definition somewhere, and I think it has to be about real people to be illegal killporn."

"Aunser really existed, you know. But I think that definition had to do with films, not written stories."

"Maybe, but one thing is crystal clear. While Aunser may be marginal, *Killroom* is way outside the campus rules for server usage. If we're caught, it'll go on our records. So why not just delete it from the boards—and delete Blissdrip's access?"

"We could do that. It would clean that crap off of our board. But it wouldn't solve the problem. All Blissdrip would need is one tech as good as ours, and he could start his own board. If the read-rate spiked, it would start a hunt that would uncover our board."

Reluctantly, Vret suggested, "Well, then close down our board and let's all just get out of this. If others want to get themselves caught doing something like this, let them."

"That wouldn't solve the problem."

"So what is the problem?

"Have you read *Killroom*?"

He wanted to say no. Oh, he wanted it very badly. "Yes."

"And...?" she prompted.

"And?"

"Does it affect you?"

"Well..."

"Ah. I see you understand the problem."

"I do?"

"It's powerfully seductive. The younger students shouldn't be exposed to anything like that. I'm not sure I'm old enough."

Suddenly the problem snapped into a new perspective. "You started this secret history board. You started the Aunser chronicle, the frank discussion of the realities behind history. If you just cut it off and walk away, that leaves Blissdrip free to victimize people who really can't handle what he's dishing up."

"If I can't handle it, and you can't handle it—and nobody I know who is reading it can handle it—who can? We have to stop Blissdrip—we have to find out who it is and make them understand what they're doing."

"We?" Vret was pretty sure the understanding was already there and the "stopping" wouldn't be merely a matter of conveying information. He wanted to run away and pretend he'd never been involved.

"I'm recruiting you into the board management team. So you're part of 'we' now. If you agree."

No, I don't agree. "What if I say no?"

Her nager whipped out of her control, turning heads of the passers-by on the path behind them. She drew a breath and reined in her showfield.

In that moment, Vret had zlinned deeper into her than he had ever intended though, and knew he couldn't refuse to help her.

"You don't have to help us. But we watched you sleuthing around, finding me. All right, I helped you a little, but you would have figured it all out. You think of things nobody else would." Her nager seemed to smile shyly while her face was all business. "We must find Blissdrip before the mainframe staff notices us. We don't want to delete his stuff and telegraph a warning—we'd never find him then. We don't know how to do this without you."

"Why can't you find him the way you found me?"

"There are a few thousand students here, nevermind faculty and second-year students. Only about seventy five are on our secret boards now but we don't know who they are among the thousands. I knew you were on the board—it was easy to figure out your nickname. Can't work that trick in reverse."

"That's comforting. If you can't, the faculty couldn't."

"Some of the Farrises on staff may be telepaths."

He laughed, only realizing how much tension that had knotted his spine when it suddenly broke. "Yeah, right, assigned to teach in a First Year Camp to sniff out wrongdoing by the hapless students."

She shrugged. "Most channels return to teach in a Camp for a few months. Why wouldn't the Endowed be included? But it's worse than that. We think maybe Blissdrip isn't on the Rialite campus. We think maybe he's logging on from somewhere else."

"How could he possibly have gotten the logon key?"

"We have no idea. One theory is that he hacked in without a logon key."

"Ilin, I know nothing about mainframes or hacking. And if this guy could be off the Rialite campus, there's no way I could find him."

"So that means you'll join us?"

Mind racing, Vret saw two futures. One where he walked away from this, cancelled off the boards, pretended he'd never heard of them. He'd become a Troubleshooter, have an exalted career, retire with the knowledge that he'd made the Tecton work for yet another generation. And die with the guilt locked in his heart that he'd let this poison spread just for his own professional advancement.

Or, he could throw in with Sumz and her friends, risk everything, probably fail to chase down Blissdrip—or at least fail to stop him or her. He would lose his Troubleshooting career, maybe more, and end his days knowing he'd done no good for the Tecton at all. But at least he wouldn't have the guilt lacing his Need nightmares.

When he'd been a child, he would have chosen to live with the guilt—because he had no concept of what Need nightmares could do.

"What do I have to do to sign on?"

"You just did it."

* * * * * * *

Finding Blissdrip and putting a stop to the *Secret Killroom* postings was all Vret could think about for the next two days. The first thing he did was to hit the library for a stack of books on how the big computers that ran the campus actually worked.

Wading into a technical area he had no background for, he missed reading four *Killroom* postings and three *Aunser* postings. But it soon became clear he wasn't cut out to run computers. This was not news to him, but it left him at a disadvantage in solving the current problem.

Though he kept slogging through the technical manuals, and even joined one of the study groups of the technically minded, he gravitated back into reading *Aunser*.

CHAPTER SEVEN
READING ADDICTION

Then he couldn't resist the lure of the *Killroom* stories. Each one took some historical fact Bilateral chronicled and twisted it around into lavishly orchestrated descriptions of the visceral joys of The Kill—and what to do to attain the satisfaction no channel could deliver. There were even detailed descriptions of ways of torturing Gens to evince the most fear.

Six days after Vret agreed to try to find and stop Blissdrip, both of the ongoing stories had regained an obsessive grip on him. And this time it was even worse. His new found reverent loyalty to The Tecton was severely threatened by *The Secret Killroom*. As deeply disturbing as the depictions of the torture leading up to The Kill were, he just couldn't stop reading them. He even caught himself re-reading them, telling himself he was studying his quarry.

But as the fascination got a deeper grip on him, he wasn't so sure at all. He knew he would never want to torture a Gen, never want to crave Gen fear and pain to complete the satisfaction that vanquished Need. He knew he would never act on the emotions stirring in him while reading these stories.

And then Vret found himself staring at a Donor in the cafeteria speculating on what his nager would be like if he were terrified—what it would be like to have that terrified attention riveted to himself. His intil spiked even though he was three days before turnover. Instantly three channels cocooned him in a cushioning nageric haze and his intil subsided. But he'd never forget the harsh lesson that split-instant of vicarious experience drove home.

Yes, he would never set out to Kill. The very idea was revolting to him. But even though he was a channel with complete anti-kill conditioning that would stop him if he went for a Kill, even though he had a channel's draw-speed control, even though he had experienced the best transfers and knew that transfer was better than any Kill could ever be—even with all that, he was still a Sime.

In that split-instant of intil flashing through his nerves, he knew that conscience, will, desire, and conditioning had nothing to do with it. There was a point beyond which he would attack in Killmode and even anticipate satisfaction from it. Wallowing in *The Secret Killroom* was making it easier for him to be driven past that point.

Someone had to stop Blissdrip before these stories produced dangerous consequences.

Once more he swore off reading the board and focused on the hunt for Blissdrip. As time passed, he found it easier to control intil around Gens.

Every day at nearly noon, he passed Sumz on the cactus lined path as she was going one way and he the other. One fine, hot spring day, only three days before they would both reach turnover, she was late. He paused, zlinning the students racing this way and that in the blazing desert sun, and finally found her coming from the cafeteria at a run.

Vret stopped her and said, "Ilin, I still don't have a single idea how to identify and locate that writer."

"The operators running our boards are pretty much out of ideas too. I want you to talk to them in person. Maybe the bunch of us can come up with a new idea. If we don't, we may just have to take this to the administration because we can't let it go on. And if I'm going to introduce you to our people at the computer center, it has to be before turnover because I'm not yet licensed for free Gen contact after turnover."

"Neither am I." He said zlinning her more closely. There was a haggard edge to her nager that hadn't been there even five days ago. He mentioned it, and she countered, "I was up late reading. This seems to me, now, to be more than we can handle. Meet me here tomorrow night, at midnight."

He could think of other reasons to be meeting her at midnight, but he just flicked a tentacle and flashed his showfield in an affirmative and dashed on to his next appointment.

About five strides away, he felt her zlinning him and it was a nearly tangible, speculative caress.

As she raced off in the other direction, he kept his eyes on the pathway before him, but zlinned her back with a silent promise.

He wanted to turn around and walk with her, but spending all his spare time either reading the boards or studying computers, he was always late.

And he was late now, too. To his immense frustration, because he'd been late the previous day as well, he was assigned a make-up Dispensary Lab session that would last until just minutes before he was to meet Ilin for the tour.

Ilin arrived right on time. It was two days before they would both hit turnover again, and she was all business and grim haste while he was still reeling with functional recovery fatigue. As if oblivious to his exhaustion, she gathered him up from the bench among the cacti and led him to the building which housed the computers that tied the campus together.

Even after a week's intense study of the matter, Vret found himself utterly bewildered by the shining and flashing walls of machinery that leaked whirling selyn fields that just increased the feeling of bewilderment. Since changeover, he'd never met a subject, except history, that he couldn't crack in a week—until now.

In the largest of three huge rooms full of machinery, people worked before a screen and examined printouts. Vret almost recognized what the people were doing but he had no clue why, nor what one thing had to do with another.

The young Gen who conducted him and Ilin on the tour was one of three people who kept their board a secret. Eventually, the Gen ushered them into a private back room, stuffed with desks and monitors, and introduced Vret to the others. There ensued a quick tutorial on how the board was kept secret, and how easy it would be for the campus administration to discover it, if they ever thought to search.

As the two Simes and the Gen explained it to him, Vret thought he understood. He was sure it made sense. He followed every word of their explanation of what they had done to identify Blissdrip, and how and why each effort had failed. "So you see," the Gen concluded, "we have only two or maybe three more things to try. I'm not hopeful, but we really must try everything."

By the time he got back to his room though, the only impression left from the whole experience was the dizzying whirl of the selyn fields generated by the selyn powered equipment.

CHAPTER EIGHT
TURNOVER

Two days later, he just barely made it to his assigned turnover lounge a few minutes before his Donor arrived.

The turnover lounge complex was on the top floor of the sprawling Transfer Mechanics building. The huge but well insulated corner window gave a panoramic view of the Field Control Labs where he had vriamic training with Kwotiin Lake on one side, and the Science Complex on the other, where tomorrow he'd be starting Mutation Physiology.

The selyn insulation gave the Lounge a preternatural hush, probably because they sometimes used the facility as a deferment suite and transfer lounge. Even the dark blue pile carpeting had selyn field insulation woven into it. The furniture was upholstered in sky blue, with a matching pattern in the draperies. The book cases, medicine cabinets, wet benches and the large desk were rich, dark wood.

As always when he entered a field-controlled environment, the sharp visual impression, stripped of an ambient nager riveted his attention.

He was still probing at the transfer lounge's swirling pattern of blues and pale greens when the door opened and a powerful Gen nager swept into the room. Stunned, he missed the first words his Donor spoke.

"...your new interest in computers."

Fortunately, as soon as the Gen had closed the door, he came forward with his hand out, reining in that overwhelming nager so Vret could think more clearly as he accepted the white special transfer assignment card.

Vret took it wondering why it wasn't green, checked the name the man had undoubtedly pronounced—Joran Nah—and noted the reason for the stunning nager. Nah was a GN-2, not a GN-3 over-matching Vret's current status as a QN-3.

Why? Had that public intil spike in the cafeteria put him on some kind of danger watchlist? Or maybe the white and red coded card indicated that maybe, just maybe, here was his opportunity to impress administration with his determination to Qualify Second. *I should pay more attention to the assigned reading and I'd know these things.*

"Computers?" Vret prompted, hoping to catch up on the conversation without appearing too overwhelmed.

"There wasn't a Third available who shares your interest, so they assigned me." He went over to the window glancing outward in approval. "Cheerful place here. I think we can manage, don't you?" He turned with an affable grin that was cleanly reflected in his nager.

Backed by the bright blue sky, his pale blond hair formed a halo about his head, accenting his searingly bright nager. According to the transfer assignment card, this Gen had given transfer only ten days ago, but already he had much more selyn than Vret would need.

"It would seem we can manage quite well," agreed Vret, trying to sound mature, not dazzled, and certainly not over-eager. "Are you sure you're only a Second?"

Joran laughed. "At the moment, yes. I'm being re-phased for a Qualifying Transfer."

He didn't elaborate whether that would be his Qualification as a First, or some other channel's Qualifying transfer as a Second. *Me?*

Joran sat down at the desk and brought up a display where he could enter his notes on Vret's condition. As he filled in the form, he asked, "So, Vret, are you planning on taking any courses in computer architecture? Over the next ten years, we'll be bringing all the Centers worldwide onto the Controller's net. Most of that work will be done by the Thirds, you know. You could make a career of it."

"I don't intend to remain a Third."

"So I've been told, but why? It's the best position if you want to work with computers."

Vret gave his now standard answer to that. "Well, life is no fun when you're so tired all the time." He suspected he might have understood more of the tour of the computer center if he hadn't been in recovery at the time. "And frankly, I'm not sure computers are so interesting. Is that your specialty?"

"Just a hobby. But it's turned out to be a useful one. I originally graduated from the Vashol First Year Camp as a Third. But after I made Second, I decided I wanted Farris training, and Rialite is *the* place for that. But there were no openings." He spun the chair around and got up, gesturing for Vret to take his place. "So I got in because I could work on the mainframe staff—and they wanted staffers and instructors more than another late Qualifying First."

"So you're here as a student too?" Vret sat.

"But I spend more time in the hole than instructing students. Still, I wouldn't be here if not for that hobby. I recommend it to you as a career move."

"In the hole?" asked Vret as he filled in his own part of the form.

"The high field area under the computer center where the whole network is powered."

"With selyn batteries and all?" Vret left off with the form and focused entirely on Joran. The mysteries of selyn batteries held an endless fascination for him.

"Yes. And I get to work with the Firsts who keep the batteries charged, as well as with students like yourself. When I graduate Rialite, I'll probably be able to pick where I want to settle down. Like I said, as a career—"

Vret felt the bottom fall out of his stomach. Joran was racing across the three strides of blue carpet that separated them, but seemed to be stuck in mid-air. The windows faded to darkness. An unreasoning, visceral panic flashed through his veins and seized his mind.

In the depths of that moment of stark terror, when all was lost and he knew he was dying, a sudden cloud of warm gold strength caught him on a pillow of pine and rosemary scented safety.

He came to himself once again, gasping. Striving for a sophistication he didn't feel, he spread hands and tentacles, summoned a smile and inserted it in his showfield to convince himself it was genuine. "I'm fine. Just turnover."

"So I noticed," agreed Joran. "Sorry, I should have stayed closer. In the future, be sure you inform your Donor when you've been through something that will exacerbate turnover like that."

Exacerbate? "It wasn't all that bad." But when Joran stepped back a few inches, he felt the howling cold winds of Need, and the yammering insistent cry of every cell in his body for the warmth of that selyn. And he was sure it was worse this month than last. Even now, only minutes past turnover, he could barely keep his laterals sheathed.

The Gen didn't say anything, just watched.

"All right, it was that bad. I don't know why, though." *Oh, yes I do.* The one thing he had been doing this month that could sharpen the impact of Need was reading Blissdrip's *Secret Killroom.* But he wasn't doing that any more, and would not... ever again.

Tentacles and fingers shaking, he made a big show of confidently filling out the form and then relinquishing the seat again to Joran, who filled out his half. When they were done, the screen presented them with their meeting schedule for the next fourteen days leading into Vret's eighth transfer.

As Vret raced to his next class, he wondered how he could exploit Joran's knowledge without giving any hint of why he wanted to understand such arcane things as computer security when he had no intention of pursuing a career in mainframe administration.

As the pessimism of Need clamped down, he began to wonder about the real reason Joran had been assigned to him. Did the Rialite administration suspect something? If so, what did they suspect?

And now, every moment, every breath, every step he took, every thought he generated was punctuated by—and enshrouded in—the recurrent, insistent throb of Need. He wasn't used to it after only seven months as a Sime. Every time he'd had transfer, he'd forgotten what the sharp claws of Need did to him.

All he could think about was his next transfer. Several times a day he spent time with Joran Nah, and Nah attended his sessions with Kwotiin Lake as well as his Collectorium and Dispensary labs. Need became the predominate schedule dictator of his life.

And with that expanded awareness came a renewed focus on locating Blissdrip. Relying on the technique that had led him to Bilateral's identity, he redoubled his efforts to chat up other students before and after every class. He hung out at the library and watched for anyone requisitioning stacks of books on Unity, the Secret Pens, or junctedness. He garnered dozens of leads, too many to be useful without the clue that had led him to Bilateral—comments she had posted from which he had inferred what she had been reading most recently.

She, however, had Halarcy, her roommate, requisition the volumes she had wanted to study.

Classes at Rialite were expected to be only a small part of the unique education here. Students were expected to investigate and master a wide range of subjects, and pass tests in those subjects to gain a variety of certifications. Vret himself had already achieved 3 full certifications just from what he did for fun and relaxation.

Rialite had been founded to handle the Farrises. The First Year Farrises often spiked a learning rate in excess of nine times Vret's own. They'd die of boredom with only classes to attend. Hence the library provided access to everything any student channel might be curious about.

There was nothing unusual in ten, even twenty students a day ordering up books on Unity or Disjunction Crisis, or Berserker behavior. Watching for the research going into Blissdrip's writings wouldn't be fast enough.

Disappointed and frustrated, he stopped Ilin on the path again as they were both late for their lunch appointments. "Joran is waiting for me, Ilin, but I have to tell you I'm not making any progress on this search at all."

She nodded. "I've been thinking. I'm not going to post any more installments," she replied. "This whole thing is just getting to me. The techs say the board readership has doubled in the last four days and the new people are not reading my stuff, they're reading Blissdrip's. They haven't made any progress identifying him either."

She doesn't look well at all. Vret asked, "You've been posting more installments?"

"And Blissdrip has too—long ones. The board usage is spiking because of that, and someone's bound to notice us soon."

"I haven't been reading our boards."

"Don't read them. We're going to have to bring this whole thing to the administration."

"Give me until after transfer. I might think of something when I can get my head clear." But now he knew there was even less time to solve this than he had thought.

That night he woke up dreaming an installment in Bilateral's *Aunser D'zehn* saga, even though he hadn't read any of her postings in five days. He had made no headway questioning Joran about how mainframes identified users, and by all reports, their own people were doing everything that could be done. But Joran's responses to his queries convinced him that the Second Order Donor had been assigned to Vret to investigate him— either because of the Secret Boards or to determine if he was a candidate for Qualification. Maybe both.

Barely twenty-four hours later, with his whole life riding on impressing Joran, Vret lied to the Donor to get away from him during the precious two hours when his roommate would be gone. He told himself the only way he would ever have of catching up with Blissdrip would be to lure him into some kind of personal correspondence on the discussion board.

Vret spent the stolen time skimming at his fastest reading speed, absorbing the episodes of both Bilateral's novel and Blissdrip's perversion of it that he had missed. Though *Aunser* was deeply absorbing, it was *Killroom* that had him panting with intil and aching with the stern effort to suppress that inappropriate, but oddly real, surge of raw Need.

He had to break away from the desk and pace to bring himself under control. Twice, he had to admit to himself that just reading this stuff brought him close to the edge of being dangerous— but thankfully there were no untrained Gens allowed onto the Rialite campus. Still, Vret didn't want Nah to see him in this condition.

He fought himself back under control and went back to work telling himself the intil would subside once he finished reading.

CHAPTER NINE

DISPENSARY LAB

But he didn't finish all the reading fast enough, and he was late leaving his room.

Then he augmented his selyn consumption rate to race to his Dispensary lab session. By using selyn at a faster rate than normal, he not only moved faster, but he cleared the headache his fight with intil had given him. And he made it by a split second as the instructor was closing the insulated door—that would not open again until every scheduled transfer had been administered.

The lab room contained fourteen transfer lounges spread in rows, each shrouded in extremely efficient insulating draperies forming tents with doors which still hung open, facing the instructors at the front of the lab.

The instructors today were two Farris channels and their Donors, none of whom were known to Vret. The impenetrable insulating drapes, even after being closed, would be gossamer thin to those channels. Every single nuance of his nageric management, his vriamic control, his selyn flow management would be scrutinized and evaluated as he worked with his client. And all he could think about was The Kill and death by Attrition after aborting away from channel's transfer.

"You're late, Hajene McClintock," accused Joran as Vret slid into position beside him trying to look as if he'd studied this material and knew what he was supposed to do.

The module next to him held his good friend Iric Chez who

had recently made Second, sternly trying not to notice Vret's tardiness. His Donor was also a Second Vret had seen around. Vret had gotten Iric onto the Secret Boards, but he didn't know his nickname. Still, he couldn't be Blissdrip. Iric had too vast a sense of humor. He was more likely author of the insanely funny but prurient *Tecton Times* gossip column articles about the doings of the Householdings before Unity.

"*Almost* late," agreed Vret to Joran's accusation. He took up the field management for his renSime client who sat on the transfer lounge, feet dangling, hands gripping the edge of the lounge.

Joran handed him the client's file. She was Banda Muoin. Vret quickly read her medical history and transfer particulars in a series of charts, graphs and tables. Each day of this course they were to master the art of interpreting one more part of the standard Tecton file on a renSime's transfer characteristics. Today's section included the effect of sub-mutation variant on disease histories with age.

Banda Muoin was twenty three years past changeover, had three healthy children and suffered from the aftermath of a bout of Shaking Plague during First Year. The table they were studying today was highlighted in green but he hadn't had time to read up on the details.

As Vret studied the sections of the chart he'd already mastered, the young woman heaved a sign of relief at his field management, then cracked a smile. "Actually, Sosu Joran, Hajene McClintock arrived ten seconds before the hour, so he's not really late—"

She broke off as suddenly, there was a huge, rock-solid, massive silence in the ambient. Vret didn't have to turn to know that one of the Farris instructors was behind him. He swiveled his stool around, summoned a smile into his showfield and waited attentively, thoughts of telepathy dancing through his consciousness.

"Hajene," said the Farris in a deep baritone, "you yourself are in Need. How would you feel if your Donor arrived only ten seconds before the appointment hour?"

Vret wiped the smile away. The feeling of panic and even terror that he would feel if his Donor were late was overwhelming. He did his best to shield his client from his field spikes, though Joran moved to intercede his own nager, protecting her. Had that wash of Need-terror come from his own imagination, empathizing with his client, or had the Mysterious Farris Talent somehow planted it inside him?

"Yes, precisely," agreed the Farris, flicking an approving tentacle at Joran. "You would not appreciate it if Joran were almost late. Now tell me, what do you think of a channel who arrives at a transfer appointment, augmenting as if some emergency were in progress?"

"Not reassuring," Vret agreed with the implied criticism. It was perfectly just, and the Farris had refrained from zlinning him—or so it seemed. A student-Third might not actually know if a First had in fact zlinned him.

The Farris consulted a roster he held crooked in his elbow, secured by one handling tentacle. "You're up for eighth transfer. We expect more of our senior students than you have given us today. Your grade for today's work will be reduced by one level and this will go on your record."

The Farris signalled Joran and turned away to check on Iric Chez and his client.

The transfer clients were all carefully chosen and heavily trained to drill students in how to give a good transfer. They knew more about interpreting the charts than the students did. Some of these renSimes taught the academic subjects and some were administrators, librarians, or even kitchen staff. Banda Muoin knew more about what Vret should have been doing and saying than he did.

Joran settled back behind Vret saying, "That was Saelul Farris. You know who he is?"

"No, never heard of him."

"Well, he's new here. If you want a chance to Qualify Second before you leave Rialite, he's the one who will authorize it."

"Oh," whispered Vret.

Banda watched Vret absorb the shock. Then she reached out a hand to touch his knee. "Steady Hajene. Saelul isn't an ogre. He wants every one of Rialite's students to develop their full potential. If you have the ability, he'll see to it you use it."

And he won't be impressed if he finds my client reassuring me. Vret reawakened the smile in his showfield, and put personal concerns aside. This was real channel's work he was doing, despite the fact his client was actually his teacher. She did need a transfer.

After the brief augmentation, he felt refreshed, even renewed, just the way Blissdrip kept describing the joys of augmentation when in Need. Assuming his best professional demeanor, he pivoted on his stool to face front while the man who held the key to his future began the lecture.

The lab proceeded through the detailed description of the chart entries, each client present an example of one or another medical situation. Then the student channels toured the room, zlinning each client and examining their charts. There was a question session, and then each of the Farris channels performed a demonstration transfer illustrating variations on the types of problems under consideration.

Vret was suitably awed by Saelul's diamond-hard, brilliant precision in transfer, but even more impressed with the Farris's nearly instant recovery time from the intricate functional. Doing anything like that would have left Vret shaking with fatigue for hours.

Then two at a time, each of the students gave their client transfer behind their closed curtains while the supervising Farrises stood outside and took notes then discussed errors with the class, using each other to demonstrate what the student had done, and then what the student should have done instead.

By the time it was Vret's turn, he was more nervous than he'd ever been in a transfer lab.

But right on schedule for his client, Saelul Farris yanked the curtain closed on Vret's cubicle. Banda leaned back on the transfer lounge and held out her tentacles, laterals extended. Then she winked, quirking one corner of her mouth in confident and good humor despite her advanced state of Need.

It broke the tension. Suddenly Vret just fell into sync with her nageric pulsing, and with an ease that surprised him, he slid his laterals around hers, smoothly bent to the fifth contact point, lip to lip, feeling his way into her system. The selyn he'd packed into his secondary system that morning in Collectorium Lab flowed easily into her, the speed regulated by her demand.

In the time it takes to snap two fingers together, it was over. Vret straightened, dismantling the lateral contact and grinning at the expression of bliss permeating the older woman's features. "Oh, Hajene, this is going to be a very good month for me. Thank you."

The vibrant tingling he always felt after giving a transfer was even more invigorating and reassuring than the after effects of augmentation had been. As he sagged back against Joran's fields, feeling the post-functional fatigue headache start, he shoved the curtain aside.

Saelul Farris's expression and nager betrayed nothing as he jotted notations on Vret's record. Vret wouldn't be able to read those notes until he logged into his account later. For now, he braced himself for the dissection before the class. If everyone else here could endure being ripped apart while in recovery, so could he.

"Excellent work, Hajene McClintock. It's a pity you had to be docked a grade level."

Then without further comment, the Farris turned to watch Iric Chez who had performed at the same time, be dissected while Banda made her way out of the room. As a Second, Iric had been given a harder problem and as a new Second he'd made errors any Third might have. In a week or so more though, Iric would be shifted to classes with his new peers. So the instructor landed on him harder when he offered excuses.

For a moment, Joran's attention riveted on the Second Order channel being chewed to bits in a class for Thirds. Vret felt the lack of his Donor's protection when every student in the room seemed to be zlinning him. Then Joran moved to counter the effect of the ambient on his channel and suddenly all attention was on the instructors again.

Neither Farris was even sweating. After all that high precision, deep zlinning through what seemed to Vret opaque curtains they were as fresh as if they'd spent a couple of hours drinking trin tea in the gardens.

And they're born that way. Farrises! Still, his own life would become markedly easier if only he could Qualify Second and get into a specialty. And that wouldn't happen if his involvement in the Secret Boards were discovered.

He would have to draw Blissdrip out by getting him to comment on the Boards.

The great gaping flaw in the plan was big enough to swallow Vret whole. It required him not only to read these deeply disturbing stories, he had to write some too, because if Ilin wouldn't be posting, then someone had to goad Blissdrip into making a mistake and revealing his identity in a comment or response on the Boards.

The day after he had so ignominiously brought himself to Saelul Farris's attention, he was waiting for Ilin to pass by the cactus garden when he saw Iric Chez galloping toward him in the long-legged stride that was just short of augmented speed. His dusky complexion was darkened by the desert sun, and his bony physique seemed etched sharply under his student Second uniform.

"Vret!" hailed Iric. "That was some performance in Dispensary Lab yesterday. The Farrises really admired your work. I don't know how you get all the reading done and still get through the class work."

"Well, yesterday I was just lucky."

"Yeah. Farrises! They count "almost late" as actually late! You got lost in the *Secret Killroom* installment, just like I did, didn't you?"

Vret quickly zlinned all around but nobody was close enough

to have heard. *He's a Second now. He'd notice if anyone were close.*

"Calm down," admonished Chez. "I just wanted to thank you for getting me onto the Secret Boards. After *Killroom* started, it became a real eye-opener. The Tecton has to re-think the legal status of the junct in today's society. I'm on my way to the library to see if there's anything on the Distect philosophy. The Gulf Territory direct transfer experiment has to be tried again with modern technology. Killbliss is the natural culmination of the transfer experience."

And with that, Chez was off down the path toward the library. Unable to read the Second's fields well, Vret could only guess the man was just shy of turnover.

He'll change his mind when Need gets a grip on him. That was when the Tecton's values really made sense, when you knew the forces within you could rip your will to shreds, pound aside your determination, and force you to the Kill no matter what philosophy you espoused, or what your conscience dictated. And just reading *Killroom* roused those inner forces from their Tecton imposed slumber.

He'll come to his senses when he knows once again the only thing between him and Killing someone he loves is his anti-kill conditioning, and renSimes can't even have that advantage.

"Vret, why are you standing out here in the sun staring at that cactus?"

Ilin came up to him, favoring him with a deliberate effervescent nager and a wide grin. It was a remarkable feat three days past turnover. Her skills were improving markedly. He told her his plan. "But how do you write this kind of thing?" His prior scribblings for himself didn't count. This would have to be posted for all to read. The thought of that left the words frozen in the back of his mind.

"It's not hard. You just pretend you're the character and write down what you would say to another character, who is someone you know."

"You mean you base it on real people?"

"A little bit. It's like you're talking to someone you know, but you have to be sure an eavesdropper would completely understand what you mean."

"I see...."

"Vret, I have to run. I'm almost late for Dispensary Lab and a friend warned me I've got Saelul Farris today!"

"Go! And don't augment on the way there!"

Curiosity burning, she didn't ask, but took his advice.

Deliberately balancing in duoconsciousness, he watched her speed on down the path, sun and shadow playing around her, primary field fluttering through her showfield in graceful rhythm.

Once again, as she walked away from him, eyes firmly front, her attention was on zlinning him watching her. With a wistful flick of her nager, she added a little sway to her stride.

Just the way she placed her feet as she strode was totally absorbing to him. *Maybe we'll be assigned for our post-reactions this month.*

The following month would be her 10th transfer, so she'd have the deferment training exercise, taking transfer a whole day late. That meant they wouldn't have post-syndrome at the same time. *Got to be this month!*

CHAPTER TEN
DISJUNCTION CLASS

He went on to his Mutation Physiology class whistling thoughtfully between his teeth. If Blissdrip were using the same system for generating his stories that Ilin used, if his characters were actually people they all knew, maybe Vret could identify the real person behind one of the characters, and get a lead on the author that way.

He spent most of the lecture reviewing what he remembered of Blissdrip's writing, studying everyone in the class with a new speculation.

He missed a chunk of the lecture when it suddenly dawned on him that Blissdrip's descriptions of the channel's experience of channeling were flat—glossed over as if viewed from outside. But the descriptions of the renSime experience during transfer or the Kill came to life in vivid and compelling detail, repeated in endless variations that evoked a reader's intil in the oddest ways.

Blissdrip is renSime? Could it be? There were many renSimes on campus as faculty and other staff, and there was Rialite's facility for renSimes in First Year adjacent to the channel and Donor training schools. He'd ask Ilin if the renSimes could have access to the same network their Secret Boards were on. He vaguely remembered something about that during his tour, but he just wasn't clear on it. Each of the three First Year Camps had their own mainframes and complete libraries, but were they connected?

Trying to make up for what he had missed while thinking, he lingered after class, talking to some of the other students and listening to the instructor chatting with the more advanced students who were discussing the disjunction characteristics of the various sub-mutations.

He'd done a lot of this kind of eavesdropping and subtle questioning while searching for Bilateral, too, and it had paid off. But now he was searching for someone Blissdrip might be using as a model for his characters. Yet if Blissdrip were a First Year renSime, he wouldn't know or interact with anyone here.

Only the senior students were sent to give transfers to the First Year renSimes as part of their graduation work, and then under strict supervision. Well, that was true for the Thirds, but what about the Seconds and Firsts? He resolved to ask Joran.

While thinking, jotting notes and chatting with his fellow students, Vret soaked up all the details he overheard the instructor discussing. The mass disjunction at the time of Unity had led to the founding of the Secret Pens, and he hadn't studied disjunction in depth yet. There was only one brief chapter in this course's textbook.

He stopped at the library to get more textbooks on disjunction. Bilateral's stories glossed over most of the ugly details of disjunction, the way Blissdrip sidestepped the details of a channel's experience of transfer.

Blissdrip wrote endless paragraphs of emotion-laden detail describing each day leading up to disjunction crisis and his descriptions of the crisis itself—which usually lasted no more than a day or two—were often longer and more detailed than his descriptions of the entire year or so leading up to the crisis.

And he wrote page after page of exacting description of life as a semi-junct, staving off the Need to Kill one more month, hoping to live just a little longer.

Disjunction and the related semi-junct state were specialties usually reserved for the Firsts, and these days not many such specialists were required so few were trained. Still fewer were really interested in the complex intricacies of the subject. But if he were going to write this stuff convincingly enough to get Blissdrip to comment in a white-heat and make a mistake, he had to know all about it.

The library at Rialite had everything about everything, so in one visit he came away with more than he could read in a month.

Outside on the dazzling white granite steps of the library building, he paused to page through the largest of the books he'd acquired. Could a First Year renSime at the adjacent camp access this material? Just skimming some of the section titles, he really didn't think they should, but he vaguely remembered something about their library having all the books that were here, too.

RenSimes had no vriamic node. The renSime had only one selyn transport system. They had no physiologic way to control the behavior of that primary selyn system. When Need reached a certain level, it triggered a survival reflex and they would attack any selyn source. The same thing could happen to any channel, but it took a lot more Need to trigger the reflex, especially when the vriamic node was developed in First Year and protected by anti-Kill conditioning then strengthened with exercise.

Without a channel's ability to control Need and all its reflexes, a renSime—especially in First Year—should be protected from intil stimulants outside of a transfer situation. Psychologically and physiologically, the renSime's only protection from their own Kill reflex was that implanted conditioning in First Year to associate intil and the satisfaction of Need with the channel's work on their fields. It was a thin protection, but it was all they had, and over the last century or so it had proven effective.

Vret went back into the library and asked at the reference desk. "Are these books available to the First Year renSimes?"

The librarian, a Third Order Donor, laughed. "No, of course not. Those are advanced medical texts. Your vriamic trainer cleared you for them."

"Oh. I see. Thank you." *Kwotiin cleared me for texts normally used by First and Seconds?*

"May I see what else I've been cleared for?"

"Oh, that information is not available to students."

"Ah. Well, thank you." As he walked across the huge expanse of polished marble floor under the echoing dome, Vret cherished the thought, *Kwotiin thinks I can make Second!*

He went back to the catalog and dug into the codes on the books' entries. At the front of the catalog there was a key to the symbols on each entry. With a bit of application, he came to understand how many of these textbooks required several instructors' clearances before you could get at them. That requirement had been sitting right before his face and he'd never noticed it.

Vret had never been denied access to any subject that took his fancy. It had never occurred to him that the marvelous library censored student reading. The only way he'd discover the limits of his own authorizations was to request something for which he had not been cleared.

And if Blissdrip is a student on this campus, he's got the same problem.

CHAPTER ELEVEN
THE MELLOW AMBIENT

A little after dusk, with brilliant stars overhead and a huge moon on the horizon, he met Ilin by the cacti again and after he reported his intuitive leaps of non-progress, she sorted through the books he'd found, pointing out the best ones. "The Farrises are great channels, but most of them can't write anything a non-Farris can understand. Stick with Lolungren and Shir. They're comprehensible."

He thanked her and came to the question that really bothered him. "So I still don't understand how this computer network stuff is set up. Can the First Year renSimes log into our main-frame and read our boards?"

She paused a long time before answering. "I don't...think...so. I'll ask and let you know."

"The library says the First Year renSimes can't get these books—at least not from our library. Would there be any other source of this material for a renSime?"

"Well, any in-Territory home might have books like this a kid could read. But what kid would understand? Or have the patience to wade through it all?"

"The child of two channels?"

"Blissdrip could be a renSime child of two channels?"

"I have no idea."

"That would narrow it down considerably."

"And the child of two channels would have a good chance to end up being trained at the Rialite Camp, no?"

"Yes. I'll find out if they have access to our boards from over there."

That was a different question than he'd asked. "Someone with knowledge of computers might do it where others couldn't."

"Might. I'll find out."

They sat a while just being quiet together in the gathering night. It was cooling off. One cactus had a flower opening into the dusk. The paths were limned in the glow of selyn fields as well as lights. It was one of those moments of sheer beauty neither could fully appreciate because of the insistent thrum of Need. But it wasn't so bad yet that they couldn't admire the beauty.

"So you're not posting more installments of *Aunser*?"

"No."

"You won't mind if I usurp your characters?"

"Why should I? Everyone else does."

Vret zlinned her. She wasn't at all upset. "Well, mostly because I've never done this before. I'm probably a worse writer than a Farris!"

That earned one quick bark of laughter. "It's all right, you can massacre away."

"If I'm lucky, I'll draw Blissdrip out."

"Don't say that name out loud! It sounds just like what it is."

"You've got a point."

"So have you. We haven't got a whole lot more time to find this crazy and nail him down."

"True. Then I'll see you tomorrow." Even though he'd said it, Vret sat there listening to her nager sing his name. He just didn't want to move, and it wasn't the lingering fatigue from the hard workday either.

"I've got an accounting class to get to," Ilin said at last. "Dynopter estimations are the bane of my existence!"

"Oh, just think how much fun you'll have teaching me next month."

"That's a thought," she grinned. "I'd like to stay here with you for hours—well, not here...we could find someplace more private—but I have to go." She pulled herself to her feet. "See you tomorrow."

Vret watched her walk away into the dark, then zlinned her as she went on around the stand of cacti and spiky trees zlinning him back in what had become their parting routine. He noted that he spent a lot of time watching her walk and never tired of the view.

Then he heaved to his feet, stretched the ache out of his back and headed for his Physics Lab. Two hours of tinkering with DeBroglie sensors and he'd have time to write the installment he'd dreamed up.

During the opening lecture to that lab, he read the two shortest books on disjunction, and as a result when he got to the bench work, he almost scorched a lateral tentacle in the DeBroglie circuit he was supposed to be energizing with a selyn charge from his secondary system.

But he went to his room full of ideas for his installment inspired by a particularly detailed and gruesome description of death from attrition in disjunction crisis. He would use a setting from Blissdrip's story, and the characters and situation from Bilateral's. That surely would draw comment from their mysterious author.

* * * * * * *

"The Mellow Ambient"

by

Asymmetric

The Tecton's ground troops were mopping up after the police action against the Secret Killroom. It had been operating from caves set into the side of a hill, camouflaged by a rambling old wooden building with a wrap-around veranda and a big painted sign saying, "The Mellow Ambient—Trin and Porstan." Now the sign hung askew, severely charred around the edges, the words barely legible.

Two chimneys were still standing at either end of the building's large common room, but the walls had fallen out, the roof had fallen in, and the back wall was no more. They could all see the black hole that led back into the mountainside and zlin the dull throb of drugged Gens being disturbed by troopers who weren't their usual handlers.

Before the attack, a wagon had been drawn up beside the building delivering the road house's supplies. Now it was nothing but a charred skeleton still emitting a plume of smoke. The scent of burning trin tea leaves was giving everyone a raw throat.

Off in the distance, several wagons were moving on the trail from town throwing a plume of dust across the fields. The wagons would collect the Gens and take them away for medical treatment.

Visually obscured by that dust cloud, other troopers, augmenting on foot, were chasing down the horses that had broken out of the corral near the road house, fleeing the fire. There had been several dozen patrons in the building at the time, and most of them had died in the first few minutes of the assault as they tried to defend the wooden structure from the Tecton force.

Standing beside the smoking remains of the Secret Killroom, Sectuib Klyd Farris argued with Aunser ambrov D'zehn. "If we do establish an official network of Secret Pens, what will happen when the out-Territory Gens discover such an officially sanctioned lie? The Contract will be no more...and then what?"

"It would be a disaster," Aunser agreed forlornly. He extended a handling tentacle and rubbed absently at a mosquito bite near its tip.

"And it will happen. There's no way so many people can keep such a secret. First it will be whispers, insidious distrust, then we'll have to issue official denials under the Tecton seal."

"'The Tecton' used to mean just the Householdings," countered Aunser, "but now it means everyone. We can't allow Householding scruples to direct public policy—not when it comes to murdering our own people so hideously."

With a nager as flat and hard as granite, the Farris stared into the hole in the mountainside. Aunser didn't have to zlin through that massive showfield to know the Sectuib in Zeor was thinking that Householding scruples had to become public policy. But the Farris wouldn't say that out loud because it was never going to happen.

Instead of arguing, the Farris sighed, coughed a little on the smoke, and paced away from the ruin, seeming much older than when he'd arrived just a couple of hours ago.

Aunser pursued, bringing up another of his favorite points again. "What if some of those Gens in there have been kidnapped from out-Territory—Wild Gens—Choice Kills. If we clean them up and send them home, they'll report that the Tecton is not keeping The Contract. Then what? Zelerod's Doom? It's better by far to keep our citizens from raiding for out-Territory Gens. Use the Gens born and raised in Pens and let them remain Pen Gens, let them meet the fate they were born to. We have a better chance of keeping Pens actually secret if we do it that way."

The impenetrable Farris nager shifted and Aunser didn't have to be a telepath to know the Sectuib was wondering how a Householder, born and raised, could possibly think such a thought.

"Your logic is compelling, Aunser. But too much of what we've done has been based on immediate expediency, clever ideas invented on the spur of the moment. Eventually all this desperate improvising will collapse on our heads—and then we may very well see Zelerod's Doom descend."

"How long would we run Pens, Sectuib? Five years? Seven? Even the healthiest semi-juncts can't live much longer than that. But we have to have them alive, healthy and working hard to train this next generation of non-juncts in how to run a civilization. Would you rather have Householding run Pens—or Secret

Killrooms? It's going to be one or the other. All juncts aren't going to just quietly accept a horrible death for a distant ideal!"

"Risa[1] never stops saying that and insisting the answer is direct Gen ransfer." His voice was low, flat, depressed by Need. He ran tentacles through his black hair which stood up in sweaty spikes, sighed again, and gazed out across the empty fields between the road house and the town of Poliston. He was still resisting the idea of Secret Pens, but seemed to view them as inevitable.

Suddenly, the Farris started, whirled back toward the cave mouth, kicked into augmentation and ran toward the cave as his showfield melted into a responsive, soft surface, as if feeling for a problem.

Aunser, stunned into immobility for two blinks of his eyes, heard a shout boom out of the cave carried on a nageric splash of urgency, "Sectuib! Sectuib Zeor!"

Aunser pelted toward the cave mouth, flying across the smoking rubble in the clouds of ash and soot pluming in the Farris's wake. Aunser's foot crunched through a blackened beam and flames shot up where he had stepped, though he wasn't there anymore. He homed on the voices.

"This way! Quickly! There's a survivor!"

Way back in the cave, inside a barred cage, they found a severely charred Sime. She was huddled in a ball beneath a pile of Gens dead from smoke inhalation. Her back was blackened, her burned clothing stuck to the skin. But she was alive...barely.

When Aunser arrived, Klyd was kneeling in the muck and ash beside the burn victim. Klyd's Companion crowded in behind Aunser, sidled past and hovered behind Klyd's shoulder. Aunser moved in to protect the renSime troopers and edge them out of the cage, though the burned Sime was so far gone there was practically no pain in the ambient.

As Aunser zlinned his own Companion approaching along the passageway, Klyd turned from his examination. "She's

---

1. See *Ambrov Keon* by Jean Lorrah

in disjunction crisis, Aunser. Semi-junct renSime. I think she crawled back here trying to find a Gen to Kill, but they were all dead. It seems she may have taken some selyn from the corpses. This is more your specialty than mine. But I don't think there's any hope here."

"Nelson!" called Aunser to his Companion. "Hurry!"

The Gen broke into a full run as Klyd relinquished the field control around the burn victim to Aunser with that incredible finesse which was the hallmark of the Farris. *It isn't something they learn*, he reminded himself. *It's just what they are.*

Nelson arrived and skidded to a halt on the slippery floor. Aunser flicked a tentacle at him, and the Donor fell into synch in the familiar and comforting way.

And then Aunser was into the problem; the world closed away from him by his own Companion's field. The woman's burns were faintly oozing selyn. She was barely breathing. Brain activity almost imperceptible.

Perforce relying on Klyd's diagnosis of disjunction crisis, he knew an ordinary forced transfer wouldn't work. He'd have to disarm her abort reflex, and with a renSime that wouldn't be harmless. *She's going to die anyway,* he rationalized what he was about to do to her. *This may give her a few more months crippled maybe but alive to get her affairs in order.*

He pulled out of the functional enough to say over his shoulder, "Nelson, on my mark, slam her. Sectuib, clear the room."

Klyd turned and scooped everyone toward the entry to the cave that held the cage full of dead Gens. To his credit, the Farris didn't even stop to ask about this novel technique of murdering a nearly dead renSime to save her life. He used that impenetrable granite field to cut all the onlookers off from the impending Genslam shock.

Aunser sank into the faint tracery of selyn circulation barely pulsing through the woman's body. He picked up the rhythm her body was using, though it was fraught with irregular stutters and lengthening hesitations.

Timing his effort carefully, he signalled his Companion and simultaneously rammed home a flash flood of selyn with merciless speed—more selyn than she could ever take in a transfer, nevermind a Kill. It overwhelmed her nerves at the same moment the Gen shocked her systems into paralysis. And the selyn went in, lighting her body's nerve pathways though not yet her brain.

A long, long pause and her heart thud-thumped into motion. He held her nose and blew into her mouth, using his showfield to stimulate her breathing reflex. Twice. Three times. And he felt her brain start to light up with circulating selyn, felt awareness begin to surface.

He dragged himself duoconscious, letting go of his selyn field perceptions and grabbing for visual and voice, for tactile and odor impressions. That last he regretted as he drew breath and shouted, "Sectuib Farris!" The Farris nager peeked around the edge of the cave wall. "Sectuib, your patient now. Burns are your specialty."

More than a little amazed, Klyd Farris approached zlinning as if he couldn't believe his eyes. "She's alive."

"If you can heal the burns she may have a couple more months...may not thank us for it though."

"I understand," he said, summoning his Companion and taking up the field management again, politely waiting patiently as Aunser's frozen grip on the fields had to be pried loose a thread at a time. "The burn scars will be disabling all by themselves."

"I have several Thirds who can manage the infection for her. Send her to me in Poliston when you've done all you can."

"I'll bring her. I want to learn more about that...um, technique you used."

Aunser stumbled a little as he rose, helped by his Companion who was wholly and totally focused on him now, trying to untangle his messed up selyn flows. Even all the experience they'd had with this technique didn't seem to help today.

Recovery from forcing a transfer was always hard for Aunser, but complicated by the slam, he battled not only the overall weakness and dizziness but a headache and pervading numbness that left his tentacles clumsy and his eyes refusing to focus.

Still, beneath it, all his systems sang with renewed vitality and a tingling warmth that could only be described as a unique and precious pleasure, a reason to live.

"You all right?" asked the Farris as he worked.

Aunser would have sworn the man shouldn't have been able to notice Aunser at that point. "Yes, Nelson will take care of me. I'm just slow to recover."

Still working carefully on the unconscious renSime's burns, Klyd muttered, "Risked your life to give this woman a few more days of misery."

"Wouldn't have had to risk myself—or my Companion—if she could have found a Kill."

The Farris turned from what he was doing, eyes on Aunser but with his attention unwavering on the renSime. "And the misery she faces would not be at all this intense."

That was when Aunser knew the Sectuib in Zeor had given up. They would get their Secret Pens in order to make Unity work.

* * * * * * *

The day after Vret posted his masterpiece, flinching from reading the message boards for comments on it, Bilateral posted another installment in her *Aunser*.

Instantly, the comment board exploded in activity. There were a few half-hearted disparaging remarks about the dry and uninteresting new post by Asymmetric. A few people objected heatedly to his destroying The Mellow Ambient and its Secret Killroom—locale of the very best episodes Blissdrip had posted.

His choice of title was even seen as a sarcastic attack on Blissdrip's fine writing by a writer with no talent, who was obviously jealous.

But Blissdrip—at least under that nickname—didn't post any comments.

But then came the comment that gave him pause. "At least that wretched trash Asymmetric posted has had one good effect. Bilateral seems to have woken up from a long nap with some new ideas, and his writing has matured remarkably. The transfer scene in Part 42 between Mirindi and Sosu Fane shows just what the semi-junct really craves in a transfer. Now if he'll just keep on developing like this, the *Aunser* stuff might become worthwhile reading."

Vret instantly flipped to the newest Bilateral installment and read, more appalled with each paragraph.

Ilin had taken his idea that Risa Tigue hadn't been the inventor of the slam-ram technique, but that Aunser had, and that Klyd Farris admired it and wanted to learn it from Aunser, and she'd incorporated that into her *Aunser*.

She had written an entire episode of close medical detail on three renSimes dying of the typical semi-junct transfer abort syndrome. Each had a complicated personal history and compelling desire to live just a little longer.

The episode delineated in vivid detail every moment of their suffering. One committed suicide, another died in abort taking a channel with her, and the third accepted being Klyd Farris's first slam-ram client to live long enough to apologize to her estranged son and turn over a treasured family heirloom. Then she died peacefully.

If Vret had been in post-syndrome instead of deep into Need, he'd have cried his heart out over the terrible tragedies. As it was, he could only respond to the descriptions of the transfers.

Vret read the description of transfer the commenter had praised so highly with horrified amazement. Point by point, the description could just have well have been of a Kill—from the Killer's point of view. It was so realistic it left him struggling for vriamic control and wishing he didn't have to.

Bilateral was a more powerful and accomplished craftsman

than Blissdrip—and so much more physically effective in evoking a total physiological involvement. *Why doesn't she save that talent for her post-syndrome scenes?*

He couldn't ask her that. And he couldn't think just how to put it—certainly would not have posted any comment to the boards after the way the readers had dismissed his work. He was just as glad he didn't encounter her on the path that day or the next. But he became worried when more of the blatantly evocative *Aunser* posts appeared. She was spending every spare minute writing, it seemed.

As if in competition, Blissdrip was pouring out ever more detailed descriptions in his *Secret Killroom* saga. He rewrote Asymmetric's episode, incorporating the attack and destruction into his story, but twisting it around so that the attack was by citizens seeking Killable Gens.

The patrons of the Secret Killroom defended the Mellow Ambient, kept the Killroom secret from the Tecton and rebuilt the way station.

In the process they reveled in and delighted in augmenting to shake off the doldrums from bad transfers from channels. The renSimes took transfer from Companions, and as a consequence lost all semblance of control around Gens. Most of the wordage consisted of repeated and detailed descriptions of hair-trigger intil, but portrayed as the natural joy of life, not a mortal danger.

The heat rose as Bilateral and Blissdrip dueled for the admiration of the readers pouring onto the comment boards. Vret spent all his spare time reading the stories and the comments, searching for clues to Blissdrip's identity.

As Need clamped down on him, Vret once again found it was all he could think about. He struggled to keep his mind on the search for Blissdrip, but easily soaked up every word of the *Secret Killroom*. And suddenly it occurred to him that Blissdrip might have the same problem. He went back over all the installments, and correlated when they were posted with the amount of Need description in each.

It didn't take long to develop a theory that nailed Blissdrip's transfer dates, but just reading these descriptions again while in Need gave him hours of struggle against his own intil. Even hours after finishing the research, he was still flying into spikes of intil at every flash of a Gen field.

Five days before both he and Ilin would have transfer, he found her in the cactus garden waiting for him. But when she turned, there was no smile on her lips or in her eyes. Her nager was ashen. She had lost weight. All his theories about Blissdrip vanished from his mind.

"Ilin, what's wrong?"

"You haven't heard?"

"Heard what?"

"Yesterday, about four hours after I posted Part 50, there was an incident at the Janroz Library—Halarcy....."

"Halarcy?"

"My roommate. She'd been reading the boards. She didn't know my nickname. I only found out she was on the Secret Boards when she tried to recruit me yesterday."

Sumz was babbling, and Vret had never heard her wander through a topic like this. Something bad had happened. "She was reading *Aunser*?"

Sumz nodded, choking back a howl of emotions so mixed Vret couldn't name it. He waited for it to abate. "And something has happened to her?"

"She's gone."

"Gone?" He sat up in alarm. "Dead?"

"No! But it's my fault."

"When you're ready, tell me what happened."

"That's just it. I don't know! They came for her things this morning, and nobody would tell me anything—just that she'd left Rialite. Vret, she was doing well. She was going to finish as a Third Order channel, but she had a good shot at Second within the year. She had four extra certificates, and had two full Specialties. There was no reason they'd kick her out of Rialite... unless...."

"Unless what?"

"It's just a rumor."

Vret's patience was wearing thin, but he could zlin how distraught Ilin was. If she hadn't been deep into Need she would have been crying her heart out. As it was, she was just zlinning into space, as if frozen on the brink of an unspeakable nightmare. *Waking Need Nightmares.* He'd read of such things. Was this an example?

Eventually, she broke off zlinning a cactus spine and turned to face him. "Vret, it's just a rumor. I don't know it was Halarcy. But they're saying that some Third raised intil and attacked a Donor. Over by the Janroz Library."

Stunned, he breathed, "I hadn't heard that."

"If it was her, it would explain why they sent her away. Or maybe she is dead. I haven't heard and nobody will answer my questions."

"Who was the Donor?"

"I don't know." It was a flat statement that would have been a hopeless wail if not for Need. Vret felt her despair pounding at her beneath the pall of Need.

"You're thinking Part 50 caused her intil to spike?"

She only nodded, the black smoke of guilt pervading her nager. People passing by on the path above the cactus garden's little glen, zlinned and then politely turned away from what must have seemed like a lovers' quarrel.

"If the Donor was a Third, we'll know soon. They'll have to juggle the schedule." His gut screamed, *Joran!* but he forced his mind away. There was some reason they'd assigned him a Second. "How do you know she was reading *Aunser*? A couple hours after you posted Part 50, Blissdrip posted his *Secret Killroom* episode, "What does it take?""

"You read that?"

Vret didn't want to admit it. That episode had focused on the details of the torture used to "work up" a Pen Gen for the Kill when the Sime was so far gone he couldn't raise intil and would abort out of any Kill over and over until he died of attrition.

According to Blissdrip, when Klyd Farris authorized

the Secret Pens, he did not allow such extreme measures, so Blissdrip made up a new character who offered that kind of service at new Secret Killrooms.

"Yes, I read every word as I fed it into a style checker I customized to score for Need terms. That's why I was looking for you. I have a new theory."

That captured her interest so he quickly explained, ending, "I think I've nailed Blissdrip's Need cycle."

"Then if we could access the transfer records, we could narrow the possibilities. I'll ask. Maybe one of our people can get the information."

She wasn't as excited as he felt she ought to be at the news. "Listen, if Halarcy was involved in that incident, and if she was reading the boards just before whatever happened happened, she was probably reading *Killroom*, not *Aunser*."

The moment the words left his mouth, he wanted to suck them back in again. He remembered how the criticism of his little piece hurt. They both knew everyone was reading *Killroom* and fewer and fewer following *Aunser* except when she posted junct transfer descriptions.

Her reaction was deadened by Need. "Yes, probably." She climbed to her feet, gathering her books. "I'll see what Morry can do about checking transfer schedules."

*　*　*　*　*　*　*

Over the next three days, Vret passed Ilin on the path but only exchanged a few words: "The boards are generating conspicuous spikes in mainframe activity every time Blissdrip posts."

"Any progress on accessing transfer schedules yet?"

"I think Morry's given up on transfer schedules. If he trips an alarm, we're caught."

And one time, he told her, "Rumor counts five intil incidents in the last two days, nothing as bad as the first one though." By some miracle, neither of them had been involved in any of the intil incidents, unless you counted Vret's indiscretion in the cafeteria that one time. Neither of them had seen a shakeup in the transfer schedule for Thirds.

CHAPTER TWELVE
ACCELERATED DEVELOPMENT

Four days before his transfer, Vret was sitting in the cafeteria staring at a bowl of stew and waiting for Joran Nah, deliberately early to recoup his reputation as best he could at this point.

"I hear you're up for Second now."

Vret turned and found Iric Chez behind him, carrying a tray with a glass of iced trin and a salad. "Not that I've heard," answered Vret.

"When they start on you, they don't give you any warning. I'm almost finished with the Accelerated Development program for First Qualification now, and they did the same thing to me again. No warning. But you can back out, you know. It's voluntary."

"Why would I back out?"

"Well, they put you through hell the last three days before your transfer. And it doesn't always work. Sometimes you go through all that for nothing."

"All what?"

"Exercises to stretch and develop your systems." Chez leaned closer and whispered, "I'll bet that's where Blissdrip gets all those gruesome ideas!"

Vret couldn't make out whether the Second was kidding him or not, even though Chez was in Need. "If it's that bad, why do it? Isn't being a Second enough for you?"

"Afterwards, if it does work, you don't have to study as hard to learn all this stuff, so there's more time to read you know what. I get another session day after tomorrow, and just in time, too. I haven't done half the changeover pathology reading for weeks because of all the long posts and I have to pass that course! But who can read textbooks when there's something so much more important waiting?"

Just then Joran Nah arrived with a tray heaped with food and Chez went off to help his Donor carry a tray.

The next day, three days before he and Sumz were both scheduled for transfer, Vret arrived at Kwotiin's vriamic functionals room ready for his workout only to find that Kwotiin wasn't there and neither was Joran. In their place were three strangers and Saelul Farris.

One of the strangers, a Gen stepped to Vret's side, grabbing control of the fields. He felt a sigh escape as the nagging thrum of Need abated under the Donor's expert ministrations. *He must be a First at the very least,* thought Vret, *possibly Farris trained.* When Joran's abilities had made no dent in the insistent pulsing of intil he'd suffered since reading that last *Killroom* installment, Vret had thought nothing could stop it. Suddenly, it was gone.

The Farris nodded. "Much better. Vret, although your work has not been top of your class, your improvement lately has prompted your instructors to nominate you to the Accelerated Development track."

Vret swallowed his excitement and allowed curiosity to suffuse his showfield.

"So you've heard of the program? It is entirely voluntary," assured the Farris. "And whatever you've heard, the reality is—worse."

Vret was sure that the man was zlinning him from behind that granite showfield while he was getting absolutely nothing from the Farris. But the way the man said *Voluntary* made it sound very bad indeed. He flipped a tentacle to acknowledge understanding though he felt as if the man were reading his mind. But of course, since he'd never had his mind read, how would he know for sure?

"If you sign into this program, from now until your transfer you will be sequestered in a field controlled environment, your class work suspended. This month, you will work to develop your secondary system capacity. If you succeed, next month we'll focus on your primary system development"

Normally, secondary system development came right after ninth transfer. "During Need?"

"This method is extremely effective and may lead to your opportunity to Qualify Second before you leave Rialite. But you are correct. It is not a pleasant experience, and there are no guarantees."

"Three days?" A lot could happen on the boards in three days. In three days, the administration might raid the boards and discover all the readers—and posters. He was now a poster.

"Three days is a long time when you are working this hard. You must decide now."

On the other hand, here was the opportunity he'd been yearning for. Here was a chance to have a real Tecton career—contribute something meaningful with his life.

Suddenly, he found himself flashing into the Killroom scenario "What Does It Take"—in all nageric dimensions. Torturing Gens to get the satisfaction that spelled life. Without the Tecton, it could become that bad again. And with the huge Sime population in the world now, Zelerod's Doom might be only a matter of months—perhaps weeks—if the Tecton collapsed. Not that it was likely to collapse, not that his efforts alone would make a difference, but Vret knew what side he was on.

But he wasn't getting any closer to Blissdrip, and with his mind dulled by Need, he probably wouldn't until after transfer. And if this program made him faster, maybe he could find Blissdrip.

"What happens afterwards? Do I get Joran for transfer?"

"Probably, but you won't be working with him in this program. And after transfer, you'll be back on your normal class schedule. Next month, we'll see."

Still he hesitated. "What about my room?" Was this what had

happened to Halarcy?

"What about it?"

"My things. Do I keep the same room?"

The Farris looked as if that were the oddest question he'd ever been asked. "Yes, of course. You'll only be gone three days. Your roommate probably won't even notice."

There was truth to that anyway. He hardly ever saw his roommate.

"Vret," said the Gen next to him. "Ordinarily Thirds don't get a chance to enter this program until after their ninth transfer unless they're expected to Qualify First before leaving Rialite, and you don't have the profile of a First. You have earned your instructors' very high opinion of you. You can do this."

"But do you choose to?" asked the Farris.

"Yes," Vret heard himself say with just a hint of repressed horror. "I want to have the skill and ability to serve the Tecton well for the rest of my life."

At that, he felt the Farris drop that impossible showfield and bring his full attention to bear. It only lasted a moment, but Vret felt thoroughly zlinned to his very core and beyond.

"Good, then you'll start immediately. Grig, take Hajene McClintock to Lelange Hall. Grig will be your Donor for this exercise. Use his abilities to the fullest."

With that, the Farris and the Gen with him left. The Gen picked up Vret's books from the table where he'd dropped them and led the way out the door.

Lelange Hall was mostly underground. By the time their elevator had descended four levels, Vret felt a strange sensory deprivation closing in. The Donor beside him, bright fire in the velvet nageric darkness, was the only feature in his whole world.

At last they reached a three room suite where Grig told him he would be living and working. It was painted soft beige and the furnishings were white. They had walked half a mile of corridors to get here. The underground structure had to be huge, but there was absolutely no sense of any other living soul in the whole world.

The next three days whipped by in a slow-motion blur. From time to time he thought surely Chez had been right and this was Blissdrip's source of inspiration. Vret felt as tortured as the Gens in a Killroom. Other times he wondered how his instructors could have been so wrong about his abilities. Then he concluded they had discovered all about the secret boards and this was his punishment.

They worked in two cubicles, the third room being Grig's bedroom. Three channels worked with him, and a constant stream of Third Order Donors presented themselves to have their fields lowered. It wasn't transfer and it wasn't the standard donation from a General Class Donor.

He had to siphon large amounts of selyn into his secondary system, and moments later, push it into a battery.

He had never been good at battery charging exercises, but he knew Seconds had the duty of charging the smaller batteries, not the big ones such as ran the campus computers. This would be a useful skill if he survived.

There were many times he thought he wouldn't. They allowed him so little time for recovery that he stumbled from room to room, reeling with fatigue. Two channels often supported him as he took selyn from the Donors.

After an uncounted number of these exercises, they stopped bringing Third Order Donors, and another channel came and presented a Third's showfield.

Vret knew by that point they didn't trust him. His Need was high, his intil higher, he was deep in recovery, and not fit to tie his own shoes. He was so tired he could barely zlin. They didn't make him stop to eat—which was good because he couldn't have swallowed anything—and they didn't let him stop to sleep—which was also good because he would have had the worst nightmares he'd ever had.

It went on forever.

He kept reminding himself he had volunteered. But he had forgotten to ask what percent of the students died during this training exercise. He was also pretty sure it wasn't doing any good.

The only thing that kept him going was being bathed in the constant attention of a First Order Donor. When Grig was sleeping, others took his place. Vret didn't learn all their names, didn't know the names of the channels who worked with him and on him either, but he was certain he'd know them nagerically if he ever met any of them again.

And then, one fine moment came when it was over. Hanging between two channels, he crept out into the relentless scorching sunshine of what the locals called late spring, and gloried in a cheerful blue sky, ugly green cacti, scraggly, shade-less trees, and realized that though his systems declared him in attrition, while the channels all said he was fine, he had survived.

Two channels and three Donors accompanied him across the pathway to the infirmary, the channels gripping his elbows so his feet barely touched the ground. He'd never been to the infirmary before, but they had set up his transfer with Joran where all treatments would be available to cover any event. They hadn't said what events.

The walk took six and a half minutes, with him staggering whenever his weight came down on his legs. But nobody seemed to notice. Then they were in a large, fancy transfer room.

It contained Joran and his exquisite nager, so Vret didn't much care what else it contained. He did notice though that it had a window, and though the insulation was incredible, that intense nageric silence he'd come to hate wasn't there. It felt like he'd come back to the living world after an indeterminate time in a grave.

"Here he is," announced one of the channels as they all opened a nageric wedge into the cubicle and gently inserted Vret into the room so that he hardly felt the transition into Joran's care. "He performed admirably, but that just means he's more tired than the usual trainee."

His escort deposited him on the transfer lounge where he sat staring ahead wondering why he was seeing double. As his escort withdrew, murmuring to Joran and handing over several sheaves of printouts, the ambient in the little cubicle dimmed and softened and ebbed into being just Joran and one channel and her Companion, wrapped in a shimmering nageric fog of not-there-ness.

A few days ago, Joran's intense brightness had seemed like a wall of dazzling cascades, impenetrable sheets of selyn fields. Now, after being marinated in the First Order Donors' fields, Vret zlinned Joran's nager as dull. But still the Donor's field wrapped him in peace. Here at last was a Donor who was intending to serve him in transfer.

Finding he'd drifted hyperconscious and was only zlinning his surroundings, he groped for duoconsciousness. Amazingly, considering his state of Need, he was able to get his eyes and ears working again. *Maybe I'm not really in attrition.* That was a frightening thought. It meant it was possible to feel worse.

The channel was saying, "...so you don't have to be concerned about Qualifying. He can't make it this time."

Blearily, Vret asked Joran, "Is there something wrong with your nager? You're not as high field as you were."

Now that is a nonsensical thing to say, he thought, but he was so tired he couldn't care very much. He just wished the channel would leave so he could have his transfer.

Joran hitched up on the edge of the lounge to sit beside him. "Actually, I'm much higher field than the last time I saw you. I've been working with Firsts in Need."

Vret scrutinized the channel and Donor in the corner, a truly high field First Order Gen, and compared with Joran.

The channel likewise zlinned her Donor and then Joran. "Yes," she said, "Joran is considerably higher field than the last time we met—what? Three days ago?"

"Something like that," said Joran, his attention centered on Vret. "Are you two leaving or monitoring?"

"Monitoring," answered the channel.

"What did I do wrong?" blurted Vret. He thought he'd earned his way out of monitored transfers.

"Nothing," assured the channel. "Standard procedure at this

point. We want a complete record on you."

Well at least she's no Farris. She wasn't going to be reading his mind during his Post reaction.

Vret's internal clock ticked closer to his assigned transfer time. The channel and her Donor were not managing his fields, leaving him to Joran's ministrations.

Drawing a deep breath, Vret reached out a tentacle to encircle Joran's wrist, and the Donor moved to ease Vret back onto the lounge. The tension flowed out of his back muscles and that somehow released his iron grip on himself.

Need blossomed, but he clamped down on his vriamic node in the way that had become a habit when his intil spiked just from reading a story. He forced himself to wait. Joran sat beside him, letting the single handling tentacle remain around his wrist. The Gen wasn't going anywhere. He could wait. Intil obediently subsided and he relaxed his automatic clamp on it.

The channel prompted, "It's time."

Joran slid his hands up Vret's arms and Vret's tentacles curled into a secure grip as Vret made the fifth contact point, lip to lip. Vret drew, and selyn rushed up his lateral tentacles, flowed in sizzling streaks into his chest, through his vriamic and this time—oh, blessed wonder of wonders, *this* time—it flashed into his primary system and washed through his whole body like golden nectar warmed to exquisite perfection.

And then it was over. Joran waited and Vret dismantled the contact, holding his breath, savoring the moment of perfect balance and vibrant life. And with his next breath the post reaction hit.

He was aware of the channel and Donor still standing off in the corner, but he couldn't stop the tide of emotion that seized him. *What if they find out?*

It was everything that had happened to him for the last two weeks coming in on him all at once. Every emotion he hadn't been able to feel when hearing of another intil incident, or having another failure in one of his schemes to locate Blissdrip, or knowing that if he couldn't flush out this writer, they would either be caught or have to confess—all of it washed over him in one gigantic tidal wave.

He felt as if he were standing off to one side watching himself writhe under Joran's protective fields. He twisted from side to side, wanting to run, to hide, to curl up and be a rock. Sweating in fear, guilt, embarrassment, panic, he identified frustration and despair too. It all warred for the upper hand, slamming him back and forth to the extreme in a dizzying whirl.

The wild emotional experience had no name other than just post reaction because it was never the same twice. *Sometimes you know what to expect—sometimes it hits you blindside because you have no idea some situation during the last two weeks had really meant that much to you.* Vret could do nothing but hang onto his Donor and wail out his anguish and terror until the incredible surge abated.

As the world came back into focus, he heard Joran urging, ". . . there, now hang on tight." His nageric grip was gentle but firm. "Just come duoconscious, focus on me, zlin me. You're going to be fine now."

Slowly, the internal storm abated.

Most of the time his Donor had coaxed and pleaded and even ordered him to talk about what he'd felt. As a student, he had no privacy at all. Ordinarily, or so he'd been taught, the content of a bad post reaction was politely ignored by a Donor, unless the Donor was a therapist trained specifically to deal with such things.

Joran just held him, washing him in kind emotions and giving him something solid to hang onto. *Maybe I've earned a new privilege.*

At some point, unnoticed by Vret, the channel and her Companion had departed. As he caught his breath, he asked Joran, "When did they leave?"

Joran flicked a glance around the room. "They're gone!" He grinned at Vret. "I have no idea. I had my hands full."

"I'm sorry. It's never hit me like that before." Then he had to say, "I've never had a transfer like that before! Joran, that was incredible."

The Donor was still smiling. "I'm glad it was good for you. After all that, you deserved a good transfer."

"It was more than good." But he knew he hadn't Qualified Second. Joran's nager seemed hardly diminished by the selyn he'd taken.

"Maybe, if you put that in your report, they'll assign us together for your Qualifying transfer."

"You'd be willing to do that? That wasn't very good for you this time."

Joran chuckled, "There's always a next time!" The Donor got up from the lounge and went to the little desk in the corner. "There's cold trin tea on the counter if you want some. I iced it down before you got here. Let's get these forms done so you can get on with your post assignment."

Ilin! It was the first time he'd thought of her at all in three days, and the first time he'd thought of her *that* particular way in weeks. The flashing vision of her warmed him all the way down to his toes.

"I have a post assignment again? When will they let me choose a woman for myself?" *Maybe they assigned me to Ilin? She's post, too, by now.*

Vret rolled to his feet. His body was glowing, replete with selyn, but oddly shaky, muscles aching, as if still in recovery from some horrendous functional. *I had transfer while in recovery. How weird.* His only desire now, though, was to find Ilin.

"Oh, you'll have the whole rest of your life for that. Right now they want you to get experience, and each of these Post Assignments you've had was to teach you something, no?" Joran twirled on the stool and handed Vret a salmon colored card.

"Yes! And I'm ready to use that knowledge." On Ilin. *Sex with the most beautiful woman in the world.* He had read about some things two channels could do in bed that he really wanted to try.

He looked at the card. It wasn't Ilin. It was some woman he'd never heard of before. A Second Order channel.

Disappointment thrumming through his veins, Vret took a glass of chilled trin tea over to the desk and began on the forms. This month they had given him three more forms to fill in. He stared at them, vaguely remembering them from some course or another. But he had to read them and struggle to remember, even ask Joran about the abbreviations before he could complete all of them.

And while he worked he felt the insistent aching, yearning, building. By the time he finished the forms, he was a lot more willing to go meet this strange new woman. Ilin would probably have an assignment too. It was only for three days, then maybe they could get together.

As he said goodbye to Joran he had to add, "And I've never been this Post before. I just have to thank you again."

"That's good to hear. It's what a Donor works for."

"Joran, I do have one more question. Maybe you don't know the answer. I know they don't tell you everything either. But was I assigned to you because they planned to get me into this accelerated track, or was I assigned to the accelerated track because I just happened to have drawn you as a Donor this month?"

The Gen sat down on the stool again frowning in thought. "I don't know and I'd never have thought to connect the two events. Lots of Thirds are inducted into the accelerated track, though not all do as well as you did, and very few get to continue. But they're not usually given Second Order Donors for transfer after the first session."

Not after the first session? What would it take to make a Third require a Second Order Donor then? Now there was an ominous thought.

But Vret had no patience left to question the Gen. "Well, that's interesting. Joran, it's been terrific working with you, and I hope we'll have another chance. The sooner the better. And maybe next time I can do a little better by you than I have this time." He grinned and they both knew he meant a Qualifying transfer.

Vret glanced at the post assignment card and took himself off to his appointment, whistling through his teeth and thinking of Ilin Sumz. He knew the post assignment trainers always wrote up detailed reports on their encounters which also included extensive instruction in the pathologies that could develop in various channel sub-mutations without healthy sex during post-syndrome. But this time he had done his reading assigned last month.

His feet bounced on a cloud of pure strength and nothing, no matter how dire, seemed too much for him to handle right now. He was in the grip of an unprecedented post-syndrome optimism, possibly to the point of complete insanity. But the pre-transfer depression was likewise a kind of insanity and just had to be ignored.

I'll deal with the whole Blissdrip mess tomorrow.

* * * * * * *

The day after his transfer, Vret was on his way to the Memorial to the One Billion where he was to meet his post assignee and attend a shiltpron concert celebrating the anniversary of the first performance of the Unity Anthem by Zhag and Tonio, the world renowned duo who had revolutionized popular music. The performers today were just students, but he'd heard they were good and he didn't want to be late. He looked forward to a very pleasant after-concert evening.

The sun was setting, shadows elongating, and the scorching temperatures abating. In the desert dryness, it was actually chilly in the shade when the breeze picked up. He was augmenting slightly as he came to the path between the side door of Lelange Hall and the front door of the Infirmary mentally calculating his selyn budget for augmentation.

He'd be penalized grade points if he didn't use enough, but it would be worse if he used too much, so he was concentrating.

As he passed the No-Augmentation sign that forbade Thirds younger than nine transfers to augment on this section of the walkways, he absentmindedly dropped to a fast jogging pace and fixed his attention on the far end of the non-augmentation zone, figuring distance and time to the Memorial Hall.

Several things happened simultaneously.

Joran Nah, carrying three metal gas cylinders and an unbound pile of printouts, emerged from the wide, air-curtained Infirmary door, turned about when someone called to him from inside and walked backwards onto the path as he shouted an answer.

The door from Lelange Hall opened and a troop of First Order channels and Companions emerged, surrounding Iric Chez, clad in one of those ubiquitous paper suits. Chez was walking on his own, which, if Vret understood what he was zlinning, was a miracle in itself. Chez was so low field he was nearly unzlinnable, and it wasn't the showfields of his escort that masked his presence. He was likely as near attrition as Vret had been after his Development session. And he was on his own feet.

Turning about to continue on his way, Nah saw the approaching group and moved to clear the walkway to the infirmary. But he spun off balance, fumbled and dropped all three cylinders and the printouts which fanned out in a long fluttering strip of paper tangling in the breeze.

Vret, speeding up to get out of the way of the approaching Chez and his escort, leaped over the rolling cylinders but without augmenting, couldn't clear the expanding mass of paper.

Feet slipping from under him, he fell backwards into Joran Nah who had staggered off balance.

Nah's right foot landed on one cylinder, his left skidded on paper, and he went down twisting to avoid Vret who was still flailing for balance and footing on the loose gravel that lined the cactus beds beside the path.

Nah's pale nager exploded with the pain of twisting and sprains. As Nah fell, Vret zlinned the bone break and slice through Nah's skin releasing pumping blood and gouts of selyn.

Too fascinated with zlinning, Vret lost his battle for equilibrium. A huge cactus frond loomed before his eyes, spiky thorns woven with cobwebs. He flung himself sideways to avoid the thorns and fell toward the pavement. The side of Vret's head hit the concrete with stunning force.

The next thing Vret knew, Iric Chez was on Nah and the ambient rang with a bizarre and macabre crescendo of selyn in sudden, rapid motion. But it wasn't just the ambient that rang—sensation extended into Vret, through him, and somehow became his own experience. He was drawing that selyn into the aching chasm of his own system.

Without transition, three of the channels came at Chez from either side and behind, battening the nageric turbulence of the searingly rapid and deep selyn draw.

Vret's awareness of the transfer turbulence in the selyn fields dopplered away. He felt the weight of that dampening force all the way through both his selyn systems, halting selyn movement in a way he'd never thought possible. He was dying. Selyn froze in all his systems.

All at once, Chez went into transfer abort convulsions. Two of the channels pulled him off Nah and pushed him down on the concrete.

Vret felt selyn move in his systems again.

Two of the Donors joined the channels working on Chez. Bucking and grunting, Chez disappeared behind an impenetrate nageric screen.

The other channel, a Farris, was deep into lateral contact with Nah. Selyn had ceased pluming from the broken ankle. To Vret's perception, Nah was dead, lifeless, beyond help. Then the other Donor joined the channel working over Nah and even that perception was cut off.

Vret sat up, nursing a crashing headache, trying to keep his showfield neutral while guilt, horror and shock warred with the ghastly suspicion that he'd just witnessed a Killmode attack by a Second Order channel, and the Gen was dead—which shouldn't be possible unless Chez's anti-kill conditioning had failed.

But Nah had given Vret transfer yesterday without being high field for a Second. Chez had been near attrition, surely needing more selyn than Nah had. Vret wished he'd paid more attention in accounting class. *Was that a Kill-abort backlash that sent Chez into convulsions?*

People came rushing out of the infirmary doors, dashing about, shouting orders to cordon off the pathway making the ambient into a dense soup of nageric communication and imposed hush. Stretchers, neck braces, and other equipment appeared. And finally a channel stopped beside Vret to zlin him deeply. The whole thing had happened in much less than a minute.

"No concussion. You're fine," she assured him. "Just sit right there and don't move while we get these two inside."

Two?

Nah was stirring, breathing weakly. Vret saw blood and selyn start to pump out of the wound again, and this time the Farris channel moved down to put hands and tentacles over the selyn plume which instantly diminished.

He's alive! It wasn't a Kill.

He clung to that through the next three hours of confusion and frantic action. As more channels descended on the scene, Nah was whisked away on a stretcher, Vret was moved into the infirmary waiting area on his own feet, but with two First Order Donors around him like a bandage, cutting off his view of the world.

He was sitting in the waiting area just inside the infirmary doors, still stunned and in shock, filling out forms when Chez was brought in on a stretcher, barely conscious, breathing irregularly, and still surrounded by three First Order channels and their Donors creating an impenetrable wall around him.

But he's alive and he didn't actually Kill. Vret clung to that thought as they moved him to an insulated treatment room. He finally managed to ask someone to tell his assignee why he wasn't at the concert, and the renSime clerk said she had been informed and they'd arranged for him to miss classes for the rest of the day, too.

Then a strange Farris channel came to examine him putting him through all kinds of tests he'd never had before as if he were the injured one. But nobody would answer his frantic questions.

There was a muttered conference outside his cubicle that he couldn't hear, and zlinning was impossible. They left him there for over an hour.

He had nothing to do but replay the whole thing in his mind again and again, seeing it was all his fault. He had introduced Chez to the secret boards, and Chez was a lot deeper into Blissdrip's spell than Vret had been during his own Accelerated Development session.

Vret had felt the wildly spiking intil surges that had started from reading *Killroom* continuing and getting worse during that whole session. He had fought them, and somehow the instructors hadn't suspected anything was wrong with him. But he knew it was.

Chez had to have experienced those intil surges too, but maybe he hadn't fought them down as hard.

Vret couldn't take any blame for Joran Nah's low field. The Donor had simply been doing his job. But Vret had not been paying enough attention to where he was jogging. He should have augmented to leap clear of the dropped cylinders and papers. Because he had obeyed that minor rule, he had slammed into Nah, breaking his leg. He hadn't been paying attention. He hadn't been thinking.

After all the reading of *Aunser* and *Killroom* and the affect of Gen pain on a Sime in Need, Vret knew he had caused Chez's attack by slamming into Nah.

He was more and more sure that he'd witnessed an actual Killmode attack. If Nah hadn't been so low field, hadn't been in such pain, stunned from the accident, he'd have been able to defend himself. Even low field, he might have fended off the attack until the channels could help.

If, if, if and *if*, was all he could think. By the time two channels and their Donors came for him, he had convinced himself he was to be taken away as a prisoner.

But they took him to another room in the infirmary, on the fourth floor. It was a corner room, overlooking the gymnasium and the large outdoor pool where channels were training for underwater rescues.

The room was designed around two large sofas that faced each other, with chairs set into semi-circles at the ends of the sofas all in soft blues and yellows matching the insulating drapes. There was even a vase of fresh flowers.

Vret curled down onto the chair they indicated and dropped his face into his hands, tentacles gripping his hair as if to pull it out by the roots. "I'm sorry!" he cried unable to take the silent tension any longer. He broke into an unexpected sob. "I'm so sorry!"

"Whoa there!" said one of the channels. "You have nothing to be sorry for!"

After that astonishing announcement the door opened again, and Saelul Farris entered alone. The granite nager was in full evidence as he came in, but then as the door closed behind him, it faded to a kind of glass effect, sparkling with reflections but revealing his primary field.

"Vret, I am so sorry about what has happened to you."

All the whirling vortex of emotion that had built up in him for the past hour slammed to a halt in utter amazement. "Nothing happened to *me*!" he protested.

The Farris came to sit in the chair at right angles to where Vret was, silent as if pondering Vret's pronouncement. The four others in the room took places on the long sofas, facing each other, the ambient reshaping itself about the expert field manipulators until Vret sat in a bubble of calm, marveling at the affect.

Farris attention settled onto Vret and the silence stretched until Vret realized he was being asked to lower his showfield. Finally, clumsily, he did.

"That's better," Saelul breathed and sat back as if relaxing for the first time that day. "Vret, I want you to tell me exactly what happened, what you saw and what you zlinned, and what you did as a result."

By now Vret had organized and memorized the litany of his sins, and he recounted the events and his moves exactly. He only left out his supposition about the reason for Chez's hair-trigger condition. That wasn't his secret to give. Strangely though, when he had finished, he had listened to his own words, and somehow the growing anguish over his own guilt was stilled.

"So you made an error in judgment by not paying enough attention to zlinning your total surroundings, but First Year channels do that often. When it was clear you were moving too fast to stop before stepping on the dropped items, you made a second error in attempting to jump over them without augmenting to clear all of them. And that's the full extent of your guilt here. You obeyed a rule that common sense required you to break, and didn't augment when you should have."

"Isn't that enough? See what happened because of me!"

"Had it not been for the decisions and actions of others synergistically exacerbating the results of your actions, there would have been no injuries. Had that been the case, what discipline do you think should be imposed for your carelessness and thoughtlessness?"

The Farris nager was still crystal clear and Vret thought he zlinned no ulterior motives, and there was no trace of anger.

Honestly he answered, "I'd say the usual reduction in selyn budgeted for augmentation for two weeks, followed by two weeks of extra hours in physical training with emphasis on spatial awareness."

"That seems reasonable. I'll see it added to your schedule. Now with guilt dispensed with, we must address the injury you have sustained, which is mainly psychological."

"Psychological?"

"Vret, a Third in ninth month of First Year should never have to experience a Second Order channel driven into a Killmode attack on a Donor. This experience has changed your life, forever."

"My anti-kill conditioning was damaged?"

"No!" answered all three channels at once. Vret was convinced.

The Farris addressed the other two channels. "Nobody told him?"

The two looked at each other. "I thought...," they chorused and looked at the Farris.

But the Farris was zlinning Vret. "Nobody told you. We've tested all your reflexes and examined your systems minutely. There have been changes, severe changes, because of this experience, but you've sustained no damage. You would have come to this level of experience early in your third year if you'd followed the usual training regimen as a Third. Or if you'd Qualified Second here at Rialite, you'd have been through this in the middle of your Second year. Physically, you have simply come to a greater maturity sooner. However, emotionally this experience may pose some difficulty simply because you are so young."

"So it was a Killmode attack, wasn't it?" Vret's voice sounded hoarse in his own ears and he wasn't sure he was hearing everything the Farris was saying.

"Yes," answered Saelul bluntly.

"It was very—*different*." *It was very horrible.*

"Yes," intoned Saelul Farris and the ambient throbbed with sadness.

"I have a question."

"Which is?"

"Can experiencing intil spikes or living constantly on the edge of intil, even when not in Need, undermine a channel's internal stability?"

"Yes, though the effect is negligible on the fully mature non-junct a year after the anti-kill conditioning transfer."

"Does undermined stability like that make a young channel more vulnerable to the Kill reflex?"

"Yes."

Vret compressed his lips over the confession he wanted to blurt out.

"I see where this is leading," said the Farris, and Vret froze, once again resisting the certainty that his mind was being read.

"Vret, everything we do for you here at Rialite, every rule and every frustrating bit of tedium, is specifically designed to bring you to your own inner strength and stability. We inculcate the strongest possible inner defense against that kill reflex—which isn't a "Kill" reflex at all, but a personal survival reflex.

"As you can't suffocate by voluntarily holding your breath—you will breathe when you pass out—you can't deny yourself selyn until you die of attrition—you will take it regardless of the consequences to anyone. There can be no guilt in that, except the failure to avoid the situation.

"We design each student's schedule to provide opportunities to encounter intil stimulating conditions interspersed with points of rest from such stimulation. That's why you are required to spend time alone in your room each day, resting from such stimulation.

"Each student's schedule is tailored to push their physical systems into the maximum development while seating and reinforcing the anti-kill conditioning.

"The Accelerated Development track is carefully metered to each student's abilities, stressing the developing systems to make them stronger, not to break them. What happened to Iric Chez was not his failure, but that of his escort. They did not protect him quickly enough from the shattered ambient.

"You may rest assured that if you choose to continue in Accelerated Development, you will not be driven beyond your personal limits, and in your vulnerable moments, you will be protected, the more so from the lesson we've learned from the Chez incident. You will leave Rialite having attained your maximum resistance to Gen pain and fear."

So minds can be misread. But it was the information he'd wanted...dreaded. Just reading the *Killroom* stories could do serious damage to a First Year channel's systems.

The Farris zlinned him again, lightly, then cast a smile into the ambient dispelling the gloom. "I think you will come to assimilate this shock and move on quickly. However, there is an obligatory procedure in these cases."

Vret sat up straighter and waited anxiously.

"For the next week, you will attend a therapy session daily. You will talk about your experience, and how it might be affecting your thinking and responses during the day, and dreams and sleep patterns at night. You will watch some films and discuss them. At the end of a week, I'll assess the reports and we'll see where you go from there."

At a shift in the ambient that seemed to dismiss him, Vret rose. "I'm sorry I disappointed you, Hajene Farris."

"Oh, you haven't done that, Vret. Not yet. It's nearly midnight, so I believe your Post Assignment appointment is waiting for you." He checked with the other channels. "We did tell her midnight?"

"Yes, Hajene," said one of them.

CHAPTER THIRTEEN
POST TRANSFER

Keeping his post assignment appointments, doing almost without augmentation, adding the therapy sessions to his schedule and catching up on his course work left Vret in a mad scramble for the next three days.

Oddly, he caught up easily. There were times when it seemed like the world around him was standing still. He seemed to have plenty of time to read and think through what he was learning. And everything was interesting, even the therapy. Chez hadn't mentioned that affect from the Development track exercise.

But the more time he had, the more he tried to do. He kept dreaming up schemes to determine once and for all if Kwotiin had been reading his mind, or was just a good guesser.

Either way, they couldn't afford to let administration get a hint of Blissdrip's activities. *Unless we have to tell them.* And he knew they'd be better off to tell them before they found out by themselves.

In the therapy sessions, he never mentioned the Secret Boards, but somehow, as they covered the ground over and over again, probed and poked at how he felt about what had happened, he came to believe that if Chez had been driven over the edge by reading *Killroom*, it wasn't Vret's fault, but there might be some responsibility he carried, simply because he suspected the involvement.

At any rate, Chez had been sent to a facility that could provide the closely supervised therapy he needed, and all anyone would tell him was that Chez was going to be fine, too. Joran Nah appeared on campus again, foot in a cast, and nager gleaming brighter than the sun though he was very low field indeed.

Vret worked on ideas for finding Blissdrip via his transfer schedule and assuming he was in this Accelerated Development track. But reviewing the *Killroom* episodes by posting date, it just didn't correlate, so he gave up that idea.

Twice he saw Ilin in the distance, racing as fast in one direction as he was speeding in another. And once he saw her with a tall, stocky Gen who couldn't keep his hands off her. He didn't blame the Gen at all.

The third time, he saw her she veered from her course and paused just long enough to pant, "There have been eight more intil incidents and administration is hushing it up. See you in the cactus garden tomorrow at noon!"

"I'll be there!"

And she took a long pull on the bottle of water slung from her waist and was off at a mad dash just short of augmenting.

He crashed down from his idyllic cloud back into the harsh reality that if he didn't solve this problem soon, they would have to confess. His post-reaction was over. Blissdrip wasn't just a distant intellectual threat anymore. He was an immediate and terrifying menace.

Vret had grunted and groaned his way through the torture they called *development* clinging to the thought that this would get him into the Troubleshooters' training program and into a really great and interesting career.

But he'd lose it all if he couldn't solve this problem. And he was out of ideas. Nothing he'd tried had worked.

The following day he rushed through his Augmentation Lab work even though he hardly got to augment any other time. He had read the textbook material for the lab the previous night, but not carefully. He had squeezed out half an hour to catch up on six days of Blissdrip's latest posts.

As a result of not paying attention to his textbook reading, when he raced around the circular track tossing heavy objects this way and that, he barely managed to identify selyn consumption rates, and wasn't always able to identify his own augmentation level. His trainer did seem to note each of his failures, too. Vret did a little better when observing the other students in the class, but not better enough. Still by the time class was over, he thought he was getting the hang of the nomenclature.

He rushed through his shower and headed for the cactus garden at noon. He had a good ninety minutes until his lunch appointment, He didn't want to be late because he would be meeting his next Donor there and wanted to make a good impression.

Ilin was waiting as he jogged up to the bench where they always met. The sun was fierce, but the air so dry he wasn't even sweaty as he dropped onto the bench beside her. "Oh, it's good to see you!"

Her nager flared rosy pleasure and she smiled. He'd lived to see that smile again. "I searched but couldn't find any mention of the intil incidents you heard about."

She sobered. "I know. They're keeping it very quiet but Vret, this morning the incidents spread to the First Year renSimes. According to Morry, the renSimes shouldn't be able to get at our boards at all, even if someone gave them the sign-on password."

He hitched over a little closer to her, basking in her nager. "I'm all out of ideas. If we had a lot more time, maybe I could come up with something." He told her about Chez's incident, just hitting the high points despite her nageric spikes of concern and curiosity. "So he's in therapy somewhere, and might just have to tell all at some point. So as it stands, I think we have to give ourselves up and ask for the administration's help to put a stop to this. This isn't the way I wanted to handle it, but there doesn't seem to be much choice if the incidents are spreading, and somehow the First Year renSimes are reading these boards."

"We don't even know for sure that Blissdrip's—or my—postings are causing these intil incidents," she countered. She outlined what he had told her had happened to Chez, point by point, arguing that he had no indication that the Secret Boards had actually been a causative factor.

"But Morry passed on one more alarming bit of news this morning which makes me think Iric Chez may have had to discuss the Secret Boards in therapy already."

There was a long silence, and he felt her attention gathering and centering on him. His nager responded of its own accord, and Blissdrip was not what he wanted to discuss. But at last he had to ask, "What was that news?"

"Oh." She shook herself and slid a little closer to him. "There was an investigator touring the computer center last night. Well, Morry thinks it was an investigator. It was a Farris Gen who works at the Infirmary. Maybe you know her. Dosry Farris ambrov Inna. Morry says she asked for usage data and seemed to know what she was looking at. He thinks they suspect something about the secret boards. He wants to close them all down tonight. I told him I'd talk to you. Vret, he's serious."

"We have to confess this afternoon then. Closing down the boards would just leave us with absolutely no way of identifying individuals who have been deeply disturbed—maybe even compromised—by all this. You've seen some of the comments on *Killroom*. Iric was talking just like that before this happened."

Her nager darkened to a bleak anguish. "Ever since *Killroom* started there's been this huge schism developing among the readers and even the other writers. And most of the new people are blatantly in favor of Blissdrip's approach. They view it as innocent and realistic—but it's not at all innocent, even though it might be the most accurate and realistic account I've ever found.

"The official historical record is such romanticized nonsense. But this—this exaltation of the Kill, this idea people have been discussing the last few days that somehow owning Gens satisfies Sime instinct...Vret, this is dangerous stuff...."

"I haven't read that discussion. I don't think I want to! And neither do most of the people who were on the boards before Blissdrip."

"We really shouldn't say that name out loud."

She always said that, either out loud or nagerically whenever he mentioned the name. "There's nobody around." And it was true. The paths were deserted.

The ambient was still and peacefully silent—and private. He put his arm around her waist and waited to see how she'd react. His thoughts filled with the lessons taught him by his post-assignment instructors who had been channels. He knew just what to do with a channel. He let his showfield caress hers with just a slight fluttering like the beginnings of a kiss.

She snuggled into the curve of his arm. With effort, she said, "I have a class at two, but I'll be free at four this afternoon. You shouldn't have to go confess this. You didn't start the secret boards, I did. You didn't write *Aunser*, I did. I'll go and—"

"I'll go with you. I bet Morry will want to come too."

"Are you sure you want to do that? They'll send us all away from Rialite—probably to separate places—to finish training. If they'll even license us at all after this."

"It's the end of what would have been lovely careers. But if they're already suspicious, or if Iric has told them anything to make them suspect the boards exist, we're better off getting it all out in the open now. And you're not going into this alone. Until Blissdrip came along, the Secret Boards really were innocent good fun with some historical facts neglected in the textbooks. It was only a little bit beyond what the rules allowed for student boards."

"The facts on the Secret Pens are varnished over for a good reason, you know. All the information is in the historical record—it's just made so dry, factual and impersonal it's too boring to learn. I tried to bring it to life. But to do that I had to get into The Kill and what it meant to people, and how they coped with Killing their own children. That's not stuff to study during First Year—that's obvious to me now. Iric has to be an exception. He just has to be."

"You were only exploring how it might really have happened."

In a very small voice, she said, "No, I think Blissdrip is

telling it like it really did happen. Vret, the Tecton is such an accident. It should never have happened—logically, it should never have survived—*couldn't* survive. When you understand how accidents created it, you see how fragile it was—and still is. If it really did happen the way Blissdrip tells it,—what if people start yearning for the good old days? For real."

"That couldn't happen!"

"Oh yes it could. People don't consider that getting what they want out of life just for themselves, personally, could affect the course of history. But it does. It has. And it will. I should never have started this!"

"History has always been your favorite thing. This isn't your fault. Someone let Blissdrip onto the secret boards—and that is the person to blame. Or maybe Blissdrip himself. But this isn't about blame, this is about preventing a Kill on this campus. I'll meet you at four at Rimon's statue. Tell Morry to meet us there."

"Morry's in a class now. I'll talk to him before my class." She turned to him. "What I regret the most is—not seeing you again. Not zlinning you again. They'll separate us this afternoon. I know they will."

He dropped his showfield and let his primary field engulf her, gradually focusing his attention here...then there...then all the way down there...and murmured the invitation that had been sizzling in his veins for three days, "We have a little time now."

Her eyes closed and he felt her relaxing and accepting his attention, felt the wash of pleasure that reached out to capture him. It was better than he'd ever dreamed.

Laughing, she broke off, and leaped up. "Lelange Hall Private Lounges three or four, whatever's open." And she raced off under lowest augmentation, calling, "Hurry!"

After a moment's hesitation, he was after her, laughing as he ran but careful not to augment, saving his ration for later. The Lelange Hall private lounges were where couples went to be alone. As they wound through campus, only a few people took notice, and they all pretty much figured what the two running channels were up to.

Ilin kept tossing little glances over her shoulder while zlinning her footing, then zlinning him while she watched her step. Vret zlinned the path and watched her body move.

He could have caught her, he realized. But he didn't want to. He wanted to watch her run. It was embarrassing how much he wanted to watch her run—and how precisely everyone who passed knew that.

They plunged into the corner door of Lelange Hall and raced around the corridors, up the stairs to the mezzanine, and around to the private lounges. It was cool in the building and pleasant in the lounges. Number three was vacant, and they shut the door behind them.

There was plenty of space, a nice wide bed, a shelf full of clean sheets. He didn't notice what all else. Books, clothes, everything went into a heap on a bench and he brought her down onto the bed feeling like the most important man who had ever lived.

Distantly, he knew that he was feeling her regard for him, possibly even something she'd learned to do for men. He gave her something he'd learned, that she had redefined the concept beauty for him.

She writhed beneath him. "Oh, that's wonderful! But let's just do this—you and me."

And she did something he knew she hadn't learned in post training. Her nager, showfield and primary, erupted into a burbling foam of bubbles of joy. Here and there he zlinned a touch of dark dread lurking at the edges. But she shoved all that aside and gave him her joy.

He let it kindle a grin in his nager, turning the cells of his body into happiness. He sank down around her, investigating every curve, worshipping her hair, her eyebrows, her ears and finding her lips waiting for him.

In perfect sync, they plunged hypoconscious.

All at once, there existed only touch, her skin a silken caress against his thighs, her tongue moist and smooth—hot within his mouth, her breath scented with cinnamon.

He slid down to explore her breasts, now taking his cues from her breathing. He knew he was hypoconscious. He knew he was not zlinning. Yet some cells deep in his body were wide open to what she was feeling. When she felt it, he felt it. When she didn't, he didn't.

He ran his hands up her sides, around her back, kneading the hard muscles between her shoulders and at the base of her neck with his handling tentacles.

She moaned, and leaned back into his grip, moving her handling tentacles on his lower back probing at the tense spots, then lower still, urging him closer.

He moved up to kiss her closed eyelids ever so gently. He followed his inner urging, caressing her shoulders with his lips, finding the hollow at the base of her neck, the peak of her chin, and her lips.

Each touch sparked fires deep within, kindled fires in her that erupted within him. Her hands moved between them, tentacles guiding him, urging him.

Without hunting or trying they found their rhythm, so perfect, so natural, effortless as it had never been before with anyone. The bright, beautiful, perfect moment flowed over them, engulfing them in concentrated privacy—just the two of them—a rare treasure shared.

The sweet warmth of that moment was cinnamon scented.

Forever afterward that hint of cinnamon would always arouse him.

He was aware of time again. And far too much of it had passed though he wished they could do it all over again.

"Vret, we really shouldn't have..."

"Oh, we really should have!"

"I just want to do that every day now."

"Me too."

"We'll never see each other again after this afternoon," she repeated with throbbing regret even greater than it had been earlier.

"Likely not. But you know the life of a channel working

for the Tecton. Our transfers are in phase here at Rialite, but when we're working—even if we worked in the same Center we wouldn't stay in phase, wouldn't have many chances like this."

She nodded silently, but there was a tear in her nager that didn't quite surface into her eyes. "You're right. But I'm afraid that we've just established a benchmark that nobody else will be able to meet for either of us."

"I'll treasure it."

"Me, too."

CHAPTER FOURTEEN
WORKING THE PLAN

They met Morry in the very welcome afternoon shadow of the colossal statue of Rimon Farris that stood before the administration building steps. He looked just like Saelul Farris. But then all Farrises had that look.

The moment they walked up, hand in hand, Morry grinned at them. He tossed his brown hair back with a shake of his head, and gave them a tentacle gesture of triumph.

"We should get this over with," said Ilin. Guilt and resignation suffused her nager.

"I don't know why we can't just close down the boards, erase everything, and forget it ever happened," said Morry. "Do we really have to do this?"

Vret explained that it's no solution if they get out of it and leave trouble behind. "The people who have been attracted into this by Blissdrip are in serious trouble. Some of them could become time bombs that could blow up, under stress, years from now because of this experience during First Year."

Vret explained he had learned that from the reading assigned by his therapy group leader, then had to explain what he'd seen Iric Chez do. What would be harmless for a full adult could be devastating to a First Year Sime. And channels were peculiarly more vulnerable even than renSimes to certain types of stress while being nearly impervious to things that would destroy a renSime's equilibrium.

Morry paced around in a circle rubbing the back of his neck, then faced them. "So Iric has this mark on his record now?"

"But most of the others on the boards don't," said Vret. "We can't abandon the ones who need help to avoid that fate or worse. You don't have to go in there with us if you can't help the administration solve this problem."

Morry didn't understand how some amateur stories could have such an effect, so Vret and Ilin took turns filling him in on some of the postings to the comment board as a few people had come to espouse the junct philosophy of life that Iric had been toying with. "So you see, there are two kinds of people here, and we owe both of them equally. We can't let this—" Vret broke off a bright sizzling idea flashing out of the depths of his mind.

"What?" asked Ilin.

Several passers-by stopped to zlin them. Vret reined in his nager and waved cheerily until onlookers lost interest.

"Two kinds of people," repeated Vret. "—innocent ones being dragged into trouble and ones who are opting to head into trouble and lure others with them."

Morry's eyes fixed on Vret, head cocked to one side as he zlinned. "But the innocent ones are in trouble too, you said, conditioning being undermined almost as it forms."

"I think there's a dividing line," said Vret. "Those who find raising intil reading about the Kill to be just fun, denying the danger they will put their Gen friends into by doing this to themselves during First Year and undermining the stability they'll one day depend on. And those like us who were involved in the secret boards when it was just historical puzzle stories with a bit more frank description of the Kill than allowed on the regular public story boards."

"Yes, I see your point," said Morry. "The former should be brought to the administration's attention. They must have more help than we could give them. And we're not equipped to judge who needs what kind of help. But the latter, the original members of the boards, they'll—we'll—be punished for what these new people have been doing. We'll all be lumped together, and we shouldn't be."

"That's my idea," said Vret. "If we could get a message to the original people, and anyone who has spoken up on the comment board against Blissdrip's endless dwelling on Killbliss as if it were a great mythical grace denied to us modern citizens—we could separate out the innocent and let the administration find the boards, and deal with those who have to get help."

Ilin shook her head. "Morry's right, you and I don't have what it takes to judge people, to decide who really has been adversely affected all on our own recognizance."

Vret thought about that. "Have you been? Adversely affected?"

"I think so."

"Have you ever said so on the comment boards?"

"Well, I've posted a few times that *Killroom* didn't seem healthy to me because it raises intil just reading it. A few people agreed, but more said I was jealous of a better writer, and that it was all just good clean innocent fun and that I take everything too seriously."

"And," said Vret, "there have been a number of posters who explained and supported the junct attitudes. What do you think of their ideas?"

"I think they're wrong. I think they're dangerous. I think the older ones are infecting younger channels here with some very bad ideas. But it's not the ideas that are the real problem. It's the emotional lure powering those warped ideas. Older people wouldn't be so—susceptible."

A few hours ago Vret would not have dared ask his next question point-blank. But now he felt he knew her ever so much better. "Do you find your intil rising when you read the *Killroom* episodes?"

"Yes, of course, don't you?" she returned astonished.

"And what do you think of that?"

"I think it's horrible that reading about torture of Gens can do that to me. I hate it."

"But you read more of it anyway?"

"Yes."

She didn't offer any excuses—no 'but I have to because I'm writing this stuff' and no 'I'm responsible for the boards.' Just plain yes. Vret admired her for that. He wasn't that strong.

"And that's why you think it's bad?" asked Vret, pursuing his original thought.

"Yes."

"There! You see? That's the dividing line. That's how we tell 'us' from 'them'."

"I don't understand," said Morry.

"We all read this stuff. We all get an intil charge out of it. Some of us think that's a good thing. Some of us think that's a bad thing. We're all having the same experience, but we have different opinions of that experience. I think that whether this stuff is doing us any harm depends on just that one thing— whether we approve or disapprove of our own reactions to it."

"Who could disapprove of satisfying Need? You'd have to be suicidal to think like that," argued Morry.

Vret explained, "It isn't reading about The Kill or striving to understand the old junct lifestyle that's bad. It isn't raising intil while reading a story that's bad. The problem comes from what you're willing to do to assuage that intil. The problem comes from what you are willing to do to survive. What personal satisfaction will you give up to safeguard others from your Kill reflexes? What will you do to avoid being pushed over the edge like Iric was?"

"People don't think that what a single person does for fun changes the course of history," said Ilin, paraphrasing herself from earlier. "But it does."

"Yes, exactly. That's where I got this idea. We're willing to give up our fun, the Secret Boards, simply because others might have their conditioning compromised by these stories."

"So tell us the idea!" demanded Morry.

Vret gestured with three tentacles, *listen,* "First, Bilateral posts that question, 'What are you willing to do to survive? What price do you put on your own life?'—maybe in an *Aunser* installment and on the comment boards, 'Does what you do for pleasure, and to sustain your life, matter to the course of history? And does the course of history matter to you?' and discuss how *Killroom* causes us to raise intil, and whether that might be contributing to the intil accidents being investigated around campus.

"Second, we make a list of who responds and how. Yes, I know some people don't read the comment boards—I don't think Blissdrip does. People who've never posted any stories or comments—well, I hate to say it, but I think we just have to pick out those who were on the boards before Blissdrip signed on, and let the latecomers be lumped in with those who need help.

"Third, and this is where Morry has to tell us if this can work—we create a board post that will appear on both the story and the comment boards, that can be seen *only* by those we have chosen. When they log in they'll see not the usual boards, but just our post. And we tell them admin is onto us and they should sign off and security-erase anything they have from the boards.

"Fourth, once everyone is off, Morry stops trying to prevent administration from finding the boards. Then just let them handle it."

"I don't like it," chorused Ilin and Morry.

Vret's shoulders slumped. "I just thought of it. It probably needs some fine-tuning."

Ilin said, "It seems to be you're saying anyone who agrees with us is virtuous and guiltless, but anyone who disagrees with us is trash not worth saving. Their careers are on the line here, too, you know. What makes us better than them? I think it would be better to just shut the boards down than to set ourselves up as judges."

Morry added, "A given user might have more than one nickname registered. Digging around, I've found a couple who do, or so it seems."

"I didn't know you could do that," said Vret.

"You can, and so some people you might want to spare the full force of Tecton censure might not get your message if they logged on with only one identity that day and it was the identity we didn't send the message to. Of course, if they logged on with both identities, they'd get the message twice."

"So it is possible to make a message like that? That can be seen only by selected individuals when they log on?"

"Yes, or rather it'll be seen by selected nicknames if you can give me a list. It'll be touchy, but I should be able to do it without anyone noticing—but just this once." He zlinned each of them in turn, catching their worry. "And yes, there are a lot of people who are better with a mainframe than I am. And the admins have tools I don't. Maybe they can trace the users on the secret boards. But maybe not. Maybe these people you're about to hand over should be identified—and won't be. I just don't know."

"Neither do I," admitted Vret.

"I'd be a lot more confident," said Ilin, "if I could meet these people in person. Sometimes you can tell a lot about a person...."

"Not," interrupted Vret, "if you're a Third and they're a Second or First. You know we've probably got a good number of Seconds and Firsts reading these stories."

"There could be Gens, too," said Morry.

They both turned to him in shock.

"Well, if the renSimes have gotten in, who's to say the Donor-trainees haven't? I don't have any indication in our logs, but I can't rule it out."

Ilin stared at Vret. Vret stared at Morry. Finally Ilin breathed, "What a ghastly thought. I've always been writing just for student channels. There are some things you just don't discuss with Gens."

"Like what it feels like to read about The Kill when it's written so...realistically," agreed Vret swallowing hard in a suddenly dry throat.

After a long silence, Morry said, "I doubt there are any Gens in favor of the junct attitudes being espoused on the boards."

"Distect Gens might be," said Vret worrying. The ambient among the three of them chilled markedly. None of them had ever thought of that. Throughout modern history, the shady underworld organization that called itself the Distect espoused a lifestyle of direct Gen transfer for every renSime on the theory that the result of any Sime/Gen interaction was entirely the Gen's responsibility. If a Gen died under a Sime's tentacles, it was the Gen's fault, and the Sime was held blameless.

But about thirteen years ago when Laneff Farris ambrov Sat'htine had discovered how to tell Sime from Gen before birth, events had conspired to bring the Distect out into the open and they were no longer the menace they once had been.

Ilin decided, "If there's any clandestine Distect involvement behind Blissdrip's supporters, then we definitely have to hand this over to the administration. Now wouldn't be too soon." She eyed the building behind them.

"Yes, it would be," said Vret, "because there are a lot of people involved here who don't deserve to have their careers ruined."

Morry asked, "How do you know the Tecton would treat everyone involved the same? Surely they...?"

Vret laughed. Ilin joined him.

Morry thought about it. "I see your point. Despite all the progress toward dissolving the Territory borders recently, the Tecton is still a very conservative bureaucracy with almost no flexibility in its rules. You don't get an out-Territory license with any blemish on your record at all."

Without an out-Territory license, you don't get into the Troubleshooter's training either.

Ilin added, "And your Tecton service record is more important than you as a person." She turned to Vret. "What if we make a mistake? What if we let someone go who should be in a medical facility? Or someone who's involved in some renewed Distect conspiracy and invading our little hobby space to recruit for them?"

"Do we know anyone," asked Morry thoughtfully, "who can be trusted...who's a First?"

"Any student who's a First already would probably be a Farris," said Vret glumly.

"Or maybe a Tigue," added Ilin. "What are you thinking, Morry?"

"In our targeted message, instead of telling people to sign off the boards and hide, maybe we should call a meeting, zlin and test the ones who respond, at least try to be sure there are no obviously unstable people we are turning loose to become a problem later. Yes, that would be setting ourselves up as judges, but this mess is our problem and we have to take some responsibility."

Vret looked at Ilin and she gazed back somberly.

Morry added, "It's too bad I couldn't get us the transfer assignment records. If we couldn't find Blissdrip from them, we might have been able to figure out who on the boards are Firsts."

"And if there are any Gens among us," added Ilin.

"But it can't be done at my level of clearance," said Morry. "Private medical records are just that, private. They are open only to those who are involved."

"Here's an idea," offered Vret. "Suppose we post this secret message to our selected people and tell them to come to a meeting. A few people who should be there will have classes or something, but we'll make the meeting long enough that everyone can get there for a while. And we'll talk to people until we find a First we can trust who can help evaluate the Seconds and other Firsts."

"That's pretty thin, as plans go," said Ilin.

"I know."

"It could work," said Morry. "The only First you could trust would be one who's on the boards."

"So how long do we have?" Vret asked Morry. "You said they're probably onto us and we should shut down tonight. But this is a complicated plan. It'll take days to get ready."

Morry scrubbed his face with his hands and turned to pace away from them, thinking. He stared up at the granite statue of Rimon Farris, the founder of the House of Zeor, and the First channel. He sighed a few times. Then he walked back to them. "You're asking for a month, maybe a month and a half, aren't you?"

"I wouldn't think it would take that long," protested Vret. "Ten days, maybe?"

Morry countered, "Where are you going to hold this meeting for several dozen people—and administration won't be curious?"

"I hadn't thought about it." He pointed to the colonnaded open space around them. "The rotunda?"

"No," Ilin said. "Morry's right. To get away with this, we need a cover story—a gathering we could normally sponsor for some ordinary purpose, but that we could keep to invitation only. And it'll take time to set that up."

Vret shook his head. "This whole thing is too elaborate. It'll never work."

"Vret," said Ilin, "do you believe that each and every individual is important to the course of history? Do you believe that some of the people we're trying to save could eventually contribute something crucial to the Tecton? Do you believe in the Tecton and all it stands for?"

She'd thrown Vret's own words back at him and he knew he deserved it. But the whole situation unnerved him, and he tried to articulate his worry. "We're standing here trying to out-fox the Tecton, to subvert the rules and escape its penalties." He looked up at the statue of Rimon, wondering if there ever really had existed such a person. "What a place we chose for that!" But his mind replayed Saelul Farris quietly scolding him for not breaking a rule when circumstances called for it.

Ilin looked up at Rimon, too. "It has always seemed to me that the people who shaped the world we live in today had the courage to do what was right, no matter what custom or law said. This is the same sort of situation—well, on a much smaller scale. I got these people in trouble, and I'm willing to take a risk to get them out, and to get help for those I can't help. It's going to cost me. But that's the price of living with myself."

Vret said, "One thing I learned about history from you. It was made by people who had to act, even though they weren't sure, didn't have the authority, and knew they didn't know what they were doing. According to one of the myths anyway, Rimon was in First Year when he changed the world."

"That sounds like us," allowed Morry.

"So," said Ilin, "if it takes another month, or more, can you give us the time?"

"The truth is I don't know. We could get caught. One of those intil accidents could become a Kill. Look how close Iric came to that, and the reason it didn't happen had nothing to do with Iric's or Joran's will, values or conscience. It had to do with the training, skills, hard won internal stability of the channels who aborted Iric out of it. If Blissdrip's posts are causing this year's class of channels to be unable to attain that kind of internal stability, where will the Tecton be?"

"Maybe they're not being caused by us," wished Ilin.

"But I do have some ideas for misdirecting the searchers," allowed Morry. "The faster you can make this happen, the better."

"I'll write up the story and discussion posts tonight," said Ilin. "I think we can do this in a week or two."

"I'll set up a database and log the responses," agreed Morry. "I have a list of the board users at the point where Blissdrip joined. I'll set up delivery for your special post."

"I'll see about a meeting place and an excuse," said Vret. "Right now I haven't a single idea, and I'm due at an accounting class." And after that he had a Language class where they were reading and comparing three versions of a play purportedly written in the archaic Genlan, but rumored to be a translation of an Ancient masterpiece. He much preferred Math where they were hand calculating algorithms to duplicate some tables found in an Ancient text.

If ever we get out of this mess, I'll never even look at another historical novel.

* * * * * * *

Ten days later, both Ilin and Vret went through turnover. Vret was beginning to get used to it, and the consequent loss of a sense of independence when his Donor for his next transfer showed up at his room and essentially moved into his life.

But it wasn't so bad this time. Ever since his last transfer, Vret had been thinking and moving faster somehow. The world just seemed easier to cope with, so he was able to get a lot more done in a short period of time.

The effect lasted through turnover and into Need. He scraped up enough time to research their prospects for holding a private meeting in public. It turned out it wasn't nearly as difficult as it had sounded at first.

He found they could reserve the Rialite campus Memorial To The One Billion for any meeting purpose as long as it was open to anyone who wanted to come. He could arrange to have the hall assigned to them from early evening all the way through midnight. And it was easy to work up a program boring enough that few would actually come, and most would be eager to leave early.

Vret only had to ask his Accounting teacher, Hajene Lassin, to give a special lecture and she came up with a topic instantly, "Gulf Territory's Failed Experiment: The Tragedy of Direct Transfer" presenting her personal theory of why the Direct Transfer experiment in Gulf had failed, using an advanced calculus method to show it wasn't possible to bring enough Pen Gens to full awareness where they could give transfer to a renSime, nor could Gens from out-Territory, be found and trained fast enough, to do any good on a Territory-wide scale.

In the end, Gulf had reluctantly turned to the same solution Nivet had found, the Secret Pens, and politics had nothing whatever to do with it. It all came down to Accounting. Quantities of selyn, distribution of it, and satisfactory delivery modes. Modeling the selyn system for Gulf during the years surrounding Unity seemed to be her main hobby and she put great enthusiasm into Vret's lecture project.

Vret was certain his meeting would draw only a scattering of attendees besides their invited group.

The lecture would last about an hour, and their message would specify that their own meeting would start an hour after the official meeting ended.

All that was left was to pick a date. He flagged Ilin down one noon as they raced past the cactus gardens.

"And," Ilin said when he told her his brilliant idea, "we can assign a password to get into our meeting in case anyone is really interested enough to stand around and talk for hours."

"Who would be interested?" asked Vret and immediately regretted it.

She just zlinned him while averting her eyes.

"Sorry," he apologized. They were both ten days past turnover and feeling hair-trigger intil surges, especially when their Donors were absent. Right at that moment, Vret was glad he'd be meeting his Donor in a few minutes, even though it meant having to eat lunch.

"Has Morry got his part of the plan in place?" asked Vret when she didn't answer. "When should I reserve the Memorial for?"

"I don't know," she muttered absently, still gazing into the distance, "but you're in that Accelerated Development program again starting tomorrow and I have tenth transfer and my Farris Screening to see if they'll let me try to Qualify Second. That's the day after your transfer. Morry has transfer right after that. He said he'll have the final list for us the day after his transfer and we should allow three days for everyone to see it."

Vret counted days and they set the date. "As I recall the schedule, the Memorial will be available then. I'll check with Hajene Lassin to make sure she's available and put in our reservation—if I hurry, I can get it done before lunch."

With elaborate casualness, Ilin turned to him sweeping her showfield around them as if about to kiss him and muttered, "Look, don't zlin, over my left shoulder. See that tall man with a green tool case studying the purple fruit on that tall cactus?"

"Yes."

"Notice anything strange about him?"

"No. Looks like a typical Farris. But it's not Saelul."

"Zlins like a channel. Carrying what seems to be a plumber's tool kit? How many Farris channels have you heard of who are plumbers?"

"Not many. Could be any number of reasons he's got that tool kit though."

Intil sizzling to the surface, she snapped, "Vret! He's watching us—maybe zlinning, but I didn't feel anything. Wouldn't though."

"You're up for Farris Screening—maybe they're starting early."

"And maybe they suspect something?"

"And maybe they're just guarding the campus against another intil incident." He wasn't feeling too steady himself. If a Gen walked by and stubbed his toe, Vret thought he'd leap as high as the roof of the gazebo in reflex.

"And maybe they're really watching us."

"And maybe if they're not watching us now, they will be if you keep that up!"

Her vriamic control seemed shaky, her showfield laced with so many emotions he couldn't read it, and she was telegraphing her intil.

"I don't see how you can just stand there like a rock," she complained. "That Farris could be reading our minds!"

"If so, then we're caught already and there's no reason to fret and panic. If not, we should work through our plan—it's not much, but we agreed it's our best chance."

"Maybe I am just spooked. I've got a training session to get through—transfer deferral this time. I'm not fit company for a mouse. I'll see you after transfer."

They parted then, and despite his bravado, Vret watched to see which of them the Farris would follow. To his immense relief, the man hefted his case and went in another direction paying them no heed.

Vret summoned all his new and growing vriamic control and

marched himself off to meet his Donor. As eager as he was for that meeting, he took time to call Hajene Lassin, fighting down intil with all his might to keep his voice from shaking.

As eager as she was to do the speech, she wasn't available until four days before Vret's next turnover. He made an executive decision and booked the Memorial for that date. He left a message telling Sumz of the new date so she could tell Morry, and raced to make his lunch appointment, carefully avoiding augmentation.

CHAPTER FIFTEEN
PRIMARY SYSTEM

And the next day he was catapulted headlong into the next phase of his Accelerated Development program.

This time they focused on his primary system, and the whole session was worse torture than anything in the Killroom stories. This was real, not fantasy, real and very personal.

Months ago, he'd thought he'd mastered the technique of the internal shunt—moving selyn from his secondary system to his primary system and back at will. Kwotiin Lake had made sure he practiced shunts until his vriamic nerve plexus just refused to function at all. What more could there be to learn?

Plenty.

While he was in serious, hard Need, Vret's Donor forced his intil into sharp peaks, and just as he was about to flip into Killmode, one of the channels would ram selyn into his secondary system and right through his vriamic nerve, into his Primary.

Every time it hurt worse than death, and every time his Donor pulled him out of it, and they'd go at him again. With each passing hour, he was deeper into Need and the torture became worse and worse.

Oddly enough, the worst part was being full of selyn, to the depths of his primary system, and still feeling that weird, off-kilter, throbbing demand of Need sans intil. He guessed that had to be what a junct felt after taking channel's transfer. It certainly matched the descriptions in *Killroom*.

Sometimes, when his primary system was full and his secondary system nearly empty, his vriamic would knot up in the most horrible spasms he'd ever felt.

One time, he had to wait an entire hour in that condition while the channel-Donor teams worked on someone else in the program who was in worse shape.

Intellectually, he understood that this training was expensive. They carefully chose only those who had a real chance to Qualify Second—or if already a Second to Qualify First—because it took so many trainers to get students through it.

But intellect counted for nothing when he was the one curled into a fetal ball on the transfer lounge, stifling screams of agony.

The three days leading up to his transfer appointment passed in a haze in which he barely remembered there was such a thing as a story posting board, nevermind the complex disaster it had turned into. Even up to his elbows in Farrises, he had no worry they would read his mind—he had no mind to read.

In the end, he finally decided it was better to be full of selyn and in Need anyway than to be empty and in convulsions. But the worst part of the whole thing was that they didn't even let him skip meals. Discipline they called it. He had to learn to care for his body no matter how he felt about it. It was all right with him as long as they cleaned up the vomit and other effluents.

When they led him into the transfer room wearing the fourth disposable paper suit of the day, he didn't even bother to greet his Donor. He couldn't remember the Gen's name, except it was something Tigue. He didn't care. It was a Gen—replete with selyn.

His primary and secondary systems were empty. Once again they'd driven him to the brink of attrition. He knew he was in Killmode, by now, a familiar state. The moment Gen flesh touched his extended laterals, he would rip selyn from the Gen system with savage glee. This time they wouldn't stop him. This time he wouldn't find a channel's tentacles twined around his own instead of the Gen arms he had thought he'd zlinned.

I will not grab this Gen.

He flung himself on the transfer lounge, reaching for the Gen he could zlin but not see—and stopped. Time slowed to a standstill, and the pulsing throb of Need went oddly quiet. He forced himself duoconscious so he could see as well as zlin the font of life that was rightfully his.

"If you would, please...," he asked as quietly and calmly as he could. "I am in something of a hurry."

The Gen grinned and thrust his arms forward, folding down onto the lounge to offer the fifth contact point.

Selyn gushed into his emptiness in rich, royal abundance. He was not conscious of drawing but of receiving a bounty.

Of course, he's a Tigue, a First. The Gen could deliver hundreds of times more selyn than Vret could ever take, and do it faster than Vret could accept. He relaxed and just let the transfer happen. And it didn't stop until he was totally full, nerves ringing with blissful satisfaction.

The First gently wafted him down to hypoconsciousness, aware only of the physical sensations, and unconcerned with the complexities of the ambient nager. Vret floated there for a while, just breathing in deep, painless, free breaths, noticing smells and temperatures, hearing sounds echo from the cabinetry around the room.

In the observer's corner, a channel and Donor he didn't remember seeing before sat at a little table and made notes. The Tigue held out a tall glass of cold trin tea. Sitting up, he took it, swiped it along his cheek to feel the coldness, and drank.

It was the most delicious tea he'd ever tasted. His post reaction was dawning gently within him, fear, anxiety, even dread, coupled to a burning sexual desire. It was the mildest, most orderly post reaction he'd ever had. *Maybe the Tigue reputation is well deserved?*

The channel was satisfied with his performance and sent him off with his Post Assignment card—not, alas, Ilin Sumz—and words of advice. "Get in some heavy augmentation practice now you've got a generous budget for it. It'll work the knots out."

CHAPTER SIXTEEN
CAREFULLY AND PERSONALLY SELECTED

Four days later, the private message was posted.

Greetings!
You have been carefully and personally selected to see this message, either because you are one of the earliest members of this group, or because you have expressed misgivings about the work of Blissdrip and his fans.

Those who started this board see Blissdrip's contributions as a problem so important it warrants partially compromising our anonymity so that we can call a private and confidential meeting.

At this meeting, we will present additional information, make decisions and take immediate actions that will affect all of us.

If you're seeing this message, we require your help. Do not miss this meeting.

You've all seen the notices for a lecture by Hajene Lassin six days from now in the Great Hall at the Memorial for the One Billion. Arrive one hour after the end of this lecture. When all the attendees have gone, we will have our meeting. If you can't make it that early, get there before midnight.

You may be asked for a password. It is: "The Mellow Ambient."

This meeting must remain absolutely private. Do not tell anyone about it, or bring anyone to it. All those who should be invited are seeing this message when they connect to the board. It is necessary that no one else have knowledge of this meeting.

This is for your protection. Your anonymity is at stake—guard it as carefully as we will. Do not give your board identity to anyone at the meeting.

Vret read the message himself, wondering if it was good enough. Would the right people show up? Would anyone tell one of the wrong people?

He alternated between knowing that this was the best way to handle the problem, and fearing he was making the most colossal mistake in history, endangering people just on his own judgment.

That was the day he was first able to meet Ilin on the path since before his Accelerated Development session.

"Vret, you look wonderful—amazingly wonderful actually."

She wasn't looking or zlinning so well, but he didn't mention that because she was very, very clearly post. She had taken her tenth transfer the day after Vret took his ninth so she should not be so haggard.

He grinned as seductively as he knew how and toyed with her nager. "I didn't know it showed, but I've been feeling pretty amazing. Maybe almost dying does something to your perspective, even if it's only a training exercise."

It had certainly done something to his learning rate. He'd whizzed through all his catch-up work and was actually ahead in most of his studies for the first time at Rialite. After three days in a hell-hole, life just didn't seem so hard anymore.

She marveled at him, walking all around him while looking him up and down. "It didn't feel that safe when they did it to me." Her appreciation of his appearance seemed to vanquish her own fatigue. "You saw the message this morning?"

"Yes, and I checked with Hajene Lassen. She's all set to give the lecture, and notes have gone up everywhere about it so we might actually have a couple people there."

"More than that, I'll bet. It's a fascinating topic—anything about the Tigues is riveting and Gulf is legendary."

One arm around her waist, he walked her to the private room they had made their own, and wooed her with details of his transfer with a Tigue Gen.

And they had a wonderful hour all to themselves. It was just so much better with her than with anyone they'd ever assigned him that at the end he complained, "When oh when will they let us pick our own post-syndrome partners?"

"I don't know—I thought we'd get that this month, but I must have disappointed them terribly."

They lay side by side on the wide bed, his foot hooked under her calf, her hand playing with his hair. Vret felt her misery surface from under the cloud of ease and comfort they had generated together. He muttered, "It can't be your fault!"

"It is."

He hitched up on his elbow to look at her more closely. "What's wrong, Ilin? What's happened?"

"I didn't pass my Farris Screening. They're not going to let me try for Second this year after all. They were all nice about it—saying I would have another chance next year, but the deal is that I'll graduate Rialite as a Third." She rolled away from him, whispering into the pillow, "They have no idea how long a year is!"

Her anguish brought up the specter of failure for him, as real and tangible as it could be. It was as if he, himself, had been told he would not be allowed to Qualify. "But you said they were very pleased with your performance in the Accelerated Development work."

"That's what they said!" The dam burst and her silent anguish turned to post-syndrome sobs of unutterable guilt, remorse, and soul-paralyzing grief. It was only three days since her transfer, but she shouldn't still be in this condition.

Vret wrapped himself around her back, scooping her into the crook of his body, stroking her abdomen with his tentacles. In moments, he was grunting out his own sobs and moans of loss and sorrow, of failure, of disillusionment over his own identity. And none of it was his own.

Still, his vriamic control deserted him, his selyn laden systems ran amok, his nager burgeoned outward reinforcing her misery, and her misery came back to him multiplied, fueling his own anguish.

Together they were helpless in the whirlwind of augmented emotion ripping at the center of consciousness.

A tiny thought erupted into Vret's awareness—ever so small a thought at the very back of his mind. *This is why they don't let us choose our post-syndrome partners yet. We can't control this.*

But there was no one to help them. Vret focused his attention inside himself at the spot that had sent him that one little, sane thought. He found a purchase, and began to drag his raging emotions to a stop, to haul it all inside, to bring his showfield under conscious control.

It was almost impossible to make himself want to do it, to believe he could, in fact, do it, to know that he wasn't helpless— but once started, he found he had strength he'd never known was there.

As his showfield finally responded to vriamic control, the escalating storm within her subsided, and they retraced the path they had traveled into this storm.

Sometime later all was quiet for them, within and without. Eyes gritty, throats raw, muscles aching in places that never ached before, they lay nested together, welded together on so many levels he couldn't assess them all.

Eventually, Ilin turned over and Vret moved back to give them both room to lie supine and just breathe. "Vret, what happened?"

"Some kind of emotional positive feedback loop?"

"How did you make it stop?"

"I don't know. Maybe it just wore itself out."

"I feel better. Nothing's changed. My wonderful historical fiction project is a burgeoning disaster that may cost lives. My ambition to Qualify Second is in ashes. There are so many Thirds applying for the Troubleshooter Training that I surely won't be chosen. I'm not going to have any kind of career in the Tecton. I'm such a failure, I'd be better off dead—and my parents will disown me for sure once I get out of here. All that is still true. But somehow it's not the end of the world anymore."

Yes, that about summed it up. "We still have our plan. If it works, we can salvage something from it all."

"Half hour ago, I wouldn't have given it a porpoise's chance on the desert sands. But right now, I can see it does have a chance, and it's the only thing that does." She twisted to sit up and look down at him. "You know what changed my mind?"

He flicked a nageric interrogative and waited.

"Yeah, just that—you're stronger somehow. You're solid. You can do this if anyone can."

He had no idea what she was talking about, but he returned her grin and pushed optimism into his showfield. She nodded and laughed. "Let's get showered. I've got a lunch appointment, don't you?"

The time finally rose into his consciousness, and he swore, "Oh, shen! Let's go!"

* * * * * * *

Six days later, they finally had the meeting They had one whole meeting hall on the ground floor of the Memorial building. The sanctuary with the names of the known martyrs and entire Householdings that had died to bring about Unity was two stories below them.

The hall was a huge space, lit in the daytime by arching windows along the sides, and a translucent domed ceiling. In the dark, it glowed with every sort of illumination, nageric and visible. Pillars, statues of historical figures, and low banisters were arranged to control the nageric noise.

It was a majestic space designed for conducting portentous affairs. To Vret's astonishment, the hall was half full by the time of the first meeting.

Hajene Lassin, a Second Order channel, mounted the high stage at the front of the room with the ponderous deliberation of an old time World Controller about to announce the acquisition of a new Territory, showfield projecting immense gravity of purpose.

She placed her notes on the podium, took a deep breath and announced, "Risa Tigue was a businesswoman who saved a nearly bankrupt Householding from ruin by integrating it into the surrounding junct society's economy.

"Given that inordinate success during her youth, she had no reason to suspect that her methods, designed for the sparsely populated area around her Householding, would not work on the grand inter-Territory scale demanded at the time of Unity.

"Tonight, I will explain why her methods could not possibly have succeeded without the Secret Pens."

The audience came to rapt attention, many poised to take notes, others keenly focused on Lassin's arguments.

Vret lost interest as Lassin went on to contrast this scholar's opinion with that one's, and wove in her own ideas backed up with slides of graphs and equations. She was a good speaker though, spilling words out at the sizzling pace the First Year channels required to keep their interest. And she brought the lecture to a close right on time, offering handouts to anyone who wanted them.

Oddly enough, many people did want them and stood around reading the handouts. The planned hour for clearing the room was not enough. Other people started to arrive and get caught up in the raging arguments about Carre's role in Unity, particularly with respect to the Logan Genfarm. Many of these young channels were from out-Territory, and Tonyo Logan was their hero.

Watching from the sidelines, Vret noted that as the crowds mingled and rolled through one another, many of those who had been there through the lecture were settling down to stay for the real meeting.

In a way this was confusing, and in a way it might turn out to be good. It would seem that the topic had brought together a discussion group that just lingered, and that was the effect they'd been hoping for, a clandestine meeting in plain sight.

The trick would be knowing when all the outsiders had left. Vret figured that would happen as soon as Hajene Lassin and the little knot of enthusiastic students left.

"Morry said there were thirty eight people invited—other than the three of us," Ilin said counting.

"We still have forty-five here, at least."

"Forty-five? I make it forty-four."

Vret flicked a tentacle. "Behind that pillar near the front door."

She moved sideways a bit. "Oh, I zlin him. He can't be renSime? How can you zlin through this soup?"

"RenSime? I don't think so." At least there were no Gens. Morry had worried about that. But still, if there was a renSime who had been invited, they were in bigger trouble than he'd thought. "I'll go find out."

"I'll come, too. I haven't zlinned any Firsts yet, have you?"

"Not sure. There's that tall blond girl over by the mural of the First Contract signing. Real tight showfield. Notice how far around her the ambient seems so smooth?"

"Hmmm. I don't recognize her. We'll check her out later if she stays. She seems to be listening to Hajene Lassin, but not willing to get too close."

With just a few dozen people in a hall designed for hundreds, they had no trouble making their way toward the suspected renSime.

The young man lurked in the foyer of the hall, an area between the front doors and a row of closely spaced pillars. He had placed himself between two pillars, a position from which he could observe but others wouldn't notice his nager.

As Vret neared, it became obvious that the fellow was renSime. "You were right. RenSime."

"I don't—" four strides closer, she said, "Yes, I zlin. Now what?"

"We have to talk to him."

"Saying what? Go away?"

"Pretty much." Vret approached the young man looking him over carefully.

He was medium height, slightly built, brown hair and dusky complexion. He wore a Rialite student uniform in the current summer colors. As far as Vret knew, the renSimes and Gens wore the same basic uniforms as the channels. As he got closer he could see the patch on the sleeve and collar was different, showing he was from the adjacent renSime First Year camp.

And now, seeing them marching toward him shoulder to shoulder, zlinning their combined channels' nager, the fellow was becoming alarmed.

Vret and Ilin simultaneously adjusted their showfields to seem more friendly and reassuring.

"I know I shouldn't be here," blurted the renSime.

"If they catch you, you could be expelled," said Vret. "Rules are there to protect everyone." *Did I really just say that?*

"If you'll help me, 'they' won't catch me until I've done what I came to do."

"And what's that?" asked Ilin.

"I have to talk to the people at this meeting."

"The meeting's over," lied Ilin smoothly, her showfield firm. "The lecturer is just about to leave. She's a Second and she's going to be walking right through here. She'll surely notice you. She's faculty. She'll take immediate action. You had better leave."

The renSime studied them carefully. He obviously knew his disadvantage against two channels. "Are you in charge of this— uh lecture? Or are you just attendees trying to be helpful?"

Vret zlinned Ilin under cover of their showfields. She was

deep in thought but flicked a nageric shrug at him.

"The lecture was my idea," admitted Vret. "I have to stay and close up. But my friend here could escort you back to your camp."

To her credit, Ilin didn't even start at that offer, but scrutinized the renSime closely for his reaction.

He frowned, inwardly gathering up his courage. "I was hoping to discuss The Mellow Ambient with Hajene Lassin." He waited for their reaction.

Vret managed to hide his chagrin but Ilin's showfield broke up enough for the renSime to zlin. He grinned broadly in triumph.

Smoothly, Vret asked, "And why would you want to do that?"

"I want to talk to the board organizers." His eyes strayed to Lassin but his attention stayed focused on them. "I thought since she was giving the lecture—maybe she's...she's not?"

"No, *she's* not," Ilin admitted with such finality it was an admission that she indeed was one of the organizers. "How did you find out about this meeting?" asked Ilin. "You shouldn't have any access from the renSime facility."

"Yes, I know. And I wasn't officially invited to this meeting. That is what I have to talk to someone about. I have information the original organizers of the boards should know and it's urgent—very urgent. It could already be too late."

At that moment the knot of students around Lassin began to move, sticking to her as she smoothly edged toward the front doors.

Vret decided. "Move over this way," he told the renSime while nagerically nudging Ilin into position to shield the renSime from the Second Order channel's notice. It wouldn't be hard. She was still fully engaged with a vociferous student who kept singing snatches of classic songs—off-key.

Meanwhile, the tall blonde First Order channel drifted in their direction, trying a little too hard not to seem to be going anywhere in particular.

"Make it quick," said Vret. "We'll relay your message. But you have to get out of here. That's a First coming toward us."

Wide-eyed, the stringy youth hunched into the shadow between the two pillars and confessed radiating guilt. "I built a secret, illicit connecting cable between the campuses so I could get into the systems over here. I stole the access codes. I just wanted to search the channels' library—there's so much they don't let renSimes read. But I stumbled into your boards by accident. And I couldn't stop reading Bilateral's stories. And now—" he swallowed back something emotionally charged and leaned forward to whisper, "Well that doesn't matter anymore. Now they've caught onto me. This is all my fault."

"They've caught onto..." Vret remembered something Morry had said about someone logging into the boards maybe from the renSime side of Rialite. It was just too unbelievable that a student could do something like that. It was far more likely Iric Chez had said something.

Ilin asked, "They've followed you to our boards?"

"If not already, then in a day or two they'll know everything. You have to shut it down and wipe out all trace of it, and if you can't handle that yourselves, I can help."

"You can help?" echoed Vret stunned.

"I've been defending you from discovery for weeks now. But they're on to me, and they're going to get through."

Lassin and her knot of students filtered past them and simultaneously the First Order channel passed between Lassin and the three of them. The First circled, much too casually keeping herself between Lassin and the renSime. This First was clearly neither Farris nor Tigue. Perhaps she had just Qualified First.

As Lassin departed, her students scattering, the First circled all around and came right up to them saying, "I've been looking for someone willing to discuss shiltpron parlor names in fictional works. Which historical novel was it that took place in The Mellow Ambient?"

As she said the words, the ambient around them smoothed out as if flattened by a massive weight.

"You *are* a First," accused Ilin happily.

"Could you use some help with this problem?" She indicated

the renSime. "He shouldn't be here."

"Why do you say that?" asked Vret aware of the sizzling alarm from the renSime. Was she just objecting to a First Year renSime wandering among First Year channels?

The First zlinned the hall with a sweeping attention and returned to the renSime. "I doubt he was invited."

Being discussed in the third person was really getting to the youth. He was fidgeting from one foot to the other.

Vret got the distinct impression the First had figured out exactly what they wanted a First for. To Ilin, he said, "Could you pass the message on to someone who can use the information while I talk to our helpful guest?" To the First he said, "Over here, please?"

When she moved in response to his tentacle gesture, and, surprisingly without argument or discussion, Ilin went off searching for Morry, he said to the renSime, "Wait here and don't move."

He led the First out of earshot and began, "In fact we had been hoping that a First would turn up because you see we really don't know if we've got anyone here who shouldn't be here."

"It seems to be a pretty uniform crowd. What would be the disqualifying trait?"

With his gaze fixed firmly on the renSime, he gave her a very quick summary of what was happening and what they'd decided to do.

"So we want to be sure there's nobody here who should be under the care of the experts before they're out of First Year. The rest of us—well, do we really have to ruin so many careers because of what other people have done and are doing?"

She listened carefully and when he stopped, she gazed at him without reaction. Was she just thinking or had she made up her mind? He couldn't penetrate her showfield. Had he trusted the wrong person?

Finally she sighed. "Well, that is what I meant about that renSime but I didn't want to say anything in front of him. I've got a lot to learn yet. I can't understand how his monitors haven't spotted what I can zlin, if it's really there. Something has damaged his conditioning. It was there—I could zlin it. I've never actually zlinned junctedness before but there was a hint, the barest flicker, of what I'd expect it to zlin like. And then it vanished without a trace, and that shouldn't be possible."

Vret hadn't zlinned that in the renSime and he'd been concentrating. But likewise, he had not zlinned an actual junct renSime, a very advanced lesson. "He's been reading the boards. Before you came over, we were discussing the boards. Could be that what you're zlinning only appears when he's thinking about those stories."

"As I said, I have a lot to learn. But I don't understand why he's still just standing there. He should be scrambling to get away from here by now."

Vret told her what the renSime had said about the authorities finding the boards by investigating him.

Ilin was bringing Morry back with her, stopping along the aisles to mutter to the people waiting for the meeting.

The First studied the renSime again. "I can't imagine why he's told you this—why he came to this meeting."

"That's another thing I want to find out. So while we ask him questions, could you circulate among these people and see if there's anyone else who obviously doesn't belong? I know you're just a student here like the rest of us, but we wanted to be sure we tried our best. If you can't find anyone else, then we're going to tell them all to sign off the boards and give directions for purging all evidence of their involvement."

"That's a very big responsibility...."

"Yes, but ruining lives unnecessarily is also a big responsibility. We want to be sure everyone here is internally stable, hasn't been badly affected by too much intil stimulation."

"I'd expect the specialists would be better able to tell who is in trouble and who isn't than I am. The Tecton wouldn't ruin...."

She trailed off thoughtfully zlinning the hall. Vret couldn't resist asking, "Wouldn't it?"

"I see what you mean. Some of those who are not here will

have been unaffected by the boards, and no doubt will get off with just a warning on their records when you let the boards be discovered. But those here don't even deserve a warning flag that could mar their chances for advancement. I, personally, would be very interested in what cleaning methods you are going to recommend." With that, she went toward the front of the hall to talk with the people waiting for the meeting. By the time Vret rejoined the renSime and Morry, the talk had become entirely technical rattled out at incredible speed.

Morry didn't believe the renSime could have done all he claimed and was making him prove his knowledge by explaining. That was fine, except they had no time.

Aside, Ilin said, "I told people to pass the word that the meeting was about to begin so nobody would leave. By my count, we have the right number of people now—except for him." She gestured toward the renSime who was suddenly animated and intense.

Vret told her what he'd done with the First and her opinion of the renSime.

"Then he's on our 'needs help' list," she concluded. She stepped up to the two jabbering men and said, "We don't have all night you know. We have a meeting to start."

Morry took a deep breath and pulled himself back to the business at hand. "This explains a lot. If it weren't for our friend here, we'd have been exposed weeks ago. So if we're going to achieve our objective, we have to set up some timing." He turned to the renSime. "How much longer do you think you can give us?"

"If you're not going to close down and erase everything, why do you want more time?"

Ilin asked, "What makes you think we won't?"

Morry and the renSime spoke at once. "I just told him the whole plan."

"But he just said you weren't."

Vret and Ilin stared at Morry. Too late.

Vret turned to the renSime, "Then I have one very important

question you must answer."

"I'll do my best."

"Why did you come here with this tonight? You obviously have the ability to erase all your own involvement with the boards, so if they do catch you, all you're guilty of is reading the channels' library. You'd probably just be sent to a different camp with a mild censure on your record. Why take this risk?"

"You're all going to get caught. And it's my fault. Isn't that enough reason?"

"For some people, maybe. But I zlin there's more to it than that for you."

With three channels focused on him, he couldn't evade. But he didn't offer anything more until Vret said, "Our First detected something strange in your nager. I think you have more to say to us."

"You want to know my board identity, don't you? I'd think it would be obvious to you. I am Blissdrip. I'm the one who ruined everything for you. I'm the one who should be punished, not you."

The guilt and remorse was thick enough to have come from a Gen not a renSime. It brought tears to Vret's eyes, but he blinked them back and said, "Why did you do it? More...why did you keep on doing it?"

"I didn't know until just a few days ago. I—I never looked at the comment boards. I stopped reading everything but Bilateral's entries. I never had time. I didn't know that people were taking what I was writing so seriously."

"You didn't care how the readers felt?" asked Ilin.

"At first...but then...I just had to finish writing it. Every night I would dream something, and I'd just have to write it all out. I just had to. And...and...after a while it wasn't like dreaming at all. It was more like I remembered it, like I was.." He broke off, staring at them.

The ambient was thick enough to wrap tentacles around. "Zlin me," said Vret dropping his showfield so the renSime could get the truth of it. "I believe you didn't know what harm you were doing. But how and why you did it matters. Tell us."

"This is going to sound insane, but I remember being Aunser, founding the Secret Pens. I wrote it the way it really happened because—because someone has to know. Everyone ought to know. And reading Bilateral's whitewashed version, I knew—I just knew—that the world we live in now isn't going to last unless people understand the way it really was at Unity. The price that was paid, the value of what we have today, the Tecton with all its shortcomings has to succeed. It just has to."

Vret felt the laughter surfacing in Morry and Ilin. He asked, "You think you really were Aunser ambrov D'zehn? Why?"

"Well, there is the theory that people do get reborn."

"I've heard that. But not everyone living today was someone so—famous."

"Maybe I just imagined it all. But that's why I did it, why I had to do it, and why I was so intent on getting the real story out that I just ignored everything else, the comment boards, the other stories being posted distorting what I was talking about, and the authorities searching for my tap into the channels' school. But now, innocent people are going to suffer for what I did. Again!" He took a deep breath. "Or maybe I just imagined it all."

It wasn't a surly challenge, nor a dodging defense. The renSime was entertaining the notion that his conviction was wrong. That, more than anything, convinced Vret.

But there was also the penetrating and undeniable reality in Blissdrip's writing. It could have been written by someone who knew first hand what The Kill was all about. Vret had felt that in the one, too real, experience of Killmode he'd had. And there was the First's testimony. She found something indefinably junct in this renSime's nager. But it was there only when he was thinking about being Blissdrip.

Vret said, "When you write, it's as if you become Aunser, isn't it?"

"Yes! Yes, that's it exactly. And all I've written is the truth as he knew it. But its done immense harm. I only knew that ten days ago after I read 'The Mellow Ambient' and the comments on it. When I let them catch me, I'm going to take all the blame for this—all of it."

Morry said, "I believe him. I don't think he meant all the harm he's done."

Ilin said, "Neither did Aunser, and in the end what he did was necessary, if not good."

Morry said, "If we let him go, I think he'll do what I've asked of him, and what he's promised. If he does, we can pull this off. His confession here has solved a lot of mysteries and restored my confidence."

Unnoticed, the First had drifted back to join them and report, "I didn't find anyone else who shouldn't be here, and you must get this meeting started before people decide to leave. I'll take this one back to where he belongs."

After Morry and the renSime had exchanged more incomprehensible words, and Vret had told the First that they'd take care of getting the innocent out of the way, she wrapped the renSime in her nager and, with one arm around his shoulders, walked him down the steps of the Memorial.

Ilin hesitated, then ran after them and shot one more question at Blissdrip and returned saying, "Come on, let's tell these people what they have to do."

As they walked up to the stage, Vret asked, "What did you say to him?"

"I asked if Aunser really was a telepath, and he said he hadn't just made that up either. Even the First didn't think he was lying, but the only thing I believe is that he actually didn't mean any harm. There weren't any Endowed channels back then. It's a new mutation."

"That's what they've been teaching us," allowed Vret.

The two of them sat on the edge of the stage, gathering the few dozen people up close and gave them the whole story, and the plan for getting them out of the fix they'd fallen into by following Bilateral's saga.

The discussion lasted past midnight, but eventually everyone agreed to the plan and drifted away as inconspicuously as possible to erase all connection with the boards according to Morry's directions. The sadness was palpable, but there was also relief.

* * * * * * *

Everything went off like a Tecton precision disaster drill. Five days after Vret's turnover, Morry confirmed that all trace of the thirty-eight innocents had been eradicated from the systems. Blissdrip and his followers were all that was left.

Then Blissdrip made the mistake he and Morry had planned at the meeting.

Within a day the campus was buzzing with questions. Students had disappeared all over, older students, some with great records and some very poor. Tallies were guessed at anywhere from thirty to a hundred, and rumors began to escalate in the absence of any official announcement.

People connected the disappearances to the intil accidents, to a minor shaking plague outbreak, to a political purge, to ever more unsavory scandals.

Finally, two days after that, came the official word, one sentence at the bottom of the daily announcements.

Sixty-seven students have left Rialite for other First Year Camps over the last four days as we have adjusted the size of the student body to allow your instructors to give you each more personal attention.

Rumors still flew, but most people believed this was the whole story. Others questioned why the announcement hadn't been made before the departures. Others said it was because it would have spooked everyone into worrying if they would be sent away.

CHAPTER SEVENTEEN
BARRIER CONTROL

By the time Vret was swept into his third Accelerated Development session, the rumors had disappeared. Vret walked into his session with a calm confidence and ebullient spirit he had never found in himself before, especially not this deep into Need. He was on his way to his life's goal and nothing could stop him now.

That lasted less than twelve hours. He had known that this session would be about transfer deferment. His transfer was set for a full day after his normal schedule, just as he'd known Ilin's had been at her tenth transfer.

He hadn't known that this session would be a drill in barrier control.

In his math and physics courses, he'd learned about discontinuities. He'd learned that renSimes, Gens and channels all had three major barriers or discontinuities within their selyn storage systems, and that barrier behavior was what distinguished the Orders. A Second Order channel was simply one whose primary system was not permanently divided into three compartments, but only two.

Some people were born with the ability to find, sense, and even control their barriers. Some never got the knack of it, or if they did, they died horribly because they didn't have the vriamic strength to manage it. Others had to learn the hard way, and many of those developed skills far superior to those with natural talent.

Until they hit him with the first barrier exercise, Vret had harbored the ambition to become one of those supremely skilled Seconds and make his mark in the world of Troubleshooting because of his precision skills. Four minutes afterwards, he was ready to give up forever.

They wouldn't let him.

Three channels and their Gen assistants surrounded him while he was strapped into a nightmarish chair rigged around with all kinds of instruments he didn't recognize. They peered at the readouts and muttered to each other, snapped instructions at him as they tailored selyn field gradients and then slammed at his Second barrier with a Gen-like selyn field, discussing his vriamic responses with an abstract disdain that seemed cruel.

That made him mad and he tried harder the next time. But with each attempt, he was left dizzy, weak, nauseated, and eventually knotted in painful muscle spasms. At least they didn't force him to eat.

Sometime during the second day his brain locked up in fear—no, it was actually terror. Real abject terror.

Kindly, they explained this was a common side effect for a Third and was certainly not nearly as bad as what the average Gen would experience if attacked by a Sime.

Patiently, they explained over and over that what they were doing was nothing more than simulating conditions a Third would encounter working as a channel, conditions that would eventually bring a Qualifying transfer.

Understanding that didn't help. The third day passed in a murky blur.

And this time there was a fourth day, the day he would have had transfer except for the transfer deferment exercise that wasn't even part of the Development session. Without sympathy, in fact with something akin to satisfaction, the channels continued to hammer at his barriers using their Gens' fields at odd intervals.

Need clamped down bringing bouts of extreme panic between peaks of torment and troughs of unutterable dread of another assault on his barriers. Through it all were the physical symptoms, but he was barely aware of his body's rebellion. All he knew was Need.

And then he surrendered to Death.

That suddenly changed everything. He came to lying in a hospital bed surrounded by opaque white curtains laced with nageric dampening fibers.

His whole body was one aching bruise, the worst in chest and abdomen. There was dried blood under his nose, and tears glued his eyes shut. His throat was so raw he could hardly breathe. His handling tentacles gripped the bars around his bed spasmodically, and his laterals protruded, wandering through the dampened ambient with fretful insistence. But padded restraints held him fast.

Outside the curtains, a tight cluster of Simes and Gens gathered, muttering and gesturing. And finally he knew what had wakened him. The unmistakable nager of Saelul Farris approached talking to a Gen who moved with him. The whole conference fell silent, audibly and nagerically.

The Farris attention raked over Vret right through the curtains and the channel announced, "He's awake. The drugs have worn off. Good, it's all arranged. And—all of you—your reports will be on my desk in the morning without fail."

Immediately the curtains were whisked aside, and Vret caught a whiff of that Farris nager retreating toward the ward doorway before the team working over him began their next attack.

But this time they only tipped him onto his feet and began cleaning and dressing him in another disposable coverall, keeping him wrapped in a nageric cocoon. "Your transfer has been moved up. We're taking you to your Donor now, so just be patient."

Moved up?! Vret had never heard of that being done on a tenth transfer deferment exercise—not unless the student had failed some key test for an out-Territory license. You had to pass deferment to get a license.

To his vague horror though, he couldn't work up any interest at all in his failure.

His time sense told him it was barely half an hour later that they brought him to a transfer suite down the hall, not one across in the other building as always before.

But as the door opened, he knew his Donor wasn't there. There was only a First Order Donor in the suite along with the channel and Donor escorting him who took the monitoring station in the corner.

But the Donor came over to him, nager open in complete welcome, falling into sync with him. He felt the monitors relinquish command of his body as the First smoothly took over, a clean, hard but precise grip that sent waves of relaxation washing through him in places he hadn't known were tense.

He was scooped onto the transfer lounge so smoothly he was hardly aware of moving, and then the Gen was sliding his hands up Vret's arms.

Vret's tentacles lashed out with embarrassing strength and his laterals flicked into place. The Gen was already coming close for the fifth contact point, lip to lip, but Vret didn't wait. He seized the Gen and his draw began of its own accord.

All at once, he was raging in Killmode, grabbing selyn from the Gen without waiting for the Gen to offer it. It was just like Blissdrip's endless, sensuous, detailed descriptions, identical to Iric's mad attack on Joran Nah. Killmode. All his carefully developed control was gone.

He drew and drew selyn faster and faster seeking that final lightening strike of pure bliss at full satisfaction, Killbliss, the sizzling shock that would leave his body strong, healthy, pain free, and in love with life for another month.

He almost had it and then something inside him broke, and Need erupted full force again. Frantic for satisfaction, he redoubled his draw. And selyn rushed into him easily, in pure abundant plenty, carrying a bright, shining joy such as he'd never felt before.

And then he felt the Gen's strength like a hand spread wide, containing and protecting, guiding the selyn flow, regulating its speed and permitting the endless abundance to continue.

He relaxed into that powerful presence, no longer drawing selyn but simply accepting it deep, deep inside himself where it spread a great, abiding peace and serene happiness. It was better than any description of Killbliss. It was what he'd really been trying for. And it went on and on for almost a minute after the selyn ceased flowing.

Awareness of the room slowly faded in. The monitors were bending over him but somehow nagerically transparent. His Donor was waiting for him to dismantle the contact. The First Order Donor was still apparently high field, bearing much more selyn that Vret now had.

As Vret repossessed his laterals, and unwound his handling tentacles from the Gen's wrists, the Gen smiled warmly, just as if he'd participated in Vret's satisfaction.

The monitors moved back to their corner to fill out their forms without comment, and Vret sat up, scrubbing at his face. "I'm so sorry. I didn't even say hello. I was...well, I was...I...." It was all starting to crash in on him, the failure, the loss of everything.

The Donor laughed gently, apparently oblivious to the gathering post-syndrome storm. "My name is Kuri Diza, a First, as you've guessed. I know your name and I've read your chart. Serving your Qualification Transfer was an honor and a privilege."

"Qualifying—transfer?" Suddenly the storm of grief, remorse, loss, and failure just dissipated. "I Qualified Second?"

Kuri and the monitors filled the room with a joyous happiness that left no doubt he had. Kuri said, "Yes, definitely a Second. Saelul will have to evaluate you tomorrow to zlin what really happened, and why, and see what we can do for you next. There was nothing in the development session that could have triggered this. The program calls for at least one more transfer before you could reach this point. I guess talent always provides surprises."

While Kuri spoke, he brought some trin tea over from the

sideboard. Sometime during all this, the monitors had finished their work and departed, leaving Vret with another Post-assignment card that did not have Ilin Sumz designated as his partner.

Internally and externally pulverized, emotionally whipsawed from total failure to complete triumph, he didn't think he could perform at all. But he'd underestimated what transfer with a First could do to him.

CHAPTER EIGHTEEN
FARRIS SCREENING

The following day he began to emerge from the whirlwind of euphoria and disbelief.

The world had changed drastically. Everything was brighter, sharper edged, and people were more complex, hiding layers within layers. Everything around him seemed to move too slowly, to splash nageric noise in swirling fountains of emotion with jagged peaks of Need mixed with other people's rich pungency of sexual attraction.

He broke a door knob and two tea glasses before he understood that the world had become a delicate place.

He arrived at Saelul Farris's office in the administration building three minutes early for his appointment for his first Farris Screening as a Second. The building was insulated for the Farris sensitivity, the exterior walls opaque to Sime senses, and the interior partitions barely allowing a Farris to sense the existence of others in the building.

To his new Second Order senses, the Farris shielding was as solid and impenetrable as it had ever been to his Third Order awareness.

But he didn't even have to touch the door signal before Saelul Farris opened the door to his office to greet him. "Hajene Vret McClintock. Come in. We have a great deal to accomplish this afternoon."

The Farris nager still seemed like solid granite but now, just like granite the surface of the Farris showfield was decorated with perceptible structures, colors, details that Vret had never zlinned before. He fell into studying the effect without realizing it.

An inordinate amount of time passed, perhaps two and a half minutes, and Saelul had seated himself behind his desk, waiting until Vret emerged from fugue like a First Month student still playing with his brand new tentacles.

Embarrassed, Vret moved to the seat Saelul had gestured him toward. The office was huge, built in an L shape, with a small treatment room in the short arm of the L.

The carpet before the desk showed signs that chairs were sometimes ranked there, and perhaps another table for larger meetings. The window behind the desk looked out on a court-yard with a fountain and lush greenery such as one never saw in the desert. There were sliding doors to one side leading to that garden.

The Farris zlinned him. Once again, Vret felt that searching, soul-reaming, total invasion all the way to his bone marrow. It didn't feel different than the first time, when he'd been a Third late for class. But this time, he zlinned back. It didn't do him any good. He couldn't get through the surface of the Farris showfield.

At length, Saelul sighed. "So tell me, Vret, how did you first get involved with the secret boards?"

Cold needles of utter dread washed over his skin and his vision went black around the edges. He had to force himself to draw a breath. "Secret...boards?"

"Yes, and posting a story too. I like the nickname you chose for yourself, Asymmetric. Nice ring to it. Good story you wrote, too."

"Th-thank you."

The failure Vret remembered feeling just as he had accepted death washed over him. It was all over. Now he'd never get an out-Territory license, never become a Troubleshooter.

"How did you get involved to begin with?"

"A friend who knew I was failing History told me a password. Said there was this terrific story I ought to be reading, but you have to sign a pledge of secrecy to get at it. If I'd known it was about history, I'd never have looked it up."

"Says here you failed that exam several times."

"Yes, I had to have a tutor." *Oh, why did I mention Ilin?* "I thought history was boring."

"So what have you learned from that experience?"

"Learned?" His mind was paralyzed by the whirlpool of emotions. "History isn't boring. And it's not irrelevant to the things happening today. It matters."

"Good." Saelul made a note on the form before him. "So what about history matters the most?"

The Farris was zlinning again. Vret made an effort and dropped his showfield, feeling like he'd just stripped naked before an enemy. "Unity. How and why it came about, but mostly what it cost, why it's so precious."

"And what about the Secret Pens? That terrible blot on the honor of the Tecton?"

"It was the only way. And lying about it was the only way. The Secret Pens and the lie were the price of Unity that makes it so incredibly, irreplaceably precious. Those people lived in a hard world and they became hard. They could do it. But we could never do it again."

Lacing fingers and tentacles together, Saelul rested his chin on his knuckles with all his attention focused on Vret. "You've heard of the rash of intil incidents across this campus?"

Vret assented with his nager, making no effort to hide his alarm at the question.

"Is there any connection between them and the stories you've been reading?"

"Could be. After you explained how riding waves of intil, using our programmed leisure time to arouse intil instead of resting from it, could actually damage the hardening of anti-kill conditioning, well, I took the whole problem a lot more seriously."

"And knowing that, you concocted a plan to hide the involvement of several dozen people? On your own recognizance?"

"Who told you that?"

"I protect my sources, just as you protect yours."

You're not going to admit you're a telepath, are you?

But the Farris merely blinked solemnly and went on. "You do realize that young channels in First Year are especially vulnerable, that the careful program of development here at Rialite has been undermined for these people, that many of them will never obtain an out-Territory license now because of these stories?"

Now he's getting to his point. I've been blacklisted.

Since it was too late for him, Vret figured he'd have his say and take the consequences. "Yes, I know some readers were compromised. But I wanted to protect the careers of those channels who had been involved but not affected like that. I learned from those stories just how potent the lure of Killbliss can be, and I decided that because that lure is so gripping, so undeniable even to non-junct channels, the Tecton with all its harsh practices is the only way to Unity—and Unity is the only way for humankind to survive."

The Farris made another long note on his form.

Vret couldn't stand the silence. "The Tecton can't afford to lose the full strength of a few dozen channels just because dozens of other channels had their anti-kill conditioning impaired."

"And it's your judgment to make—what the Tecton can and can't afford?"

Well, all is lost anyway, why not? "If it's not my judgment to make, then whose judgment is it? I learned from those stories that each and every one of us, Sime, Gen, renSime, channel—is personally responsible for the course of history, for the fate of all of us together. It's not that it isn't my place to decide what the Tecton can or can't afford—it's that it's not my place to *not* make this choice.

"Hajene Farris, I dare not refuse to do what must be done, not with my knowledge of the price that has been paid by my ancestors so that I can live. I will accept the consequences of my decisions without protest."

For a long time, for a very, very long time, the Farris just sat there staring at his notes, still as a granite statue both physically and nagerically. Vret again became convinced the Farris could hear him thinking.

"Hajene McClintock, why do you think you Qualified Second on this transfer?"

Suddenly worried, Vret answered, "Because Sosu Diza said so?"

A small smile flicked across the Farris lips. "Oh, you did Qualify. What caused that to happen prematurely? What caused your Second barrier to collapse?"

"The Accelerated Development program?"

"No."

"I don't understand."

"Think like a channel. Analyze it. You've spent a lot of your time lately fighting intil spikes caused by reading those stories during what should have been your rest periods. For you, that has strengthened your vriamic control. You've spent a lot of your time imagining yourself living in the semi-junct world, facing the kinds of channel's functionals the other students here won't face until a year or two after they leave. Because of those stories, you've been exercising your systems in ways we—don't recommend in First Year. As a result, your development ran about a month ahead of schedule."

"I'm sorry."

"You're going to have to live with the consequences."

"Yes."

Saelul made another note on his form. "What do you think we should do with you?"

"I don't know. I don't know what the options are. I've always had my sights set on a career as a Troubleshooter for the World Tecton. I never looked at what a channel with such a blemished record could expect."

"Blemished record. You could put it that way. So you think we should consign you to an in-Territory Center in the back of nowhere and forget about you."

The image of such a life sprang full blown into his mind. It was a horror he had been unable to contemplate for so long the reality of it was paralyzing. "You should put me where I can do the Tecton the most good with the least risk of damage."

"Regardless of how you feel about the assignment?"

"Regardless of how I feel about the assignment, yes."

"I see."

Again the Farris zlinned him deeply. Vret did his best to keep his showfield dormant and his barriers quiescent.

"So, if you had it to do over again, what would you do differently?"

Vret hadn't thought of it that way before. "Nothing. If I hadn't signed onto the boards to read those stories, I wouldn't know what I know now. If I hadn't tried to help the innocent protect their careers with the Tecton, I wouldn't be able to live with myself. If I knew how you found out about it anyway, then maybe I'd know what I shouldn't have done."

Smiling, Saelul made another note. "Maybe someday you will know. So, then, I have your permission to use you for the good of the Tecton and ignore your personal wishes?"

"Yes."

"And you still believe you must act on your own judgment for the good of the Tecton?"

"Yes." Mentally he was already packing.

"And you do understand the content of this interview is not to be discussed with anyone, student or faculty."

"Yes." Well, nobody else ever discussed what went on in a Farris Screening. He'd always assumed it was just a deep zlinning.

The Farris pulled a folder out of the stack on his desk. He tapped it on the desk to align the papers within, and handed it over, thumping it with one tentacle. "Here's your course schedule for the remainder of your year here." He stood up, ushering Vret toward the door.

Stunned, Vret found himself out in the corridor with the door closing behind him. The door opened again, and the Farris said,

"Oh, and I don't ever want to hear about you being late for class again."

Opening the folder to find a list of Second Order courses, three of them labeled for out-Territory License Requirements, and one on exercising of authority in the absence of a supervisor's orders, he didn't dare let himself be happy.

CHAPTER NINETEEN
GRADUATION DAY

Two months later, Ilin Sumz graduated and left Rialite on the train that had just brought new students. As far as she knew—or admitted—there had been no repercussions from the secret boards to any of their chosen innocents. Vret wasn't so sure, but as far as he knew all of them were going about their academic tracks in the most routine ways.

As much as he'd wanted to be there for her graduation, Vret could only pause on his way between classes to watch the brief ceremony on the concrete platform and wave as she boarded the train. He already missed her.

They had been assigned to each other for post-syndrome, and it had worked out beautifully—the best ever for Vret. As a Second while she was still a Third, he'd been able to prevent the kind of feedback they'd experienced before, even though both of them had been horribly torn over the inevitable parting.

"You'll be graduating in another month. Maybe we can find a way to get together then."

"That would be a rare accident," Vret had replied while his heart was breaking. And they said goodbye again, all night long. It wasn't enough.

Four weeks later, Vret stood with his class on that same concrete train platform, resplendent in his new working channel's uniform, a small carry-bag at his feet and the sun twinkling on his new Tecton ring.

He hadn't heard a word of the faculty speeches. In his hand

was a folder with his first assignment for the Tecton, and it was an appointment to the Troubleshooters Training school in Heartland Territory—out-Territory. His out-Territory license nested in his pocket next to a letter from Ilin giving her new address as that same Troubleshooters school.

The ceremony broke up, and the class headed for the train but Vret circled around to corner Saelul Farris one more time. He waved the folder at the Farris. "Why? What did I do to deserve this?"

"I thought you weren't going to complain about where the Tecton sent you."

"I'm not complaining—just confused."

The Farris relented, showfield softening. "You acted on your own recognizance to solve the problem created by Blissdrip's postings to the secret boards. If you're going to insist on behaving that way...the Tecton is going to use that predilection to maximum advantage.

"You will be trained to make such judgments when lives and careers depend on your being right. Once you have completed that training and gained a few years experience in the field, you will have the chance to attain the authority to act for the Tecton. In the meantime, the Tecton would be best served if you rein in your eagerness to protect the Tecton from itself—just temporarily, you understand."

"Thank you," said Vret not sure if he was thanking the Farris for the explanation or for sending him to training.

He gathered courage to ask Saelul if he was a telepath but just then the train began to move. He turned and ran, just catching the last car and swinging aboard as the door was closing. He was still unsure if he was being rewarded or punished. But he did know that Saelul Farris didn't want him to change the way he did things.

THE STORY UNTOLD

Tonyo Logan and Zhag Paget are the stuff of legend. Their music is the soundtrack of the turbulent period after the signing of the Unity Treaty, when Simes and Gens must figure out how to live as their leaders have decided—together! When from time immemorial Simes have killed Gens in order to live, and Gens have murdered Simes to keep from being killed, how can they change literally overnight? And how can music help?

The three stories told here span the first fifteen years of Zhag and Tonyo's partnership, from their beginnings as starving musicians to their heyday as international superstars, a supreme example of the creativity that happens when Sime and Gen work together. But theirs is also a personal story of tragedy and triumph, and the scars left by growing up in an insane world poised on the brink of destroying itself.

THE SIME~GEN SERIES from The Borgo Press

Other Jean Lorrah Books from Wildside:

THE STORY
UNTOLD

AND OTHER SIME~GEN STORIES:
SIME~GEN, BOOK TEN

JEAN LORRAH

THE BORGO PRESS
MMXI

THE STORY UNTOLD

DEDICATION

All my work in the Sime~Gen universe must first and foremost be dedicated to Jacqueline Lichtenberg, who many years ago invited me to come and play in the Sime~Gen universe. We have long since become business partners and best friends, and it is sheer delight to have the opportunity to continue these stories at last.

Both of us must acknowledge the fans who kept the dream of Sime~Gen alive after all the books went out of print—I can do no more than sincerely agree with Jacqueline's sentiments below, both about our fans and about Karen MacLeod and Patric Michael. Without their help, we would not have simegen.com, and without simegen.com it is highly doubtful that there would be the opportunity to write new Sime~Gen stories.

Jacqueline and I believe in interaction between writers and readers, and invite comments on our work. Send them to simegen@simegen.com or simegen@gmail.com and we will both receive them. If you just want the latest news about our work and activities, though, see http://whatsnew.simegen.com (*Note:* no www, as it's a blog).

I am grateful for the encouragement my readers have given me over the years, and sincerely hope those of you familiar with my work will enjoy these new adventures. If you've never read anything else I've written, welcome! I hope you'll find something new and exciting in *The Story Untold*. To old friends, welcome back! I hope you also find something new here, along with whatever has brought you back for more.

Note: If this is your first venture into the Sime~Gen universe, I respectfully recommend that you read the three short stories in *The Story Untold* before reading *Personal Recognizance*. The stories introduce the background for the reader new to the Sime~Gen universe, and are set in the Year 1 after Unity, while the novel assumes you already know it and is set in the Year 245 of the official chronology: http://www.simegen.com/CHRONO1.html

If you have read all the other Sime~Gen novels over the years, though, feel free to plunge in anywhere! If not, there will be reprints available soon. Watch or drop us a note on the blog:

http://whatsnew.simegen.com

CONTENTS

CONTENTS

ACKNOWLEDGMENTS

Firstly and most importantly, we have to acknowledge the extraordinary effort put forth by Karen MacLeod in meeting absurd copyediting deadlines during the final moments of production of this manuscript.

Over the years, Karen has taken skills learned in fanzine editing and honed and then applied them to become a professional copyeditor in the ebook field. With the October 2003 trade paperback release of *Those of My Blood* by Jacqueline Lichtenberg from BenBella Books, Karen has begun working on "tree-books."

Cherri Munoz enthusiastically volunteered to use her talents as a publicist to line up autographing appearances at various bookstores for us, and has done other publicity work and even proofreading into the wee hours.

Beyond even that, as Cherri and Jacqueline accidentally ended up neighbors in Arizona for a while, Cherri saved Jacqueline a lot of writing time by helping her pick out a house, teaching her to navigate around town, and pointing out the best places to shop. Cherri even raced around town finding a copy of one of Jean's novels, *Survivors*, when it was suddenly needed for show-and-tell because the producers of Trekkies Two, the sequel to the documentary Trekkies, (www.trekkies2.com) asked to interview Jacqueline.

Jean Lorrah & Jacqueline Lichtenberg

SIME~GEN:
where a mutation makes the evolutionary
division into male and female
pale by comparison.

CHRONOLOGY OF THE SIME~GEN UNIVERSE

The Sime~Gen Universe was originated by Jacqueline Lichtenberg who was then joined by a large number of Star Trek fans. Soon, Jean Lorrah, already a professional writer, began writing fanzine stories for one of the Sime~Gen 'zines. But Jean produced a novel about the moment when the first channel discovered he didn't have to kill to live which Jacqueline sold to Doubleday.

The chronology of stories in this fictional universe expanded to cover thousands of years of human history, and fans have been filling in the gaps between professionally published novels. The full official chronology is posted at

http://www.simegen.com/CHRONO1.html

Here is the chronology of the novels by Jacqueline Lichtenberg and Jean Lorrah by the Unity Calendar date in which they are set.

-533—*First Channel*, by Jean Lorrah & Jacqueline Lichtenberg
-518—*Channel's Destiny*, by Jean Lorrah & Jacqueline Lichtenberg
-468—*The Farris Channel*, by Jacqueline Lichtenberg
-20—*Ambrov Keon*, by Jean Lorrah
-15—*House of Zeor*, by Jacqueline Lichtenberg

BEST OF FOOLS

"Why do you introduce me as Tonyo?" demanded Zhag Paget's young protégé. "My name is Tony."

"That's a Gen name," Zhag replied.

"In case you hadn't noticed, I *am* Gen."

"I mean, it's an out-Territory name," Zhag explained.

"In case you hadn't noticed...," Tonyo repeated, voice and energy field dripping sarcasm.

Zhag sighed. "It makes you sound like a Wild Gen."

Annoyance resonated in the boy's field as he threatened, "You want to see wild? Dammit, Zhag, I'm *me*, you don't own me, and you can't change my identity!" Abruptly he got up and stomped out, a frequent response to their disagreements. Was Tonyo used to someone who wouldn't listen?

The Gen went only as far as the woodpile. Zhag picked up his shiltpron and went to sit on the rickety steps of his house. Snatches of melody churned up in his mind, disconnected phrases that would not form a tune. He plucked the notes anyway, knowing that music often soothed away his Gen's annoyance.

Tonyo was chopping wood for the cookstove Zhag had never used—the extent of his "cooking" was to make tea over an oil burner. The Sime had learned to avoid disparaging comments about Gens and sharp instruments. He didn't want to provoke the boy again, but he was relieved when Tonyo carried the wood inside and returned to sit at the other end of the step. Tonyo's nager—the field of life energy that surrounded all humans, Simes like Zhag and Gens like Tonyo—precisely echoed the notes Zhag played.

Zhag let go of the senses he shared with Gens, except for hearing, and zlinned the boy with Sime senses. Perhaps Tonyo's golden field would provide the inspiration to compose something. Anything. Just one more song before he died.

Or killed.

Zhag was prepared to die, but if he were to kill again—

That's need depression talking, he told himself. The loss of creative energy was the worst effect of Zhag's chronically unsatisfied need. When Tonyo was nearby—and not frustrated—he could almost...almost...feel normal.

But normal for Zhag was creating new music, not merely playing at Milily's Shiltpron Parlor. Since Tonyo had joined him, he frequently felt well enough to improvise—as the Gen was doing now, vocalizing variations around Zhag's new riff. But Tonyo had not warmed up his voice. He reached for a note—and missed. His field followed his voice out of tune, a jolt to Zhag's wide open systems. When he next skidded flat, Zhag stopped playing. "Follow your nager with your voice."

"What?" Gen confusion.

"Your nager has perfect pitch," Zhag explained. "You think of yourself as a singer, Tonyo, but it's your field Simes 'listen' to."

"I know that," the boy said.

"You *know* it, but you don't *feel* it," Zhag told him. *The way I know I will never kill again, but can't feel it—can't trust that I'm not deluding myself.*

"Well, I'm Gen!" Tonyo protested. "I can't zlin."

Zhag searched for words. "When you were listening, your field matched every note—before you started singing."

Tonyo pondered. "I was thinking those notes."

"That's it, then, isn't it?" Zhag suggested. "Follow your *inner* voice."

The Sime played the riff again—then deliberately raised the key. The Gen met the challenge nagerically, but when he tried to follow with his voice, it cracked. He waved a hand. "I know.

I'll get it. Play it again."

Zhag did...and Tonyo's voice sailed up the scale, well above his normal range before it cracked again. Unmindful of Zhag's wince, the young Gen laughed. "This is wonderful!"

"Not to me!" Zhag said through gritted teeth. "You're still thinking about your voice."

"But it's my voice I'm trying to improve," Tonyo said with impeccable Gen logic...something that theoretically couldn't happen when he was speaking Simelan. The boy frequently managed to be equally dense in either language.

Zhag had no words to explain what he could have demonstrated to another Sime. "Try again," he said, "and...focus on your field instead of your throat."

Tonyo echoed the riff in different keys, voice and nager in synch until he ran out of his range and again shredded Zhag's nageric comfort. Oblivious to the Sime's reaction, he asked, "What's the rest of the song? Does it have words?"

"There isn't any more," Zhag told him. "I haven't been able to compose since— For a long time now. At this time of month it's not possible anyway."

"Maybe after your transfer," Tonyo suggested. "When's your appointment?"

"Day after tomorrow."

"No wonder you don't feel creative." Tonyo got up, stretching. "We're out of food." This close to hard need, the boy's hunger made Zhag faintly ill.

"It's market day," said the Sime. "Come on—let's get you something to eat."

Zhag had to wonder how he could keep the Gen. It wasn't so much the risk of having a high-field Gen nearby—Tonyo was as easy to be near as a Householding Companion. But Zhag's earnings at the shiltpron parlor would not pay his Pen Taxes— Selyn Taxes, as they were called since Unity—and also feed a growing Gen. Until there were new laws, Tonyo was here only as a visitor. Since using up his small supply of money, he was dependent on Zhag...unless he became a selyn donor.

It was the obvious solution. Tonyo had donated twice before arriving in Norlea, but donating selyn, the life energy that Gens produced and Simes needed to live, would reduce Tonyo's glorious field. No low-field Gen Zhag had ever zlinned could hold a roomful of Simes spellbound.

They had been performing together for over a month now, drawing more customers each week. Zhag had wangled a raise out of Milily, but not enough to keep his Gen fed, let alone clothed. The denims he wore today were practically threadbare.

In the public forum of Norlea's market, Tonyo kept his nager carefully neutral. Nevertheless, when the boy stopped at a citrus stand Zhag sensed bristling annoyance in Sime customers. Tonyo picked up a lemon—

"You!" It was Zhag the proprietor addressed. "Make your Gen stop squeezing the fruit!"

Feeling outrage rolling off Tonyo, Zhag stepped between him and the vendor, saying, "He's not my property."

Zhag won a smile from Tonyo—but sneers from nearby Simes. One muttered, "Don't *look* like Householders," for Zhag referred to Tonyo with the pronoun for a male Sime...as, despite protests, he called the boy by the Simelan version of his name.

Zhag said, "Tonyo is a guest in Gulf Territory. Under the law he has the same rights as a Sime."

"Shenned *Tecton* law!" said a woman in bright calico. "Can't kill Gens anymore, but we don't have to live with 'em!"

Mutters of agreement were backed with nageric static. Tonyo, wide-eyed but with his field under tight control, put the fruit back and edged away.

Zhag shared the boy's consternation: there were always Gens in Norlea's streets. Usually they were ignored, but today the ambient nager rang with hostility. These juncts didn't care where the boy came from—to them he was need denied.

Life denied.

Zhag had not killed for far longer than most Simes, nor did he want to. He had chosen another way two years before Tonyo wandered into Milily's and brought that shining nager to brighten Zhag's ever-bleaker existence.

Simes always gravitated toward Tonyo, but usually it was a positive response. The only Gens his age they saw were breeders on the Genfarms, Companions in the Householdings, or the few living with disjunct or nonjunct families. Until very recently, most in-Territory Gens were raised on Genfarms, sold for the kill as soon as they began producing selyn...and never allowed to learn Gen defenses against Sime attack.

While many Simes wished nothing had changed, most acknowledged that it had to: even by capturing Wild Gens, Sime Territory governments could not provide sufficient kills. Raids across the border brought retaliatory strikes by the Gen army. If nothing changed, eventually all the Gens would be killed...and the remaining Simes would die.

There was a solution: Simes called channels could take selyn from Gens without hurting them, and transfer it to other Simes so they did not have to kill. But for those addicted to the kill—the vast majority of Simes alive today—channel's transfer meant never knowing true satisfaction again.

And...it meant an early death.

Zhag trailed Tonyo through the market. As long as his Gen was near, he could avoid feeling life draining heartbeat by heartbeat. But his comfort was an illusion—he would never draw Tonyo's selyn, unless the boy became a Companion in a Householding. If he were ever tempted to attack the untrained boy...one or both of them would die. What a shidoni-doomed choice: to satisfy his selyn needs, he must give up the musical partner of a lifetime. But he had so little time—how could he part with the one thing that made life tolerable?

Besides, Tonyo had come to Gulf Sime Territory in pursuit of music. The way he told it, when he donated at Keon, the Householding near the north territory border, they had done everything short of locking him in a killroom to make him stay. So he had avoided Norlea's Householding, Carre.

Tonyo stopped at the stand run by the local Genfarm. Here he was waited on by another Gen, a breeder male by the look of it, well fed, strong, and alert enough to total prices with an abacus. The local farm produced healthy Gens. Prime kills.

But those days were over. For now, the Genfarmer could sell his Gens' selyn. But if, as the Tecton wanted and everyone else feared, Gens were made free citizens of Gulf Territory, they would be paid for their own selyn. The Genfarmer would lose his means of earning a living.

Verl, the Genfarmer, was a patron of Milily's—but while he might appreciate Tonyo's performance, Zhag could zlin that he didn't like him acting as good as a Sime.

Tonyo chose the cheapest goods, but still had too little to cover the cost. If Milily would pay Tonyo—

Well, that was not going to happen. The boy counted out his coins, and Zhag handed him as much as he dared put toward Tonyo's keep. The boy understood Selyn Taxes; he knew Zhag was not holding out.

With a frown, Tonyo set aside nut butter and cheese. Zhag said, "You require protein, Tonyo."

"Pasta and rice are cheaper," the boy said. "I'll go fishing tomorrow—cook and eat 'em down by the river, so you don't have to zlin it."

But you'll be gone for hours! Zhag forced down panic. Tonyo's field unconsciously locked onto his own, soothing and steady. "That's...a good idea," Zhag managed.

"We'll talk about it later," said Tonyo, and turned back to his purchase. Their funds would almost cover it now.

Selyn fields reflected emotions, not thoughts—Tonyo was making a decision, but Zhag assumed it was what else to put back. Then the Gen said, "Verl, we're good customers. Let us have this for the money we have, and we'll buy you a porstan next time you come into Milily's."

The worker Gen gasped. To suggest that a Gen buy a drink for a Sime— Even Zhag was shocked.

"Control your Gen!" Verl said through clenched teeth.

When Zhag made no move to discipline Tonyo, Verl added, "Get away from my stand. I don't sell to Gens or Genlovers!"

Nager hard as diamond, Tonyo began, "My money's as—"

"*Your* money?!" The furious Genfarmer pulled a whip from his belt. The worker Gen hid under the table, emanating fear—emotion every junct Sime craved.

"Tonyo—don't!" Zhag warned as Simes gathered.

But the boy had had enough. His field drew in upon itself, as if drained from within. Zhag knew what was coming and forced himself to stop zlinning.

Three Simes dropped bonelessly to the market floor.

Verl flicked his whip, caught Tonyo around the upper arm, and sent him careening into Zhag. The musician did not have the mass to hold him, and they went down in a heap.

The Sime sat up, wincing at the pain of Tonyo's whip cut. Tonyo immediately focused inside himself. His pain left the ambient, but blood trickled down his arm, pluming selyn, as he helped Zhag to his feet.

Without Tonyo's brilliant field masking it, the worker Gen's panic throbbed a siren song. A man with an eyepatch knocked the Genfarm table over—but a woman snatched up the cowering Gen. It squealed in terror as Sime tentacles grasped its arms—and then in pain as the one-eyed man tried to tear it from the woman's grasp.

Zhag's attention was torn between the kill about to happen and Tonyo's reaction to it. The boy had grown up in Gen Territory—had he ever seen a kill?

Zhag had to zlin, every sense alert to get Tonyo out of the market alive.

Tonyo froze, nager damped almost into nonexistence. *Keep it that way,* Zhag willed.

Verl's whip snaked about the Sime woman's arm, lashing her lateral sheaths. Zhag shared her gasp of pain—but she hung onto the Gen's other arm. The one-eyed man slashed the edge of his hand down on a sensitive nerve point.

As the woman bent over her injured arms, Verl flicked his whip back—

The man gripped the keening Gen from behind, tentacles

lashing Sime and Gen arms together. Zhag felt Tonyo's relief. *He thinks a Sime can't kill from that position!*

The Gendealer raised his whip—

The one-eyed Sime pressed his lips to the back of the worker Gen's neck. The keening became a screech—

The whip came down—

Killbliss split the ambient. Juncts screamed frustration.

Zhag howled in despair as pain/fear/ecstasy ripped through his nerves.

Tonyo's skin crawled.

Verl's whip slashed the killer, who dropped the corpse to turn and fight. Other Simes converged, some lashing out at one another, but more turning toward—

Dizzy with denial, Zhag lurched toward the luscious fear borne on the golden field he knew as *his*.

Another Sime cut between Zhag and his prey. A growl rose in his throat. He knocked the other aside, reaching for the promise of satisfaction denied so long, so long—

Something inside Zhag whimpered. But something else exulted.

His hand found the Gen's arm, tentacles seeking killgrip. *Mine!*

Zhag's laterals licked out toward perfect terror. *Tonyo!* He recognized sole satisfaction—as his soul rejected it.

His knees gave way.

The Gen went down with him. Zhag couldn't let go—he needed the selyn, the fear, the pain.

But not the kill! Never again! On a wave of sheer shen, he fell into blackness.

Zhag fell unconscious, pulling Tony Logan down with him. Shaken out of his shock, the Gen realized: with any other Sime, he would be dead—and it would be his own damn fault!

If a Sime attempted to draw selyn from a frightened Gen, the resistance burned out the Gen's nervous system. Zhag had torn himself out of the commitment caused by Tony's fear.

But Zhag's frail old systems could not take many such shocks. Shame replaced panic. *My fault, my fault.*

Abruptly turned from protected to protector, Tony looked up at converging Simes. *I know how to handle Simes*, he reminded himself. Their laterals licked out of their sheaths, zlinning him... and that made them vulnerable. Zhag was out cold—he couldn't hurt him any more than he had already done.

Tony slammed the ambient again as he had learned to do at Keon. All around him, Simes fell unconscious.

But those still on their feet were angrier than ever. He had only moments before they were on him—

Tony slung his mentor over his shoulder, wincing at the pain from his whip cut, and sought an escape route.

"This way!" called a voice.

Tony slid through a tent flap that was raised, then closed behind him. As his eyes adjusted, he made out two Sime women, calm, dressed in neat shirts and trousers, no weapons visible.

He laid Zhag down on a grass mat. The older woman exclaimed, "He's unconscious! Greet, run to the pharmacy for some fosebine."

The younger woman dashed out the front of the tent as Tony knelt by Zhag. Their rescuer lowered the front canopy, but there was enough light for Tony to examine his friend.

The musician had the beginning of a black eye, scratches and whip cuts on his neck and hands, nothing that looked serious. But what about internal damage? "Zhag?"

"Stop that!" the woman scolded. "Wait for the medicine. What kind of Companion are you?"

"I'm not," said Tony. "Zhag's been sick, and I'm afraid he's badly hurt." He looked up. "It's my fault. I know how powerful my field is, but I panicked when I saw the kill."

"You're a Wild Gen!" the woman said in astonishment.

"I'm Tony Logan, from Heartland Gen Territory. Can you tell why Zhag isn't coming to?"

"You moved him while he was unconscious."

"They were trying to kill us."

"*You* they want to kill," the woman corrected. "*Him* they just want to murder. He may want to murder *you*, though."

The Simelan word "kill" was reserved for what Tony had just seen in the market—caused not merely by Sime need for selyn, but by the addiction to Gen death agony. Zhag had overcome that addiction, said to be harder to break than the worst drug dependency, long before he met Tony.

And Tony had triggered the craving for Gen fear today, when Zhag was in need. *What a fool I am!* "It was the first kill I ever saw," he said. "I still shouldn't have reacted. Zhag shouldn't have had to—" he realized that he had the right to say the forbidden Simelan word, as it was what had literally happened, "—shen himself to protect me."

"He'll forgive you for that," said the Sime woman. "It proves his disjunction is true. But then you moved him."

Tony still did not understand, so he just sat back on his heels and radiated confusion.

Sure enough, the woman explained. "Unconsciousness disrupts a Sime's sense of where he is—I can't explain it in Gen terms. Worse than the worst hangover you've ever had. And your friend will have disorientation on top of shen."

"Should I have left Zhag to the mercy of that crowd?"

The woman sighed. "Obviously you couldn't. And you didn't move him far. You're lucky they're fighting among themselves instead of hunting for you."

Tony looked around. Although he could hear shouting, the booth must be selyn shielded. Most of the market booths had canopies, but this one was a complete tent. Again he didn't have to ask. The woman told him, "My other daughter is Gen, as is Greet's husband. But we had the sense to leave them home today."

Zhag moaned. Tony focused his attention on his mentor, knowing his field soothed the fragile Sime. He pushed damp dark hair off the musician's pale forehead.

The frail body shivered, then arched into a convulsion. Tony pulled Zhag's belt off, doubled it, and wedged it into the Sime's mouth so he would not bite or swallow his tongue. The only other thing he knew to do was to examine Zhag's tentacles.

At full extension, the four handling tentacles on each wrist would reach the tips of the fingers. Normally they twined in graceful patterns about the hands, but Zhag's now stuck out stiffly over and under his clenched fists.

The small, pinkish gray laterals moved, though, retracting into their sheaths on either side of the Sime's wrists, then thrusting out on a gush of ronaplin, the selyn-conducting fluid. Zhag dripped the stuff when he performed, for shiltpron music required nageric as well as physical manipulation.

But Zhag was not performing now. "He's voiding selyn!" the Sime woman informed Tony.

Zhag had no selyn to spare. "Tell me what happens," Tony said, and held his hands close to, but not touching, Zhag's forearms. *Rest on my field. You're safe. No one will hurt you. You don't have to fight anymore.*

"That's amazing," said the Sime woman. "You say you're not a Companion?"

"Has he stopped voiding?" Tony asked, although as Zhag's laterals retracted and stayed in their sheaths, he was pretty sure he had achieved his goal.

"Yes. He's coming out of it."

The younger Sime woman returned with a vial of liquid. "The police are breaking up the fight."

Zhag's eyes opened a crack and immediately shut again as he groaned, putting both hands to his head. Tony followed Zhag's hands with his own, thinking soothing thoughts. The Sime gagged as he pulled the belt from his mouth, but after a moment whispered, "You're still here."

"I'm so sorry!" Tony told him. "I never meant to hurt you. Here—this will make you feel better."

After a moment Zhag allowed Tony to support his head and accepted the vial. "Fosebine?" he asked, wrinkling his nose.

"Yeah—that's what they called it."

Zhag upended the vial and swallowed the contents in one

gulp. He made such a face, Tony was almost tempted to laugh.

But the medicine worked. Tension drained from Zhag's face and body. His eyes finally opened beyond slits. "How did you manage not to get killed?"

"I was so worried about you, I forgot to be scared. Zhag, I'm sorry I lost control. I never meant to hurt you."

"I meant to kill you," said Zhag.

"No you didn't. The others did, but you shenned yourself rather than harm me." Seeing Zhag ponder that, he repeated what the woman had said, "It confirms your disjunction. I would trust you anywhere. I just hope that after this, you can trust me."

"You got us both out alive," Zhag replied. "You'd never seen a kill before, had you?"

"No."

"I hope you never do again." Then the Sime looked past Tony to their rescuers. "Where are we?" he asked.

"Halpern's Ironmongery," the older Sime woman replied, introducing herself as Eliza Halpern, her daughter as Greet. Then she demanded, "What were you thinking, to bring a Wild Gen to the market today? Any Gen, for that matter?"

"What's special about today?" asked Tony.

"It's turnover day for half of Norlea!" said Greet.

Turnover occurred when a Sime used up half a month's supply of selyn, and began the descent into need. It made Simes edgy and irritable—and explained why once the temptation disappeared they had turned to fighting each other rather than hunting Tony for selyn they didn't actually need. "Why would so many Simes be on the same transfer schedule?" he asked.

"The Last Kill," Eliza replied.

"Of course," said Zhag. "I'm sorry, Tonyo—I forgot about that. I'm on a different schedule."

"What's the Last Kill?"

Greet explained, "When the Unity Treaty was signed, the Tecton set a date after which no more kills would be allowed. That was two and a half months ago."

Tony still didn't understand. "Why would so many kill on

that one day? They couldn't all be in need at once."

Greet said disapprovingly, "Every junct who could afford to pay for an extra kill wasted enough selyn to...enjoy it."

Eliza took up the story. "Juncts hate channel's transfer—'fake kill' they call it—and put it off as long as possible. Most of them have stayed on the same schedule for the past two months—so today they all hit turnover."

"It will happen every month," added Greet, "until their cycles drift apart."

"Or till they all disjunct," said Tony. He had studied up before coming in-Territory: juncts would reach a physical and psychological crisis six months or so after their last kill. Then there would likely be worse scenes than what had happened in the market. If not for his fight with his father, Tony might have stayed home until that time was over.

Some Simes, he had been told, would die, forbidden to kill but unable to accept channel's transfer. But most, he understood, would come through as Zhag had....

The two women stared at him...and then at Zhag. Eliza asked, "Tony, when do you plan to go home?"

He sensed something in the unexpected query, so he answered honestly. "When I can show my dad I'm making a living at music. Maybe I'll visit for Year's Turning."

"Visit?" the Sime woman questioned.

"My work is here, with Zhag. He can't go into Gen Territory—it'll be years before people trust that Simes don't kill anymore. Even my mom was scared when I came into Gulf, and she was born here! If she'd seen Zhag today, though—"

Eliza turned to Zhag. "How long do you think you can lie to this young man?" she asked. "If he finds out the truth from someone else, how can he continue to trust you?"

"What...truth?" Tony asked. "Zhag?"

His Sime friend swallowed hard, and then answered, "For most junct Simes...disjunction is not possible."

"But...the Tecton promised—"

"It was the only way to get the Gen governments to sign the

Unity Treaty," Greet said.

"You can't break the treaty in less than a year!" Tony protested.

Zhag shook his head, gasping at the pain the movement caused him. "We won't break the treaty. Four or five months from now...junct Simes will start to die."

"Why can't they disjunct?" Tony asked. "You did."

"So did my husband and I," said Eliza, "but it's only possible in First Year. Our youngest Simes will survive...but juncts who changed over more than a few months ago will die."

Her daughter took up the story. "My sister and I never worried if we turned Sime or Gen—we wouldn't kill, and we wouldn't have to flee across the border like your mom did, Tony. We turned out one of each, and I married a Companion from Carre, so we have two Gens in the family."

Eliza added, "Our whole Territory would have disjuncted in another generation or two. Then we could have made a sensible treaty with the Gens. But last year, before we were ready, we faced the extinction of the human race. It's a bad choice, Tony... but it's the only one."

"Oh, my God," Tony whispered. "No wonder the juncts want to kill me—and murder Zhag. We're going to be alive in a few months, when they're all—"

Milily was junct. Their customers—all his new friends, the women he had—

"You let me make friends with people who're gonna be dead in six months!" Tony accused. "When were you planning to tell me, Zhag—when the shiltpron parlor was empty?"

"They won't all die," said Zhag. "Not that soon. I'm still alive after more than two years."

Tony realized...Zhag was far too old to have been in his First Year as a Sime two years ago. "...what? You don't kill. You certainly proved that today."

"That's right." Zhag's eyes fixed on Tony's. "It's almost a year since I killed, and I never will again."

"You said two years."

"I decided to disjunct two years ago. I didn't know I was too old. A year ago, to save my life, the channels tricked me into killing. I made them swear never to do it again—I would rather die. Eventually...I will."

Tony's head was spinning. Not knowing what to ask, he settled for, "What happened six months after you killed?"

Zhag frowned. "I'm not proud of it, even though Thea says I should be."

"Thea?"

"A channel in Carre. She ceded me her Companion. Janine. I burned her. I...couldn't overcome the junct need for pain."

"But you didn't kill this Janine?"

"No. She says Companions expect a burn once in a while. I still hate what I did—I don't want to crave pain, Tonyo!" Tony saw tortured truth in Zhag's eyes as he continued. "I don't know if a Gen can comprehend, or even a nonjunct Sime. I am disjunct. My mind. My heart. I *will not kill*. But my body demands it. My mind and heart are stronger than my body."

Had Tony found his music in Zhag—the music just out of reach his whole life—only to lose it so soon? "How long do you have?" he asked, harshly controlling his sense of betrayal.

Zhag shrugged. "Months. Maybe another year. I don't think about it. Your field helps immensely, as does my music. You... will be my legacy. The music will live on in you, Tonyo...if you are willing to stay with me."

Tony wasn't surprised at the time frame—Zhag had that pinched, tired look Tony's grandmother had developed in the months before she died. If Zhag had a year, how much he could learn in that time! "Of course I'll stay," he replied. "Just—don't hide anything else from me, all right?"

Zhag managed a weary smile. "All right."

Someone raised the front tent flap—a Sime in the uniform of the local police. "Miz Halpern? You all right?"

"Yes, thank you, Officer," Eliza told him, "but we've got injured customers who require transportation to Carre."

"There are some channels here—" the policeman began.

"Zhag has all the help that can be given here. Waiting for a channel would just delay getting him to the infirmary."

"Sure thing, Ma'am," the officer agreed, and a few minutes later a buckboard pulled up before the tent. Tony squeezed himself between his friend and some barrels and boxes, and took Zhag's hands. Warm, dry handling tentacles lashed around his fingers. When Zhag's small moist laterals licked out of their sheaths, the Gen slid his hands up toward the Sime's elbows to allow them to connect.

"Zhag? What else can I do?" His friend was growing steadily weaker, and Tony bent close to hear him.

"Sing...to me." Zhag's soft voice trailed into silence.

Tony tried to ease the tightness in his throat before launching into one of the songs they performed every night:

"Taxes goin' higher,
Last month I sold my horse.
Border's too far for raiding—
How could things get worse?
Ol' Mizipi rising—
Flood and hurricane—"

His voice cracked, and Zhag gasped.

Tony remembered what Zhag had tried to teach him that morning: let his voice follow his field. But his "inner voice" was as agitated as the Sime he was trying to soothe.

Zhag could zlin through the enforced calm Tony had pasted over his worry. He saw his anxiety reflected in the Sime's pinched features...just as his anger and annoyance—the tone of his inner voice in the market today—had triggered anger and annoyance in surrounding Simes.

With shocking clarity, he recognized his power and responsibility. He had started the fight in the marketplace... out of sheer ignorance. His stupid pride in being what Simes called a Giant Killer Gen. Did he want a Sime to die at his hands? That would make him...as junct as any Sime.

His enemy was neither Sime nor Gen: it was ignorance. Ignorance had nearly killed him today, and badly hurt Zhag.

Tony determined to end his ignorance as rapidly as possible.

Putting his mind at ease set Tony's field at ease. Zhag relaxed, tentacles loosing their frantic grip.

Tony began to sing again, following his now-peaceful inner voice. Zhag's frown melted, although Tony knew it was less from the clear notes than from the peace in his nager.

When they pulled up at Carre's infirmary, two women ran out, one Sime, one Gen.

"Zhag!" gasped the Sime woman, jumping onto the wagon. To Tony she said, "Don't move," and extended her laterals to zlin the interaction between the two men.

She turned a brilliant smile on Tony. "Oh, thank God! Zhag—where did you find him?"

Zhag opened his eyes. "Thea," he whispered.

"What have you been doing, you fool?" she asked.

"It's my fault," Tony replied. "Can you help Zhag? He's awfully weak."

His Gen Territory accent once again drew that curious reaction. "You're not a Companion?"

"I'm a musician, like Zhag," Tony replied. "Will he be all right?"

"He will now. Can you relinquish him to me? We'll take him into the infirmary. Janine will care for him while I do a deep contact on you—but I'm sure already."

Tony followed the channel's instructions as they carefully moved Zhag inside. Thea deep-zlinned Zhag, then gave him more medicine and left him in Janine's care. She took Tony into a treatment room, where she dealt with his cuts and bruises.

"Zhag will be fine once he has transfer," Thea told Tony. "He's off-schedule by almost two days—his injuries aren't enough to account for that much loss."

Tony told her about Zhag's convulsions and voiding.

"You shenned him?"

"No—he did it to himself. I take full responsibility, though. Now that I've seen a kill, I'll know better than to react if it happens again."

"Shen!" she swore. "How many Gens were killed? How many others saw and were traumatized?"

"I only saw one kill, and I was the only other Gen there."

Thea frowned, her eyes unfocused as she zlinned Tony's reaction when he remembered. "You were frightened."

"It was the first time I actually saw a Sime kill a Gen."

"How did Zhag react? To your fear?" Thea asked.

"He...started to attack me," Tony carefully recalled. "Before I got control of myself, he shenned out."

"You're sure? You didn't shen him?"

"No." He searched his memory, knowing details were important. "I wasn't exactly afraid when I saw the kill. Not for myself. It was—a chill up the spine because what I'd only heard about was really happening."

"It doesn't matter," said Thea, "especially with a field like yours. Simple startlement can provoke killmode."

Tony nodded, looking down at the bruises on his arms. "I know now. But in the market I didn't understand—I certainly wasn't afraid of Zhag—I never have been."

"You have no reason to be—today Zhag proved our worst fears: he'll suicide-abort before he'll kill."

"Suicide? Is that why he was voiding selyn? Thea...what did I do to him?" Tony asked.

The channel put a hand over his. "You provoked him—but if he were in good health, he could have handled it. Now, though, his systems are so fragile that aborting sent them into chaos." She gently squeezed his hand. "What I zlinned in that wagon is that you are the only reason he survived."

"Yeah, but I'm also the reason he's so sick. I didn't know I shouldn't move him."

"You didn't know? Where are you from?"

"Heartland Territory."

"How in the world did you get to Norlea? The Tecton is doing out-Territory Companion training in the Sime Centers."

"I'm not a Companion," Tony repeated. "I know, I know—every channel that zlins me wants me to move into a

Householding, but I came here looking for Zhag's music."

Thea looked into his eyes. "Would you be willing to be *Zhag's* Companion?"

"What would I have to do?" he asked suspiciously.

"Give him transfer. Otherwise, not much more than you're already doing. Less, actually, as he will get well with the right transfer mate."

"Get well? You mean he doesn't have to die of disjunction?" Tony asked eagerly.

"That's right."

"Yes!" Tony said at once. "I mean, we can work together? I don't have to live in a Householding?"

That smile again. "We'll train you, but Zhag needs you with him. He's a junct channel, so he will have occasional problems—but if you can bring him through psycho-spatial disorientation, you can handle just about anything. I know you can do the job. What concerns me is your commitment. What if you decide to go back to Heartland Territory?"

"Hajene," Tony said, using the term of respect for a channel that he had learned at Keon, "I'm young, but I know what I was meant to do with my life. Zhag is the music I came here for. I can't think of anything to keep me from staying, but I have to be sure I understand. Why me? Why hasn't Janine or another Companion already done what you say I can do?"

"Because Zhag is a channel, like me. It's much harder to find him a matchmate than it is for a renSime." RenSimes were the majority of Simes, who were not channels.

"And a matchmate," he wanted to be sure, "can keep a junct Sime from dying if he's too old to disjunct?"

"Yes. Keon and Carre are trying to match as many Simes as we can before people begin dying. But we are at a huge disadvantage."

"Not enough Gens," Tony realized.

"Not enough Gens who are not frightened. The least fear, the least resistance, and there will be a kill."

Tony thought a moment. "And not necessarily of a Gen. I

nearly killed Zhag today."

She didn't correct his terminology. "It's Zhag's responsibility, not yours. But when you give him transfer, you are going to have to take some responsibility."

"Just tell me what to do."

"In transfer, Zhag has to be completely open to your feelings. It doesn't matter if your fear is *for* him rather than *of* him. Fear will trigger killmode—and Zhag will abort. Weak as he is, he won't survive shen a second time."

"I'm not afraid. Zlin the truth of it."

She nodded. "It's hard to believe you didn't grow up in a Householding. But can you handle the paradox? Zhag needs a killmode transfer—it's the only way to satisfy him physically. But emotionally he will reject it—if you trigger killmode, he will abort," she repeated.

"Then what should I do?" Tony asked in frustration.

She sighed. "How often have you given transfer?"

"I've donated twice."

"Donated?" Thea asked. "Your field is in synch with mine, responding like an experienced Donor's—and you're telling me you've never given transfer?!"

He shrugged. "I can do it. I met kids twelve or fourteen years old who are Companions in Keon. I'll bet you've got some here, too. All the Companions say transfer's the best thing—"

But Thea shook her head vehemently, hands out, palms toward him, tentacles tightly retracted. "No, no—you can't force killbliss on an injured channel in disjunction crisis as your First Transfer! Shen and shid! I was worried about convincing Sectuib when I thought you were experienced! We'll find someone appropriate for you today, train you over the next four weeks, and next month you and Zhag can try it."

"What happens to Zhag this month?" Tony demanded.

"We've brought him through crisis before. Janine is his closest match here, but we'll probably want to overmatch him." She sat back and looked Tony up and down, shaking her head as if what she saw contradicted what she zlinned. "You slightly overmatch him now, but we'll give you a conservative match this month—no risk of knocking you out of synch with Zhag. But you've got to experience a channel's draw without having to control the transfer at the same time."

"Thea—I'm young and strong and healthy. Zhag is old and weak and sick. He can't hurt me."

"You may be right—but Sectuib won't risk Zhag's hurting you...and *I* won't risk your hurting Zhag."

Tony remembered his decision on the way to Carre. There were too many things he had to learn. Thea continued, "Don't go near Zhag before his transfer, so he won't fix on you again—but I want you there, high-field, immediately afterward. Then we'll tell him you'll give him transfer next month."

"Why didn't he ask me?" Tony wanted to know. Then he realized— "Oh, shit. I told him I didn't want to be a Companion. I meant that I wouldn't go off to a Householding, not that I wasn't willing to give him my selyn."

This time Thea's smile was wistful. "Self-destructive attitudes are typical of disjunction crisis. Zhag surely recognized a potential matchmate...you did, too, and just didn't know what you were feeling. Well," she shrugged, "we have to deal with the existing situation. Zhag is always terrified of hurting his Donor. You'll have to seduce him—but I expect that will be easy enough. Sectuib should be back soon. He'll verify my readings and schedule your training."

Thea gave Tony a clean shirt. "I'll put your old one in the rag bin. Go wash up before you meet Sectuib. Can you read Simelan well enough to follow the signs to his office?"

"Sure. My mom made sure that if I changed over and had to run to Gulf, I wouldn't be illiterate."

"Smart mom," Thea told him.

He didn't tell her how angry his father had been—or that his mother regretted making it easy for her son to leave home.

Tony took advantage of hot water and soft towels, and felt much more ready to be presented to the head of Householding Carre. It wasn't much of a presentation—the Sectuib in Carre stole a few minutes to deep-zlin Tony, confirm Thea's diagnosis, and assign his first lesson after he had transfer with a channel named Sansee. Apparently he wouldn't even meet Sansee until their appointment.

"Now go over to the refectory and have something to eat!" Sectuib told him in dismissal. Tony suddenly remembered that he was still hungry.

But he hardly noticed what he ate—his mind was on Zhag. The Sime musician was more than a skilled shiltpron player. There were others who played amazing music...but not the music of Tony's soul, the rhythm and harmony always just beyond his reach...until he touched its reality in Zhag Paget.

It was an hour till Zhag's transfer. Tony wanted to see his friend, but understood that he would make matters worse. Still, he couldn't help wandering back toward the infirmary.

Simes were leaving, bandaged, provided with transfer if necessary. Householdings had first gained wary acceptance among juncts because of channels' healing ability. Local Simes came to rely on them, got to know the Gen Companions, and some, like Zhag and the Halpern family, chose to leave the kill behind. But most of these Simes were junct, and in months or a few short years would be dead. But what could Tony do, other than save the one Sime he could?

He entered the infirmary through the twisting corridor that served to buffer nageric fields. Nevertheless, he held his own field in tightly, not knowing whether he might encounter injured Simes around the corner.

The lobby was empty except for two channels: Thea and the Sectuib in Carre. Their backs were to Tony as they bent over a chart—Zhag's chart, he realized as he heard the Sectuib say, "He's fixed on Tonyo. Neither you nor I can imitate that field of his, and it's a sure bet Janine can't."

"Then it has to be Tonyo," said Thea.

"No," said the Sectuib. "We could lose both of them." He raised a tentacle to forestall her protest. "You zlinned the potential in that boy. Zhag managed a clean abort this afternoon, but he has no strength left. A botched abort would surely kill him... and it could leave Tonyo crippled for life."

"Nerve damage," Thea agreed with a sigh. "He might never regain nageric control."

I could lose my music! Tony realized, and clamped down hard lest the two channels zlin his reaction.

But...if Zhag dies, I lose it anyway, he realized.

Could he make the Sectuib understand that, or was the man a Sime version of Tony's father, unable to comprehend music as a sacred vocation? Zhag understood. But Zhag was dying.

Before he could gather courage to try to make his case to the stern Sectuib, though, a Gen came running from another corridor. "Sectuib—Hajene! That woman with the torn lateral is voiding—Jaramee can't stop it!"

The two channels disappeared down the corridor with the Gen. Tony went to the desk and picked up Zhag's chart. The clipboard was thick with pages of hasty penmanship, but on the top sheet he made out a list of medications. He recognized only fosebine—and a note that "patient resists intil and trautholo," whatever the hell that meant.

And at the bottom, "Condition: critical."

There was a mark beside the word "Prognosis:" as if someone had started to write something. *Terminal,* Tony realized. *Zhag's life. My future. It all hinges on this moment.*

Nobody trusted his commitment—not even Zhag. Consciously, Zhag had been trying to train him so that he could go on after the musician was dead...but unconsciously...Thea had said Zhag recognized his matchmate, but dared not hope—

Zhag has to trust me always to be there for him. That's why he wants me to use the Simelan version of my name—to show I'm not some Wild Gen who will go running across the border at the first provocation. Zhag's the other half of my creativity. Our lives are lived to the same rhythm, the same harmony. If I deny him...I deny myself.

Tonyo put down the chart, and went to Zhag's room. Janine still sat by the bed, concentrating. Zhag was asleep or unconscious, barely breathing.

Janine looked up. "Go away!" she whispered sharply. "You'll ruin the work we've done!"

"Thea needs—uh, requires you, Janine. She and Sectuib are trying to help a patient with a torn lateral."

"She wouldn't send *you*!"

Tonyo looked into the Companion's eyes. She had to understand. "Take your time finding her," he said, "and then say you believed me."

"Tonyo—leave, please!"

He stood his ground. "Tell me you can save his life, Janine. Swear you believe it, and I'll go."

She bit her lip, and tried to stare him down...but she couldn't. "And if you die?" she asked.

"My conscience, not yours. But I won't die, and neither will Zhag. You're Gen. You understand what Simes can't."

After a long moment, she nodded, and rose carefully from her chair beside the transfer couch. Tonyo ignored the chair and, relying on Janine's experience to ease the transition for Zhag, sat in the channel's position on the specially-constructed couch. He was supported in position to grasp Zhag's forearms, and, when the time came—

Janine bent and kissed Tonyo's cheek. "Good luck!" she whispered, and was gone, leaving Tonyo once more where he belonged. It reminded him of sitting on the steps of Zhag's house as they had that morning, but with their roles reversed. Now it was Tonyo who had to find the way to make Zhag understand, by that same instinct with which Zhag had taught him to follow his field with his voice.

Before Tonyo even touched him, Zhag's chest rose and fell in a deep breath. *Yes,* Tonyo willed, *I have what you need, Zhag— I'll share it with you, just as we share our music.*

He played their music in his mind. His joy when he heard new sounds from Zhag's shiltpron, the lessons he had learned— What music they would make—new music they would compose together, the whole greater than the sum of its parts.

Perhaps Zhag sensed the music in his field...Tonyo took heart when a small smile touched the corners of Zhag's mouth.

He slid his hands forward, aligning their arms in transfer position. Zhag's tentacles lay under the skin along his forearms, sheaths visible because he had almost no flesh to hide them. But they did not emerge from the wrist openings, nor did his hands grip Tonyo's forearms.

Tonyo felt for the tentacle roots. Where was the reflex point—?

He pressed gently around the root of each tentacle. The handling tentacles emerged and wrapped around his arms, but the laterals remained stubbornly sheathed. It seemed cruel to heighten Zhag's need—worse, he'd been told, than any Gen hunger—but he was there to assuage it. Zhag should feel something like the pleasure of hunger just before a good meal.

Tonyo conjured up his hunger of an hour ago, along with the music that always drew Zhag's laterals forth. In his mind he played the sad and difficult songs that demanded all of Zhag's virtuosity...the songs of need.

The small, sensitive laterals licked out of their sheaths and settled on Tonyo's arms. He smiled. *Now—let's do this!*

Zhag's eyes opened, at first unfocused, then fixed on Tonyo. All his effort could not take his voice above a whisper. "Tonyo—no!" Weakly, he tried to pull his arms away—but his tentacles remained seated.

"Shut up, Zhag," Tonyo told him. "Just feel it!"

He ignored the protest in Zhag's eyes, his feeble attempts to escape, keeping the Sime under control by sheer power of will. Something inside him erupted with anticipation. *This is even better than our music!* it told him, and he leaned forward to touch his lips to Zhag's.

It was not a kiss. Twice Tonyo had performed this act with Tecton channels, an impersonal touch that completed the circuit for the transfer of selyn. In those transactions he had felt nothing except vague disappointment. With Zhag he felt hope and exhilaration.

When need turned him inside-out, he rode the music like an ocean wave. He was pure energy, blissfully pouring life and warmth into the welcoming void. It was perfect harmony, exact counterpoint— A peak of pleasure, another, and then— What—? Poignant ebb— *No! Not enough!*

He struggled, needing more, denying that need in crashing discord.

What more could there possibly be?!

He caught the panting, terrified Gen in a woodland clearing. Need clawed at his vitals—need for the fear of the Gen writhing and screaming under his tentacles. He pulled it to him, glorying in anticipation of the kill.

He pressed his lips roughly to the Gen's whimpering mouth. Terror sang through his nerves—pain—sweet death agony burned away his need. Giddy with satisfaction, he let the husk of the dead Gen drop carelessly from his hands and tentacles....

He was alive!

Warm hands loosed their grip on Zhag's arms and fell away. A head rested heavily against his neck. Fresh, clean, soap scent filled his nostrils. He was brimming with life, but—

His vision was obscured by fallen sunlight. It took a moment to recognize Tonyo's blond hair—he never looked at the boy, always consumed in his golden nager. But now...nothing.

The door opened. Thea and the Sectuib in Carre entered— and stopped so abruptly that Janine, behind them, almost ran into the two Simes.

Tonyo raised his head, blue eyes wide with awe.

"You're alive!" Zhag gasped.

The Gen grinned. "I've never been so alive!"

Carre's Sectuib stepped forward, laterals extended. "What the shidoni-doomed shen happened here?"

Zhag was too busy taking stock of himself to answer. His pain was gone, along with his need. He had a sense of well being so alien he couldn't respond to it. He wanted to laugh and cry at the same time, and...he couldn't zlin.

"Tonyo—what have you done to me?" he asked. "I haven't felt like this since—"

"The last time you killed?" Tonyo asked. "You can say it, Zhag. You don't ever have to do it again."

But that wasn't it. As Zhag changed focus to the trio on the other side of the room, a wave of vertigo swept over him.

"What's wrong?" Tonyo gasped.

"Nothing serious," said the Sectuib, zlinning them. He shook his head. "God protects fools and children."

"Zhag's alive!" Tonyo protested. "That's more than you could promise."

"Tonyo!" Zhag put a hand on the boy's arm...and felt his ability to zlin return as he sensed the pulse-pulse-pulse of selyn production. He had been wrong—Tonyo was storing far less selyn than before their transfer, but his field was no less vital. He would be able to perform tonight.

"Thea," the Sectuib was saying, "zlin this. You will probably never see anything like it again."

"What's wrong with Zhag?" Tonyo asked anxiously.

A chuckle escaped the channel's attempt to be stern. "You burned him!" he told the Gen.

"...what?" Tonyo and Zhag spoke at once, then looked at one another.

"How could a Gen burn a Sime?" Zhag asked in confusion.

"Tonyo is what the juncts call a Giant Killer Gen," the Sectuib explained.

"I know," Zhag said. "Otherwise I wouldn't allow him to work around the juncts at Milily's."

"Here we call them Natural Donors—Gens who instinctively control transfer. Being in control eliminates fear. Of course they still require training," he added with a sharp glance at Tonyo, "because they can harm Simes."

"Zhag needed pain," said Tonyo. "I...felt it."

"I don't doubt it," the Sectuib replied. "But next time deliver something like your pain when the whip cut you today."

Tonyo blushed. "Oh. Zhag, I'm sorry. I'll learn to do it right."

"It couldn't have been more right," Zhag told him.

"Tonyo," said the Sectuib, "you know that, as a channel, Zhag has a dual selyn system?"

"Yes."

"You filled his primary and secondary systems, and when he wasn't satisfied, you forced more selyn into his primary system against his resistance. It's only a slight burn—and Zhag, you feel strange because your fields have never been unbalanced in this particular way."

Zhag's secondary system, which Tecton channels used to provide transfer and he used to play the shiltpron, often contained more selyn than his primary system, which stored selyn for daily living. He couldn't remember ever having it unbalanced in the other direction. "Tonyo, I can correct the imbalance if you'll let me touch you again."

Immediately, his Gen reached out to him. Zhag settled his tentacles, laid his head on Tonyo's shoulder, and let the two systems level. The movement of energy erased the effects of the burn, and Zhag felt even better.

Had he ever felt this good in his life? He wanted to run, to dance, to play his shiltpron—but first, "I'm hungry!" he announced in astonishment.

Tonyo laughed. "Let's go to the refectory—I was too worried to eat much earlier."

"I'll have to have an accounting first," the Sectuib said, and Zhag's good cheer disappeared. Numbly, he submitted to deep contact, unsurprised to hear that he had received more selyn than last month. "You're still in the same category," the channel reassured him.

"Yeah—but early," he grumbled. He counted out the carefully hoarded coins while Janine made notes. The Sectuib deducted the collection fee, and held out the rest to Tonyo.

The boy made no move to take it.

"You were paid for your donations, Tonyo," said Thea.

"I can't take money for what Zhag and I just did. I'd feel like a whore!"

"Take it," said Zhag. "You can eat for the next month."

Tonyo frowned. "Can't we have a private arrangement, with no money changing hands?"

The Sectuib explained, "The government will collect Zhag's taxes, no matter what. We never used to do accounting inside the Householdings—I've got couples who've been transfer partners for years. But the new laws apply to everyone."

Tonyo reluctantly accepted the money, but did not put it away. "It's your money," he said to Zhag.

"You earned it, Tonyo."

"Zhag, it's not right. We did it together—the way we play music together. At least take half."

"Shen it!" Zhag snapped. "I'm beholden to you for my life! Isn't that enough?"

Thea said, "Zhag! That's post syndrome talking."

Zhag felt guilty at the boy's crestfallen look—but he also felt the anger, along with a hundred other emotions he had been incapable of expressing for nearly two years.

But Tonyo was in the grip of Gen post-syndrome, unable to feel bad for more than a moment. "Zhag," he said, "I know it bothers you to need me to stay alive...but isn't it more important that you don't need me to keep you from killing?"

At the boy's words—he felt it, no more doubt or questioning! The most important thing was completely in his own control. Zhag's mood flipped back to exhilaration, carrying him even higher than he had been a moment ago. Tonyo grinned—and Zhag realized it was in response to his own expression.

And when he thought his mood could not go any higher, Janine held out the receipt form for Tonyo to sign...and he saw the boy write "Tonyo Logan." The Simelan version of his name. *He's going to stay!* And Tonyo looked up at him as if he felt and shared the overwhelming emotion it caused in Zhag.

The Sectuib left Thea and Janine to explain to Tonyo what to do as Zhag's pent-up feelings surfaced.

"I know what Zhag requires," said Tonyo. "He'll work it off on stage tonight." He turned a charming smile on Thea. "Why don't you and Janine come to the performance?"

Zhag expected an automatic refusal—Householders did not frequent shiltpron parlors—but to his surprise Thea said, "I can't promise...but I'd love to see you perform."

After a stop at Carre's refectory, where Zhag actually enjoyed eating, they started walking home. Zhag had had to conserve energy for so long, had been so weak, that he wanted to run—almost felt he could fly. As his steps speeded, Tonyo scurried to keep up. "We have time to get there," the Gen protested. "We don't go on for nearly two hours."

"I'm ready to play right now," Zhag told him. And just because he could, he turned cartwheels down the street, then backflipped back to his Gen.

Tonyo laughed delightedly. "Are you gonna do that on stage tonight?"

"Maybe. I don't know what I'm gonna do."

Tonyo watched him with a puzzled look. Out of the blue, he asked, "Zhag...how old are you?"

"Six," the musician replied.

"Oh. Well, how old were you when you changed over?"

Out-Territory Gens figured age from birth, Zhag remembered. "Almost fifteen."

Tonyo was wide-eyed. "I thought you were at least my dad's age. You're only four years older than I am!"

Zhag laughed at his astonishment. "I feel like a child—as if I didn't even know the kill existed."

Tonyo pondered for a moment. Then, very seriously, he said, "That's because you gave it to me."

"Gave what to you?"

"The kill," Tonyo replied. "During transfer. Thea said you'd shen out if you felt killmode, so I guess you made me feel it instead. Was that your First Kill?"

"Tonyo, what are you talking about?"

The young Gen frowned. "I was Sime," he said, "chasing a Gen through the woods. I caught it...and I...killed it."

Zhag zlinned Tonyo's emotions, the rush of anticipation, the glee at his victim's terror, the bliss of the kill....

"Shen," he whispered. "Tonyo, you can't know those feelings!"

"I got them from you."

Zhag shook his head. "I've never hunted. All my kills were... regulated." A chill ran up his spine. "It doesn't matter," he decided, not wanting to know how a Gen could get such a feel for Sime experience. "It was what you...needed...to be able to give me that transfer. Lucky for me you have a vivid imagination, yes?"

Tonyo nodded, accepting. How long would he continue to accept Zhag's word, especially when the Sime had no idea what he was talking about?

"Come on!" said Zhag, as they entered a lane overhung with ancient oaks. He caught a branch, and swung from one tree to another. When he hung upside down by his knees from the last one, he finally got the laughter he wanted from his Gen.

"You're not even out of breath," said Tonyo. "I could use some of that Sime energy for singing."

"You sing just fine." Zhag chuckled, landing on his feet beside the Gen. "Tonight I'll be able to hear you without working at it. I hope Thea can come."

"So do I," said Tonyo.

"You think she's after you, like all the others?"

"Not Thea!" Tonyo protested. "Can't you tell she's in love with you? I knew it the minute I saw you together."

The Gen's words made Zhag feel warm. The ravages of disjunction might not be erased with one good transfer, but—

Suddenly, his mind and heart were flooded with melody. Tonyo's field responded in harmony, and Zhag laughed in pure joy. They were about to create something unique—something he could never have composed alone. "Come on, Tonyo!" he urged, eager to have his instrument in his hands. "We have a new song to finish before showtime!"

THE STORY UNTOLD

Music swirled through the saloon. Dust motes danced in the shaft of sunlight pouring through the roof where green wood had warped in the heat. Out here on the high plain, farther from home than he had ever been before, Zhag Paget clung to the familiarity of his shiltpron, plucking notes with practiced ease. His partner, Tonyo Logan, stood on the platform that passed for a stage, and vocalized for the gratification of the saloon owner, two Simes passed out at a table in the back, and a hound dog lolling in the patch of sunlight.

Tonyo was exercising his voice for the evening's performance, implementing nageric skills—his ability to project emotions via his field of life energy—only as required to guide his voice. The technique, suggested by Zhag in a long-ago moment of serendipitous frustration, had turned Tonyo from merely a very good singer into a great one.

Zhag closed off his other senses, appreciating with hearing alone as the singer's voice rose to a pitch no grown man of either larity should be able to reach, descended to his natural tenor for the verse, and then dipped easily into the baritone range. Zhag wondered if that was where his protégé's voice would eventually settle—or would he maintain and even extend his incredible range and control?

Not that it mattered: it was not Tonyo's vocal pyrotechnics that charmed Simes. What moved the vast majority of their audience was the way his life energy field expressed emotions that Simes perceived directly, rather than filtered through the senses Simes like Zhag and Gens like Tonyo shared.

The saloon owner shooed the hung-over Simes out of her establishment, along with the hound dog, who responded to the indignity by sitting outside the door and howling. "Critics everywhere!" Tonyo observed, pouring water from his canteen into a crude clay mug. The dry air out here was very different from the humidity they coped with back home in Gulf Territory.

After draining the mug, Tonyo picked up his guitar, an instrument developed in Ancient times and a favorite of Gens, who had no tentacles on their wrists with which to play the multiple components of a shiltpron. Tonyo was not a virtuoso, as Zhag was on his instrument, but he was good enough to play accompaniment to his powerful vocal and nageric performance. He glanced at the thin walls, the insubstantial roof, and shrugged. "Our rehearsal's a free show for anyone out there."

The hound dog nudged the ill-hung door open, plodded over to Tonyo, and leaned against the Gen's knee until Tonyo scratched his ears. Zhag extended his lateral tentacles—the small sensing organs on either side of his wrists—and let his Sime perceptions roam beyond the walls. "Not many people in town," he reported. "They'll come later, for the concert."

He didn't expect a crowd tonight, in this town so small that the Tecton Ambassadors, as Zhag and Tonyo were termed here in Pueblo Territory, were staying behind the saloon in rooms which they joked must usually rent by the hour.

There was no hotel, but the hopefully named Dis Junction was the only good stopping place on their journey to Red Rocks. At that natural amphitheater, people from all over this newly-created Sime Territory would gather for what was billed as the most important concert of Zhag and Tonyo's career. Their manager and the Tecton representatives, including Zhag's wife, had gone ahead to make the final preparations.

The hound dog turned around twice and settled to sleep at Tonyo's feet. The Gen strummed his guitar and began to sing.

"My brother, he turned out wrong,
   had to run for the border.
I'll never see his face again, never—"

"No!" said Zhag. "We are not performing that song!"

"But it's the perfect—" Tonyo began the familiar protest.

"It would be perfect for Pueblo Territory if you sang it the way you wrote it," Zhag explained. "Tonyo, that song used to move everyone's heart. But now—you go too far!" He recalled the near riot in Nivet's Capital City.

"If you wouldn't fight me," said Tonyo, "if you would work with me, we could create a catharsis."

"Create killmode, more likely," Zhag told him flatly.

"Zhag, killmode is a natural state."

"For juncts," Zhag agreed.

"For Simes," Tonyo insisted. "You're hung up on the word. Call it intil, and it's perfectly acceptable."

"It's not the same thing," Zhag said, frustrated at the way his young singer thought he understood things no Gen could experience. "Intil is merely the commitment to draw selyn. Killmode is the quintessential junct emotion. Almost everyone in Pueblo Territory is junct...and will be until they die."

Tonyo held his energy field under tight control as he tried to make Zhag understand. "That's why you and I are here: to show them that 'junct' doesn't have to mean 'killer'!"

"You and I cannot control the number of Simes who could fit in this room, let alone the thousands at Red Rocks."

"We don't have to," said Tonyo. "They'll control themselves."

"Are you crazy?" Zhag asked. "Everyone in this territory is in some phase of disjunction crisis!"

"And every single one by free choice!" Tonyo reminded him. "The Tecton didn't force it on them—they formed Pueblo Territory to separate themselves from the Kill." The Gen's blue eyes were bright with admiration. "They all have the same incentive you had, Zhag—or they wouldn't be here!"

That was true: Pueblo was formed out of land unclaimed

for many years, belonging to neither Simes nor Gens when the Unity Treaty five years ago ended the threat of Zelerod's Doom. Now the two forms of humanity had to overcome the harsh realities of the Sime~Gen mutation: Gens produced selyn, the very biologic energy of life itself, Simes needed that energy to live, and until recently there had been no way for Simes to survive except by killing Gens for their life force.

It had taken the collapse of Northwest Territory five years ago to make most Simes understand that the threat the mathematician Zelerod had warned of was real. If both larities could not overcome their nature, eventually the Simes would kill all the Gens, and then the Simes would die of attrition. In order for the human race to survive, Gens were learning to give selyn to Simes freely, even joyously, as Tonyo did for Zhag...and Simes were breaking their addiction to the Kill.

What Tonyo could not understand, what no Gen could, was how close the killer instinct remained beneath the surface. Zhag would never kill again—he would die first—but he knew as the Gen could not how the memory lurked in the blood, in the nerves, a life-long stamp of shame.

"You'll never understand," Zhag repeated. "The last thing these Simes need—" he deliberately chose to use metaphorically the word usually reserved to mean only the Need for life force "—is to be reminded of their junctedness."

"No, Zhag," Tonyo replied in the identical tone of voice, echoing Zhag's nageric tone beat for beat, "it is the first thing they...need." He pushed his blond curls out of his eyes and said, "We know what it means to be junct."

Exasperated, Zhag shook his head. "You can't—"

"I can, and you know it!" Tonyo told him. "Any Companion is capable of killing a Sime with a flick of his field—but we don't. Zhag—" the Gen's field told him how serious it was to him "—you are less likely to kill than I am. I have the strength. I could underestimate it, or simply be so angry or so frightened that I overreact. I don't know my limits—but you know yours. You've been tested, and I haven't. You drove the Kill from your life. Why do you act as if it were something shameful?"

And all Zhag could fall back on was, "You'll never understand."

"Well, *make* me understand!" Tonyo insisted.

For answer, Zhag picked up his shiltpron and began to play Tonyo's song. A channel—a Sime with a dual selyn system—Zhag also performed on the nageric level, imitating Tonyo's performance of the song that had become the Gen's signature.

The song was about the old days, and the old ways of...only six years ago for Zhag, less than four years for most of the Simes he knew. And for the Simes here in Pueblo Territory, the days since the Last Kill were measured in mere months.

Tonyo began to sing, his selyn field leading his voice and Zhag's shiltpron, throbbing with sorrow. It was the first melody Zhag had composed after Tonyo had rescued him from slow and agonizing death. Restored to health by a transfer mate whose field characteristics matched his own, Zhag had also found the musical partner of a lifetime. He had known the boy could sing, but not that the young Gen could write lyrics that wrenched the heart of any Sime post enough to hear them—while his nager worked even more effectively on the rest.

Simes zlinned the world with special senses that enabled them to hunt down Gens, and the closer they came to Need, the more they relied on those senses. Very few Gens could handle a Sime in Need the way that Tonyo did, and none could without training. The current solution was for channels to stand between the Sime and the Kill, taking selyn from Gens without hurting them and transferring it to Simes to assuage their Need. The problem was, junct Simes craved the sensation of the Kill, and very few channels could duplicate that feeling. Especially those who themselves had never killed.

Zhag's own wife, Thea, a channel who had never killed, could not really understand—so how could a Gen like Tonyo? Untrained Gen reaction to a Sime's attempt to draw selyn was fear and resistance—and when Simes drew against that resistance, they killed Gens by burning out their nervous systems.

Once a Sime had known killbliss, the Sime's body would crave it forever after, no matter how much his mind abhorred the idea of killing.

Zhag shuddered. The vibration of his field affected the drone strings of the shiltpron, producing eerie notes that Tonyo echoed—and then mutated from fear and shame into—

"Stop that!" Zhag ordered.

"I'm following *you*!" Tonyo protested. "Zhag, every time we reach this point, you project shame. It's been worse with every performance since we left home."

"But what you are projecting—"

"—is Gen response to Sime Need. You won't finish it, and you won't let me finish it. You break off when everything is hopeless."

"That's what that song is about—the days when it was hopeless if someone turned the wrong larity. You never had a brother turn Sime, but I had a brother turn Gen."

"I know," said Tonyo. "And you didn't look at it as hopeless! You tried to take him to the border."

"He was killed anyway," Zhag said bitterly.

"Yes," Tonyo said, laying a gentle hand on Zhag's shoulder. "But getting caught doesn't change the fact that you tried. You were just a kid yourself—never mind that Sime law says you're an adult the moment you change over. You had the courage to break a bad law. That's what the song is about: the courage to say, 'No, I will not kill my brother, my sister, my son, my daughter.' And for Gens, 'No, my brother, my sister, my son, my daughter does not deserve to be shot down like a mad dog just because they turned Sime.'"

Perhaps the ultimate cruelty of the Sime~Gen mutation was that no one knew until adolescence whether they would be Sime or Gen. One-third of children born to Gen parents became Sime, one-third of children born to Sime parents became Gen, and there was no way to know which larity a child would be. There was no family, Sime or Gen, untouched by this tragedy.

"Never again," Tonyo was saying. "That's what every Sime

says who has come to Pueblo Territory. No one should live in fear of puberty. No parents should be afraid to love their children."

"Perform it that way," said Zhag. "Perform it the way we always have, Tonyo."

"I will. But if you put fear and shame into it again, I have to counter. I have to, Zhag! We're symbols of hope. The people of Pueblo Territory know that 'junct' doesn't have to mean 'killer.' They are ready to die for that belief."

"Most of them will die," Zhag reminded him. "Or else be forced to—"

"No," said Tonyo. "That's the past. For the future there is only hope—the reason they are here. We have to show them what we really are."

"Junct?"

"But not killers."

"I can't do that!"

"Why not? Why not, Zhag?" His Companion's dark blue eyes bored into Zhag, the Gen's field probing, trying to draw from him the shameful truth—

"No!" Zhag took a deep, shaky breath and closed himself off from Tonyo's field. "We won't perform the song, then. Do you understand me, Tonyo? If you can't do it the way we always have, leave it out of the setlist!"

Tonyo nodded. "I hear what you are saying, Zhag. But I still don't understand why."

By evening, the little town of Dis Junction was crowded with Simes. Although there were two other bars, the saloon was the only one that could accommodate live entertainment. Designed to seat fifty people comfortably, tonight it was packed with over a hundred patrons, all Sime except for a few children. The single Gen on the premises was Tonyo Logan, for the only other Gens in town were Companions to the channels at the local dispensary. Two channels and their Companions were supposed to be here, but one pair had gone to attend a changeover, and the others were detained with the extra work.

It was the first time on the tour—the first time since they had begun performing outside small, intimate shiltpron parlors—that there was not at least one other Sime~Gen pair to help control the crowd. They had required help only once, in Capital City. But that, Zhag reminded himself, had been a crowd of more than five thousand, their biggest audience ever. Still, it had been fortunate that there were channel~Companion pairs all through the crowd. They had done two more concerts in Nivet, to crowds nearly as large, without incident...but also without performing Tonyo's signature song.

Zhag quelled his pre-show jitters and followed Tonyo onto the platform. A Gen who walked confidently among Simes meant Companion to these people, but although Tonyo was technically Zhag's Companion, that was not how he thought of himself, nor was his approach to Simes the least bit clinical.

"Good evening!" he greeted them, his field throbbing a warm welcome that was instantly projected back at him. He grinned, as if he could feel it—and Zhag, seated at the back of the platform, suspected that in some way Simes could not understand, he actually did.

They started with some workers' songs known on both sides of every border, music to raise spirits and encourage everyone to pull together. They served equally well to bring their audience together for the concert.

It was an easier crowd to please than any in Nivet Territory, where they had had to win over some tough skeptical audiences. But they had given their all, and even the Capital City concert had ended in triumph despite the shaky middle. Tonight, though, everyone present had come to have a good time.

Porstan flowed, and combined with shiltpron music had its usual intoxicating effect. When everyone was feeling mellow, they moved on to the old Sime blues songs that Tonyo performed so well. Zhag grinned to himself as his partner sang of Pen taxes and being shorted, with appropriate nageric accompaniment. Those in the crowd using the senses they shared with Gens kept having odd moments of realization that they were seeing and hearing a healthy young Gen, while they seemed to zlin a jaded old Sime.

The applause shook the crudely constructed building until Zhag feared the floor might collapse under them. It didn't. Tonyo bowed, and gestured Zhag out from behind his instrument. The roar of appreciation was backed with nageric approval. He bowed shyly, feeling naked without his shiltpron. Without the flamboyant Tonyo Logan to front for him Zhag would never have sought star status.

At this point, they usually played "My Brother, He Turned Out Wrong" before taking a break. With that song out of the setlist, Zhag left the stage, assuming his Gen would follow as quickly as the crowd allowed. Thirsty, Zhag worked his way toward the bar. He tried not to shy away from people who reached out to touch him, explaining that no, he could not accept offers of drinks, the house was supplying them—

Suddenly the notes of Tonyo's guitar rang out. The crowd instantly lost interest in Zhag.

Zhag was trapped at the bar, where the hostess shoved a glass of porstan into his hand and whispered, "Shen—never thought a Gen could be sexy before!"

But Tonyo's appeal to women was not Zhag's concern—the Gen was singing "My Brother, He Turned Out Wrong"!

I've got to stop him! Zhag thought, looking for a way to reach the stage before Tonyo started another riot. The crowd was caught up in the familiar tragedy—Zhag remembered the first time they had performed this song, to an audience much like this one, nerves raw with disjunction, reminded of why they endured for the sake of son or daughter, sister or—

Would Tonyo stay with the original song? Zhag prepared to grasp the fields if necessary.

But to control fields, Zhag had to zlin...and when he zlinned Tonyo as he sang,

"My brother, he turned out strange—one day we just didn't know him—"

"Stop!" Zhag shouted. "Tonyo! Stop it, right now!"

But the Gen continued singing.

Zhag fought his way toward the stage as Tonyo built and built toward the only possible end: pain—grief—fear—*shame*—

"Noooo!" Zhag howled, trying to stop Tonyo—stop him before the Kill!

Hands and tentacles held Zhag back. Losing touch with any but Sime senses, he threw off some people, but others closed in like water, their fields a miasma of grief, pain, and fear.

Killmode seared Zhag's nerves—raw Need for Gen pain. *Not again! No! Never again!*

But before Zhag regained control, those least in Need among nearby Simes surrounded him, held him back—

—to protect Tonyo!

He was pushed to the floor and literally sat on by junct Simes intent on protecting his Gen partner. No whips were drawn, no punches thrown—

But, Zhag realized as the music stopped abruptly, all Tonyo saw was his partner disappearing under a mass of Sime bodies! Tonyo flared fear—not for himself, but for Zhag.

But Gen fear was Gen fear. Simes near Tonyo turned—

Ignoring them, Tonyo barreled through the crowd by using his field as a bludgeon, charging to rescue his fallen partner.

Zhag tried to call out that he was all right, but there was too much weight on his diaphragm. Tonyo pushed through the last row to where he could actually see—

Zhag zlinned Tonyo's field pull in sharply and knew what was about to happen. He stopped zlinning, his voice a croak too soft for the Gen to hear him warn, "Tonyo, don't—!"

The Simes piled on Zhag collapsed—as did the first rank of those surrounding.

Tonyo pulled limp bodies off him. Zhag sat up, gasping for breath and trying to calm the turmoil in his selyn systems. "I'm—all right," he managed. "You shouldn't—have done that."

"I'm sorry," Tonyo responded contritely—but he meant for the song. What had them in big trouble now was the Genslam.

For Zhag had seen what Tonyo had not: the sheriff's badge

adorning the shirt of a Sime now slumped on the floor.

The law officer moaned and dragged himself to his feet. Unsteady, tainting the ambient with a sick headache, he nonetheless did his job.

"Show's over, folks. Everybody not hurt, go on home."

He looked at the bodies on the floor, extended his lateral tentacles, and zlinned. "Nobody's dead." Zhag let out the breath he had been holding, realizing he had been afraid to zlin for himself. "Be mornin' 'fore we know who wants to press charges."

Zhag still sat on the floor. Tonyo knelt behind him, hands on his shoulders, laving him with his field.

"I'm all right," Zhag said. "Help these other people."

The sheriff turned sharply. "Don't either one of you touch them! Not with your fields, neither. I've sent for a channel. You two are under arrest for inciting a riot, reckless endangerment, assault and battery, and you, Tonyo Logan, for assault on an officer of the law."

There were only two cells in the Dis Junction jail, and no other inmates, but the sheriff followed the tradition of caging Sime and Gen separately. Handing the keys to the deputy on duty, the sheriff gulped down some fosebine to ease his headache and returned to the crime scene.

Tonyo came to the bars between them. "Come here, Zhag. Let me help you!"

But Zhag was pacing off the dimensions of his prison, locked in his own emotions as much as in the cell. The Gen's words were mere noise. "Zhag! What's the matter with you? Talk to me! Tell me it's all my fault. Say something!"

Zhag ignored him. If he zlinned the Gen held in the next cage while he descended into Need, he would go mad.

And the way of madness led to the Kill.

So he paced, maintaining control by closing himself off to everything outside his own mind.

After a while, Tonyo turned his attention to the female deputy. Zhag became peripherally aware of a flirtation, and some small, sane part of his mind wondered if his partner, who always had his pick of women, seriously thought that he could influence an officer on duty.

But Zhag dared not think of anything except control. *Must not zlin. Must not zlin the Gen in the next cage—*

There were words he didn't listen to, shared laughter.

Then the Sime woman left.

The Gen came to the bars again. "I asked her for food. We have a few minutes of privacy, so tell me what's going on!"

Zhag heard the concern in the Gen's voice. He resisted, moving as far away as he could get, only a few paces in the small cage. Throwing himself down on the bunk, he stared at the ceiling.

The jail cells were old Gen cages, with wooden roofs of the same rough construction as the rest of this thrown-together town. Such cages could easily hold a Gen, but—

Zhag leaped to his feet, swarmed up the bars separating him from the Gen, and punched a hole in the roof.

"Zhag! What are you doing?!"

With Sime strength, he ripped boards off, leaned down into the other cage, and held out a hand. "Come on!"

"Are you crazy? We're in enough trouble!"

"I won't hurt you!" he reassured the reluctant Gen. "We'll run for the border. Come on!"

The Gen gave him a puzzled look, and Zhag grabbed his arm, wrapping his four handling tentacles about firm Gen muscle. The Gen stared at his captured arm for a moment, then accepted Zhag's help to climb out.

There were lights in all the bars, and horses still tethered up and down the single street. Zhag snagged two that appeared to be in good condition, far enough from the activity that they wouldn't be heard. Protest in every move, his Gen nevertheless followed.

Once out of town Zhag finally dared to zlin. They rode at breakneck pace, no time to talk now, time to run, to escape—

Just over an hour later they crossed the border. Zhag pulled his tired horse up, and zlinned for someplace safe to rest. Moonlight revealed a rock formation. They dismounted, and Zhag led the way to the sheltered area.

"Now you're safe," he told the Gen.

"*I* may be safe," said Tonyo, "but if they catch *you* here, we're in big trouble."

Zhag blinked owlishly at the Gen in the light of the waxing moon.

"Do you think I can't read a map, or don't know which direction the moon rises?" Tonyo asked him. "This isn't the way we came from Nivet. You headed for the nearest border, Zhag—we're in Green River Gen Territory."

"You're safe here," Zhag repeated.

"I was perfectly safe back in Dis Junction!" Tonyo said, concern overlaying everything else in his nager. "Zhag—what did you think they were going to do to me?"

"They're junct," Zhag said grimly.

Tonyo said firmly, "They are good people overstressed with the effort of disjunction. Just exactly what you were when we met—and you didn't kill me, did you?"

Slowly, alone with his best friend, both of them alive and free of the cages, Zhag began to see their situation more clearly. "I'm sorry," he whispered, slowly realizing that he had made matters much worse.

"Don't apologize," said Tonyo. "Tell me what happened back there. What's been happening every time we play the song you used to love. Zhag—we can't go on like this. What's setting you off—it's something about your brother, isn't it?"

The Gen was far too perceptive. Zhag turned away and began to unsaddle his mount. "We have to cool down the horses," he said, "and then find them some water."

"Don't change the subject," said Tonyo, although he, too, set about caring for his panting mount. "Talk while we walk them." When Zhag remained silent, the Gen began, "You lived near Lanta. Your dad died soon after your little brother was born. You had just changed over into a Sime when your mom died, and left him in your care. Two years later, he established as a Gen—and instead of turning him over to the authorities, you decided to take him to the border."

"That's right," Zhag agreed. This much he had told Tonyo early in their acquaintance, when the Gen had startled him with the lyrics to the song that had been so right, and now kept going so wrong.

"The Householdings were too far away?"

"I never even thought of the Householdings," Zhag admitted. "There was no Householding in Lanta. Simes and Gens living together—it didn't sound possible. Gen Territory seemed the only place Remmy could be safe. We stayed off the roads as far as the West Eyeway. But we couldn't get across it without someone zlinning Remmy—he was high-field by then."

When Zhag stopped, Tonyo prompted, "And so you got caught." At the Sime's continued silence, the Gen added, "Remmy was confiscated and killed."

"Yes," Zhag whispered.

"There's more to it," said Tonyo. "Zhag...did they force you to witness it?"

"Yes," he managed around the tightness in his throat.

But Tonyo had come to know Zhag too well in the four years they had been partners and transfer mates...and he had also learned Sime history. "They wouldn't let you get away with aiding a Gen to escape, would they? Remmy was killed—but you were also punished. What was it? Attrition?"

Zhag nodded, hoping that horror would be enough to satisfy Tonyo's curiosity. It should be enough—it was the worst punishment Simes had: for depriving a Sime of a month of life, which was the way junct Simes of that day perceived escorting a Gen out of Sime Territory, the perpetrator was caged on display, deprived of a Kill for a full day beyond hard Need.

Every Sime going by zlinned his sense of encroaching death, while in the next cage, separated by bars that neither Sime nor Gen could reach through, was held the Gen he had tried to rescue—until the Sime no longer knew brother, sister, son, daughter, best friend. Not a person. Only a source of life.

Zhag realized he was standing frozen, leaning against the horse that had, without human guidance, led them to a spring bubbling through the rocks. Tonyo led his horse up to drink, then tossed the reins of both animals to the ground. He took Zhag by the shoulders, turned him back to where they had left the saddles, and made him sit down.

Tonyo took the water bag hanging from one of the saddles, and returned in a few moments with fresh water. "Drink," he instructed, and Zhag did, glad the Gen was satisfied. Even Tonyo must never know—

"Did they force you to kill Remmy?" Tonyo asked.

"No!" Zhag gasped, all the horror rushing back.

"But that was the standard punishment, wasn't it? Zhag, I understand. It wasn't Remmy to you anymore—just a source of selyn. That was the lesson you were supposed to learn."

Unable to bear having Tonyo think that, Zhag whispered, "It was Remmy—the way you are you when you give me selyn. They tried to make me kill him. I...couldn't."

Warm pride Zhag didn't deserve flowed from his Companion. But Tonyo had to ask, "Then...how did you survive?"

"When they put Remmy in with me—he tried to make me kill him! He kept trying to take my arms—" Zhag choked to a halt, drew a breath, and added, "It wasn't supposed to be a death sentence for me. I was supposed to be taught a lesson, not executed."

"But you and Remmy were teaching a lesson that junct society wasn't ready for," Tonyo added.

Zhag nodded. "Finally they took us off display, took Remmy away, and brought me another Gen."

There. Tonyo should be satisfied with that.

But the Gen shook his head, his blond hair white in the moonlight. "That's not the end of the story."

"Of course it is," said Zhag. "I had to kill to live."

"Don't lie to me, Zhag—killing a nameless Pen Gen is not what ties you in knots every time you think about Remmy. I've known from the beginning that our song reminded you of your brother, but there's something new. What has changed?"

"The way you sing it."

"No. Your response has changed. I tried it without you—if you weren't performing, I thought you wouldn't react. I was wrong. But Zhag, I have to know *why* I was wrong. What has changed?"

"You...have changed," Zhag told him.

"How?"

"What you said at rehearsal. You think like a junct."

"I certainly understand more than I did four years ago. And I have more control."

"It's not the control. Remmy had no control."

"Remmy?"

"I think...you remind me of him more than ever because you think and act like someone raised in-Territory."

"So," said Tonyo, "now when I start to sing 'My Brother,' it's not just that you remember Remmy. It's as if you are back in that cage with him? "

Zhag nodded.

"Then...why the shame, Zhag? You shenned out to save Remmy, right? I know how secure your disjunction is. You nearly died shenning yourself to protect me, remember?"

Early in their acquaintance, when Tonyo had witnessed a Kill for the first time, the Gen had spiked fear and triggered Zhag's Sime instinct. Tonyo could handle such an attack today without a thought, but then—Zhag had aborted out of the commitment to the Kill, sending his selyn systems into nearly fatal spasms.

With Remmy...he had also shenned out. When he had come to with his brother leaning over him in wide-eyed terror for Zhag's life, that fear had no longer been appealing. It was as if he could not feel his Need.

"I shenned Remmy twice," he said, "but after that...I didn't care anymore. He couldn't entice me, though he tried, Tonyo. He wanted me to live."

"Of course he did," Tonyo said. "He loved you as much as you

loved him. Zhag...is what's bothering you that, if you had coop-
erated...he might have been able to give you transfer? Neither of
you had any way of knowing that."

"If he had, they'd have slit his throat," Zhag said grimly. "No,
Tonyo—the moment we were caught Remmy was as good as
dead."

"But...you couldn't kill the other Gen either, could you? What
happened, Zhag? You're no ghost—so how did you survive?"

"They couldn't let me die over a simple one-day Kill delay.
So they replaced Remmy with another Gen. They even tried a
Prime Kill, I'm told. I don't remember it. They were desperate
to save me because I had shenned Remmy while we were still
on display. People were curious."

"Nothing like the power of public opinion to get officials
to do the right thing," said Tonyo. "Did they finally call in a
channel?"

Zhag nodded. "A consult—they wouldn't let her try to give
me transfer. Against the law, of course."

"Of course," Tonyo agreed flatly.

"All she could do was suggest a cascade. Do you know what
a cascade is, Tonyo?"

"It's what nearly got me killed that time we saw a Kill in the
marketplace—zlinning that Kill provoked killmode in every
Sime around."

"Yes—one Kill sparks another. They brought in another
Sime and her Kill. Her killmode triggered mine, and I...killed
too. I survived for another month."

"...but?" Tonyo prompted.

Zhag felt the apprehension in the Gen's field, and knew his
Companion had already guessed. "The Kill...rang with my
brother's death. The other Sime...the one whose Kill triggered
mine...was given Remmy. To me...it was as if I had killed my
brother."

Zhag turned away, sick with shame. Reborn out of his brother's death, for that one supreme moment he had been—

"You're not junct anymore." Tonyo's voice was quiet, as was

his field, supportive, not accusing. "You left the Kill behind—"

"I tried," Zhag told him. "I tracked down that channel, found out she was from Carre...but when I went there—"

"They told you you were too old to disjunct," said Tonyo. "And you proved them wrong."

"I proved them right. I wasn't able to stop killing."

"Zhag—you *have* stopped killing. You disjuncted before we ever met. If you hadn't, I would have died that day in the marketplace."

"You don't understand. I've just told you my greatest shame—"

"No," his partner said gently. "You have just told me your greatest *fear*—your Need nightmare. It's not shame that is causing riots at our concerts, Zhag. It's fear."

"Fear of losing control."

"You? Lose control?" Tonyo laughed. "Tell me, what has been going on tonight?"

Before Zhag could respond to the insult of the Gen's thinking any of this funny, Tonyo continued, "You are within four days of hard Need, but in the jail you refused to zlin, so I couldn't affect you! What killer Sime could do that?"

Zhag stared at his friend in the moonlight, zlinned him, searching for any nuance of either dishonesty or disgust. But there was nothing in Tonyo's field but admiration and concern... tinged with amusement. "Zhag—you have so much control it's pathological. Finally I know why: to you, killmode means experiencing your brother's death. Worse than that—it means tearing your own life from his death."

Zhag nodded, unable to speak.

"But that is what makes you disjunct."

"What?" He often found it difficult to follow Tonyo's strange Gen logic.

"You wouldn't learn their junct lesson, would you? That your life depended on not caring who the source of selyn was or what you had to do to get it? Be ashamed of the juncts who tried to teach you that, Zhag...not of yourself for denying it—for knowing, painful as it was, that Remmy was still your brother." Tonyo put his hands on Zhag's shoulders again, letting his lush field wash through the Sime's depleted systems. "Gens are people. To know that in your heart is what makes you disjunct."

"I still...killed," Zhag pointed out. "That Pen Gen was a person, Tonyo. And...I had to kill again, months later—"

"And then you stopped killing altogether."

"But even after I knew better—"

"—you still had to learn how," Tonyo told him. "Remember the patience you had with me while I learned how not to get myself killed, and how not to hurt Simes in the process? What are you afraid of, Zhag?"

"That others will know my shame."

"They should know it," said Tonyo. "It is your badge of honor."

"What...?" Zhag whispered.

"It's a battle scar," Tonyo continued. "Zhag, you are stronger for what you've been through than luckier young Simes who have never killed."

"How can you say that?" Zhag asked. "The taint of junctedness is seared into my nager. You can't know what nonjunct Simes zlin in me."

"I can't zlin it, but I know what it is. The shame you feel at having your life at the expense of your brother's is also your sure and certain knowledge that you will never kill again. Junct Simes can aspire to attain that knowledge of themselves one day. All the young nonjunct Simes can do is hope that the situation never arises."

"I...never thought of it that way," said Zhag, wondering again at his Gen's perception.

"Well, think of it!" said Tonyo. "That is what you have to give the Simes of Pueblo Territory: your field says, 'This is what is possible. You don't require some channel or Companion to protect your Gen loved ones from you—you, yourself, can protect them until they learn to protect themselves.' You bear scars, Zhag—but scar tissue is stronger than unblemished flesh.

You are a perfect example of why disjunction is worth the pain."

Zhag sighed. "I don't know if we'll get the chance to show anybody anything. I really shenned us this time."

"Yeah," Tonyo agreed, "you certainly did! Jailbreak, horse theft—"

One of the horses whinnied, and both animals raised their heads, shifting uneasily.

"Someone's coming!" Zhag whispered, zlinning.

"We're already here," a female voice called, as two figures came between the rocks that had shielded their approach. They were Gen, one male, one female.

Tonyo jumped up, placing himself in front of Zhag before he realized who the only Gens who could sneak up on Zhag could be. "You're not the Border Patrol. You're Companions from the Dispensary at Dis Junction."

"Yes," replied the man. "We had to leave the Simes at the border. It would be wise if you came back with us now."

"We're ready," said Zhag. "I'm sorry—I shouldn't have broken us out of jail."

"We'll do whatever's necessary," added Tonyo. "Pay for the damage—or I'll fix the roof myself so no other Sime can go through it."

"You can take that up with the sheriff," said the woman.

The ride to the border was brief. There a channel and three other Simes waited with the sheriff. But when Zhag and Tonyo tried to surrender, he said, "I had no right to arrest you. I'm sorry. I forgot you had diplomatic immunity."

The grim annoyance emanating from the Tecton channel, Vohar, told Zhag that he was none too pleased with either the sheriff for forgetting that fact, or Zhag and Tonyo for their antics, either. But Tonyo's burst of laughter as the tension eased put all the other Simes into high good humor.

Nevertheless, both Zhag and Tonyo apologized and insisted on paying for the damages to the jail. "And if anyone was badly hurt—" Zhag continued, fearful that someone might indeed have been injured by Tonyo's genslam.

The sheriff, his headache gone now, chuckled sardonically. "Everybody's mad at me for breaking up the concert. No one got hurt, not even what they'd get in a barfight."

"It hit you pretty hard," Tonyo observed. "I didn't mean for anyone to do more than pass out for a minute."

"I dunno," the sheriff replied. "Maybe I was closer, maybe I was wide open because I was zlinning everything—"

"Or maybe," Zhag said, "the Tecton hasn't bothered to tell you you're a channel."

"What are you talking about?" Vohar demanded angrily.

"This man is obviously a third-order channel," Zhag told him. "Why aren't you training him? You're going to require hundreds of thirds to disjunct this territory."

"That's why you were so strongly affected," Tonyo told the sheriff. "You're more sensitive than a renSime."

Vohar was none too happy about being told his business by a shiltpron player. "Vohar," Zhag said, "Out here on the frontier you can't wait for a first-order channel. I'm a second, like you. Didn't you suspect the sheriff was a third?"

"No—but I just arrived here last week. I haven't given him transfer yet."

"Well, see about getting him a Companion instead," said Tonyo. "You've got a huge job to do here, and you need every channel you can find."

Despite all that had happened, it was still only a little after midnight when they rode back into Dis Junction. The saloon was open, as were the other bars, for people who had come all this way were making a night of it. Only the families with children had left—and when Zhag and Tonyo announced that they would finish the concert, nearly seventy people crowded back into the saloon.

They took the stage once more, and Tonyo called the sheriff to come forward. When he told the crowd that one of their own was a channel, a cheer went up—to these people channels were the heroes who stood between them and the Kill. Not only forgiveness for spoiling their fun, but practically worship poured over the beleaguered man, who escaped, blushing, only when Tonyo picked up his guitar and Zhag returned to his shiltpron.

Tonyo addressed the audience once more. "This is a show, folks—no matter what happens, there's no call for you to protect me from Zhag—all right?"

The crowd response was laughter, perhaps a little embarrassed, but mostly understanding, intimate, the accord of shared experience.

They started the interrupted song, "My Brother, He Turned Out Wrong." Despite his trepidation, Zhag let his feelings flow when they reached the point where the memory of Remmy's death rose to haunt him. Need—fear—

Grief rose from the audience—few of them, living as Raiders until they banded together to form Pueblo Territory, had escaped such loss of child or friend turned suddenly Gen. Then came the dangerous part in which Tonyo drew Zhag, and with him the whole audience, toward the feeling none of these Simes wanted to feel—toward killmode. Zhag's shame rose—

—and then Tonyo's response: strength, pride, confidence. They reached the refrain, "And I will never see his face again," with the audience weeping openly in the agony of denial—acceptance—love—sharing—joy—triumph! *Life!*

No one wanted the song to end, so Zhag played a variation of the refrain, while Tonyo vocalized wordlessly. And then... the Gen's field changed. Zhag zlinned, but could not believe his own laterals. Every Sime in the place was caught up in it, for even those who had had transfer very recently were zlinning this performance.

Terrified, Zhag began the outtro of the song, trying to force Tonyo to follow, to end what he was doing.

The song ended. Silence fell. The audience remained spellbound, gripped in the ambient nager. Zhag set his instrument on its stand and moved carefully to his partner's side. "Tonyo!" he whispered, still not believing what he zlinned. "You are broadcasting Need—hard, junct Need!"

And Tonyo simply turned to him. "You're a channel," he replied. "Do something about it."

When Tonyo held out his bare Gen arms, Zhag realized the only thing he could do. He grasped them, wrapping his tentacles around Tonyo's forearms, almost seeing the non-existent tentacles of a Sime in Need coming to the channel who could provide life—life without the Kill.

Using every skill he had as both channel and nageric performer, Zhag projected the transfer of selyn as Tonyo projected acceptance. To the audience it was as if they zlinned selyn flowing from one to the other, filling, warming—wrenching life out of death—

—but there was no death. Satisfaction rang through the crowded saloon—and people gasped in joyous disbelief.

The arguments would rage for years afterward about what occurred in the Dis Junction saloon that night. Had Simes really witnessed a Gen in hard Need? Had they zlinned a channel's transfer so perfect that it had given them all hope for their own lives? Or—and the consensus was that this was the only possible answer—had Zhag and Tonyo actually taken transfer on a public platform, while patrons drunk on porstan and shiltpron were completely confused about what they zlinned?

In later years, that concert became the stuff of legend—more so than the much larger one four nights later at Red Rocks. At least a hundred people would claim to have been the ones whose horses Zhag and Tonyo stole, while a thousand, maybe more, would say they were in the Dis Junction saloon that night. As for what they claimed to have witnessed, no two stories were identical, but all agreed that they left the premises with such determination to disjunct that nothing ever shook their resolve again.

Only Zhag Paget and Tonyo Logan knew the truth—that Tonyo had given Zhag proof in the only way he knew how that he understood what it meant to be both junct and not a killer. From that day forward their performances became ever more daring, more outrageous, as they left fear and shame behind forever, to pass into legend.

REFLECTION OF A DREAM

The concert was reaching its peak. Police Lieutenant Carla Stenner, in charge of security, had seen no sign of anyone trying to disrupt the concert or harm the Sime shiltpron player.

It was the first time since Unity that a Sime performer had appeared in Gen Territory. The audience, half won over before the music began, were in total accord now, absorbing the most moving music Carla had ever experienced. Such performances would do far more to promote Sime/Gen Unity than any laws or treaties.

Tonyo Logan and Zhag Paget's recordings could not even half convey the experience of seeing, hearing, and...somehow *feeling* them in live performance. Tony, Gen like Carla, sang and danced and pranced in denim trousers tight enough to provide evidence of how inspired *he* was by the music...or was it by the young Gen woman in a pink dress, dancing before the stage? Echoing each other's movements, they appeared oblivious to the crowd.

But Tony was not truly oblivious. He never missed a word or a note—and now he danced to the other side of the stage, where Carla stood near the barricade separating stage from audience.

Despite the backlighting that silhouetted Tony and turned his blond curls into a halo, Carla saw the wink he gave her. When she smiled in return, he grinned and bounced back to center stage as the brief instrumental interval concluded.

Tony wore a sleeveless shirt, open down to his belt. A white enamel chain about his neck supported a black-and-white starred-cross of a design Carla had never seen before. Against his plain dark shirt, Zhag Paget, the shiltpron player, wore an identical emblem. His hung just beneath his closed collar, so as not to interfere with the instrument from which he brought forth a variety of sounds.

The girl in pink, as well as most others pushing their way down front, might be trying to attract Tony's attention, but Carla saw as many eyes fastened on the shiltpron player as Tony concluded his vocals and danced once more into the shadows. The light came up on Zhag.

The Sime's dark hair and pale skin made a strong contrast to Tony's golden mane and suntan—they were like the sun and the moon, emblemizing the roles of Gen and Sime, producer and receiver of energy. That was the theme of numerous interviews they had given throughout their triumphant tour. Logan and Paget might be the first, but they did not intend to be the only Sime/Gen ensemble to perform in Gen Territory.

The press was here in force. After this experience, Carla could not imagine even the most conservative journalists rejecting the cultural exchange. The eyes of the Gen audience fastened on Sime tentacles in admiration. Tonight that outward mark of the difference between the two kinds of humans produced not fear, but pleasure.

The shiltpron solo swelled out into the auditorium. The light on Zhag dimmed. A faint green glow developed around the Sime performer, brightest near his hands, where his tentacles emerged from their wrist openings.

Carla looked away and back again, trying to locate the source of light. The girl in pink was pressed against the barricade. A taller girl with eyes made up to look twice their size nudged her and pointed toward the Sime performer.

Carla also looked back at Zhag. The glow was stronger now. She made out Tony behind him, invisible except where his pale hair picked up glints of green light.

Zhag seemed to control the glow with his music. Tony's voice joined the rising crescendo, no words now, an organic instrument playing counterpoint to the shiltpron. A pyramid of green light formed around the Sime, expanded, took in his Gen partner. The music pulsed, as if the hearts of the performers beat with those of the audience.

More than two thousand people participated in a celebration of pure life energy! Carla looked around at the enraptured faces—and saw the gasp that overcame them as her own insides were startled by an orgasmic shock of pleasure.

Her eyes caught movement at the other side of the stage. The girl in pink and her friend had slipped around the barrier.

Carla shifted instantly back to security mode.

A hand touched her shoulder. She turned to face Madson Quint, a channel from the Sime Center. "You've got to stop them!"

"Those kids won't get backstage," she assured him.

"No—stop the *show*! That idiot is raising Paget's intil in an auditorium full of untrained Gens!"

Carla didn't understand all the Sime jargon, but she saw that the channel sensed danger. Yet stopping this incredible show would surely start a riot.

The pyramid of green light pulsed in changing patterns. Notes and rhythms intertwined in ever more complex combinations—

—and shattered!

The instrument stopped abruptly. Tony's voice continued for a moment as the pyramid of light collapsed and disappeared.

Carla barely made out movement on stage by the glitter of the strings and frets of the shiltpron and the pale mass of Tony's hair. The Sime thrust his instrument into the Gen's hands and dashed offstage on the opposite side.

Quint made as if to leap over the barriers, but subsided, gasping and rubbing his forearms where his tentacles were trapped in their sheaths by the retainers he wore. Someone had the presence of mind to bring the house lights up. Tony was just disappearing backstage, charging after his partner.

Carla displayed her badge and shouted "Police!" so the crowd would let her through. As she could not leap over barriers like a Sime, it would be fastest to go around the far end.

Quint kept pace with her. A Sime like Zhag, he could have practically flown past her, but he didn't dare provoke Gen fear.

Or was it the retainers that slowed him? He had worn them for almost three hours. They made ordinary Simes sick and dizzy in far less time than that, and Quint, a channel, was more sensitive than most.

They heard the first shrieks as they reached the door to the backstage area: two screams, followed by one voice alone, building in hysteria.

Thank goodness the crowd was buzzing loudly in suprise at Zhag's abrupt departure—the screams would be covered.

Carla pushed through police and Sime Center Gens, and pounded down the steps to the hallway leading backstage.

Halfway down the corridor, the girl in pink pressed against the wall on one side. Zhag Paget was pressed as tightly against the opposite wall. Between them, on the floor, lay the motionless form of the other girl, the one with the painted eyes.

The dead girl's face was frozen in the rictus of fear indicative of the kill—attack by a Sime to strip a Gen of selyn, the life energy Simes consumed to survive. Except for channels like Quint, no Sime in need could control the kill reflex.

But Zhag Paget had not been in need. According to the carefully negotiated agreement for permission to perform tonight, Paget had filled up only yesterday with a month's worth of selyn.

Paget stood, as pale as the dead girl, clutching his starred-cross. All six tentacles on either hand were extended. His lateral tentacles—the ones with which Simes drew selyn—were slimed with selyn-conducting fluid. The stuff smeared his hands, too, and the front of his shirt. The Sime was shaking, his eyes closed as if to shut out the sight of what he had done, and he was muttering something.

Placing her trust in Madson Quint to intercept if Zhag tried to attack her, Carla allowed the channel to go first, but stepped closer to hear what Zhag was saying.

"I couldn't stop her! I couldn't stop her!" His fingers were pale at the knuckles from his grip on the starred-cross.

From the stage end of the hall, Tony Logan arrived, followed by two of Carla's officers, Similla Gordon and Rafe Belius.

Belius sealed off the scene, calling to other officers to hold Logan and Paget's crew back from one side, the audience and the press from the other. Gordon went to the girl in pink, and began to talk soothingly. The girl's screams subsided into sobs.

Tony went straight to Paget and put his hands on the Sime's shoulders. At once Paget's eyes opened. "Tonyo!" he whispered. "I couldn't stop her!"

"It's all right," said Tony. "I'm here. You're safe." He placed his hands over the Sime's, prying the clutching fingers loose from the talisman, bloodied from Paget's frantic grip. Then he slid his hands gently up the Sime's forearms. Handling tentacles lashed around muscular Gen arms, binding the two men together as the small moist laterals seated themselves.

But Paget made no attempt to create the fifth contact that drained a Gen of life. He rested his head on Tony's shoulder for a moment, gave a shuddering sigh, and let go, withdrawing his tentacles into their sheaths. "Thank you," he said softly.

Neither musical magician nor killing monster now, he looked like nothing more than a rather frail, ordinary man. Tony put an arm around his partner's shoulders and turned. "What happened here?" he demanded, as if he were the one in charge.

Carla said, "Zhag Paget, I am taking you into protective custody until you can be transported into Sime Territory."

"No!" exclaimed Tony. He looked down at the corpse. "Zhag couldn't do this!"

"After what you did to him?" Quint spoke up. "Of all the irresponsible Gen power plays I have *ever* witnessed, that was the most blatant, the most—" He ran out of words. "You don't even know what you've *done*, do you? How horribly he's going to—" Again the channel stopped, looking with pity at Zhag Paget.

Carla didn't care what the Sime government did to Paget. She had a corpse, a killer Sime in custody, and a mission to get them all out of there before word reached the audience.

And the press! It was a diplomatic disaster.

"Tony," she said, "go out on stage. Say Zhag's been taken ill. Make up something. But tell the audience the concert is over, and ask them to leave quietly."

"I can't—" Tony began.

Zhag said, "Carla's right—the audience can't be allowed to know there's been a Kill. But the concert isn't over. Go out there and perform, Tonyo."

"Zhag!" Tony gasped.

"I'll join you as soon as Carla finishes investigating. Now go!" he insisted, unwrapping Tony's arm from around his shoulders. "Sing to them. If they see you they won't panic."

But Tony insisted, "Two songs. If you're not back on stage, I'm going to end it there." He turned to Carla. "Don't take him anywhere till I get back!"

She followed him for a few steps, out of Zhag's hearing. "Tony—there's no choice. If I don't take Zhag into custody, when people find out what he's done they'll murder him."

He stopped, turning to stare at her in astonishment. "You think he did it!"

"Zhag was the only Sime here."

"When *you* got here. Why aren't your people looking for the killer? That girl provoked someone. It had to be her spike of fear Zhag sensed from the stage—he certainly wouldn't be attracted to some out-Territory groupie!"

"You've lived in Sime Territory too damn long if you blame that poor child for getting killed!" Carla exploded.

Tony's face showed a mix of frustration and bewilderment. Then, "You're as bad as the rest of them. Zhag's the nearest Sime, so he has to be the killer." His blue eyes were dark with fury. "Go conduct your shendi-fleckin' investigation—but for Unity's sake, get a channel to search the building! And when you're through, send Zhag out on stage to me."

Carla stared after Tony as he disappeared backstage. He was so close to this...Sime...that he could not accept the evidence of his own eyes.

She pulled herself together, realizing that on one level Tony was correct: she had to keep an open mind. Both Tony and Paget seemed certain it would clear him...but then, they were probably thinking of Sime Territory law. Simes were not allowed to kill, but she was sure there were plenty of technicalities. In the Sime courts where Paget would be tried—if they bothered to try him at all—the death would probably be ruled accidental.

Whatever happened later, Carla had to investigate now. "Seal this corridor," she told Rafe Belius. "We know no one left at either end. Check for any other exits."

Rafe went to the door to the auditorium and returned with three uniformed officers. They started checking the length of the corridor.

Meanwhile, Paget turned to Quint and asked in Simelan, "You didn't zlin what happened?"

"Retainered, from the middle of a crowd of Gens you had whipped into a frenzy?" Quint demanded angrily. "The Tecton opposed this foolish experiment all along—look where it's led!"

"If you didn't zlin what happened, zlin *me*!" Paget said, now in English. "And once that poor girl calms down, ask her."

The girl in pink sat on the floor now, her back to the corpse of her friend. Gordon had put her jacket around the shaking girl, and was still talking to her.

Although his annoyance was obvious, Quint turned to Carla. "May I?" The channel indicated his retainers.

"You're taking evidence at a crime scene," said Carla. "I'll take responsibility."

Retainers could not be removed quickly. With the help of a Sime Center Gen, Quint began the slow process. Muffled sounds of the shiltpron reached them. Carla hadn't known that Tony could play the Sime instrument. His voice rose, a sad song in a minor key, but she could not understand the words through the walls.

She focused on her job: to find out what had gone wrong. The channel could go very far toward telling her. One by one, the four small handling tentacles of Quint's left hand emerged from the openings at his wrist, and stretched to full length—only reaching the tips of his fingers, two over the back of his hand, two under the palm.

Sime handling tentacles were actually quite small, less than the diameter of a finger and covered with ordinary skin. Gen drawings of Carla's childhood had made them appear as huge as rattlesnakes, dripping venom, glowing with some strange magnetic force. In plain fact, they were just little extra appendages.

As the slow process continued, Carla reviewed what she knew of Zhag Paget. She had known him less than a day. But Tony Logan she had known all her life, and she didn't understand him at all. How could she possibly know Paget well enough to place the trust in him that Tony did?

She thought back to their meeting, only a few hours ago, at the police station.

"Hey, Lieutenant—I hear you know Tonyo Logan."

It was going to be much worse than the last time Tony had visited. He had been moderately famous then, a minor celebrity.

Now he was a star. And he would have that Sime with him.

Carla turned, saying with careful casualness, "We went to school together. He was just Tony in those days."

Individually misfits, together they had made one of their school's most popular couples. She had tutored him in literature, and he had brought her out of her shyness into the spotlight that always shone where Tony was. They had shared their first fumbling sexual experience, planned to share their lives...and then Unity had changed everything.

Tony lived and breathed music, but to make a living from it was so far from their working class upbringing that Carla never took his dream seriously. He also had a talent for mathematics— she recalled his explaining something called the Numbers of Zelerod while her head was spinning with his proposal that they get married and move to Sime Territory.

It had seemed worse than insane at the time. Simes might have signed a treaty by which they agreed to stop killing Gens—but who could trust Simes? Could you trust a hungry wolf not to attack you because his pack leader signed a treaty?

But Simes had indeed stopped killing Gens—or rather, accepted being prevented from doing so. In her police duties, Carla often worked with the channels at the Sime Center built here after Unity. Channels were Simes with the ability to take selyn from Gens and transfer it to Simes, with no harm to either. Every month she herself donated selyn, law officers being expected to set an example.

But fifteen years ago, when Tony had left her to pursue his siren song in Sime Territory, Carla had never expected to see him again. She cried herself to sleep, imagining him dead...until his letters started coming. He begged her to join him in Norlea, where he claimed Simes and Gens lived peacefully together. There he had met Zhag Paget, shiltpron player extrordinaire.

Today he brought his Sime partner to meet Carla. Seasoned cops separated into fawning fans and alert officers on crowd control when the two men arrived with their entourage.

Carla's eyes went to Tony. With new lines of maturity in his face, he was even more handsome than she remembered. His wide dark-blue eyes sought hers, and he smiled the smile that left women swooning in the aisles.

He needs a haircut, Carla noted, remembering Tony's mother forcing order to his mop of curls. Now his hair was longer than Carla's, a lion's mane that he tossed back as he glanced around the police station before striding up to her. "Carla," he said.

She felt her toes curl just from his undivided attention.

"You're looking good, Tony," she managed to get out, aware of the stares of her fellow cops.

"Oh, I *am* good!" Tony replied with innuendo that was new since the last time they had met. Or perhaps at that time he had saved it for his performances.

He dropped the sex-god act, though, as he introduced "My partner, Zhag Paget. Zhag, this is Carla Stenner."

"I feel as if I know you," the Sime said. "Tonyo has told me so much." He spoke perfect English with the Simelan accent Carla remembered from Tony's mother. Gulf Territory Simelan, the same language but a different dialect from that of the channels at the Sime Center.

Zhag Paget was almost as tall as Tony, but with the thinner-than-slender Sime physique. He was in good health, his dark brown hair thick and shiny. The hand he held out, allowing her to decide whether to touch him, was merely slender, not skeletal like those of Freeband Raiders—outlaw killer Simes who still occasionally marauded through Gen territory.

Carla took the proffered hand, careful to look into the Sime's hazel eyes rather than at his forearm. She had studied Sime physiology—mostly in autopsies. If Paget could coolly shake hands with her his tentacles were quiet in their sheaths, not writhing with the need to capture her in a death grip.

Not that they could—the retainers the Sime wore about his wrists prevented his tentacles from emerging.

Tony asked, "Is there somewhere we can talk privately?"

"The detectives' office," Carla offered.

"Selyn shielded?" Tony asked.

"The interrogation room, then," Carla amended. Tony took out a "Sime Diplomatic Territory" sign and hung it on the door. Carla ushered her guests inside and pulled down the shade, preventing her colleagues from watching through the one-way glass.

As the three seated themselves, Paget asked Carla, "Do you mind?" indicating his retainers.

"Take them off," she replied. "You should be able to tell I'm low-field." She had donated selyn yesterday.

That earned her a smile from Tony. "You look good," he said, reaching to help Paget out of the retainers. "How are the girls?"

"Dorrie's at school in Central City. She wants to study Interterritory Law. Mattie...."

He raised his eyebrows, waiting for the news about her younger daughter. Carla explained, "Mattie's living at the Sime

Center. They're training her as one of those special Donors—like you." It came out accusatory, despite her best efforts.

Tony smiled radiantly. "But that's *good* news, Carla. She'll get the best education, a secure future, and...well, until you do it, you don't know the thrill of giving transfer."

"You always were the thrill-seeker," said Carla, "and Mattie was always so damned impressed with 'Uncle Tony.'"

"Perhaps," he replied, "but you encouraged her to donate."

"I support Unity," Carla replied. "But plenty of people still think the only good Sime is a dead Sime. Security will be very tight tonight." It had been tightening ever since the announcement of the concert. The Church of the Purity contingent would be kept across the street with their picket signs, and the League of Gen Businesses had been prevented from buying up all the tickets, leaving the performers to play to an empty hall.

Personnel at the hotel where Logan and Paget were staying had been checked and rechecked. When two maids and a cook disappeared two days ago they had been replaced with police officers, not the conveniently available applicants with perfect credentials. Tails on those applicants had led the police to confiscate a bomb that could have blown out an entire floor of the hotel. They also rescued the three missing hotel employees, still alive—presumably intended as hostages for the escape of the bombers had their plan worked.

Carla was proud of her security team. Paget took off his retainers as they discussed how her Gen officers and the channels and Donors from the Sime Center were to be deployed.

Free of the retainers, Zhag stretched his handling tentacles. "Could we have some tea?" he asked.

"We don't have—" Carla began.

"We always carry trin tea," Tony replied. "Where can I find hot water...?"

"There's a kitchen back of the coffee service," she told him.

No sooner had the door closed than Zhag said bluntly, "You know Tonyo's still in love with you, don't you?"

Carla blinked and tried to control her racing heart. Simes

could read Gen emotions in their selyn fields—there was no use trying to hide it from Paget.

"You're all the women he sings about," Paget continued. "Sad songs—the ones all the women love, on both sides of the border. Do you understand Simelan?"

"Fairly well. Tony's mother taught both of us, in case either of us changed over and had to run for the border." It served her well in interrogating both the occasional Sime and Simelan-speaking Gens who had escaped from Sime territory at adolescence and, unable to adapt, drifted into a life of crime.

"Tonyo writes lyrics in both languages," said Paget, "but his greatest song is in Simelan. Do you know when he wrote it?"

"After his mother died?"

"Ah. You know how hard he took that."

"Yes. She and I both let him down. Neither of us would go with him into Sime Territory. His mom loved his dad very much, you know. Mr. Logan's a good man, but he never understood Tony's love of music, or his fascination with Simes."

"He still doesn't," said Paget. "He sent back the concert tickets Tonyo sent him. Are you going to disappoint him too?"

"Disappoint him? I haven't heard from him in five years!"

"You shattered his dreams. Carla, the way you treat him may inspire his music, but it is shen on the man himself!"

"Why should you care? I know you're friends, but—"

Paget shook his head. "Tonyo literally keeps me alive. And sane. To do that, he has to be sane himself."

"I've never led him on," said Carla. "I've seen him twice in fifteen years. At his mother's funeral, when his father shunned him, I invited him to stay with my family. I was pregnant and trying to handle a two-year-old! Tony got along really well with Matt. My husband. I thought he was completely over me."

Paget shook his head. "That was when he wrote—" he spoke a phrase in Simelan that Carla didn't recognize. "A rough translation is, *Love Stronger than Need.* In-territory, it's considered his greatest composition. Until Tonyo, I don't think most Simes realized that Gens could feel anything that strongly."

"So he did come back to see if I would change my mind after Matt died. I wasn't sure. He waited a year, and he said he was only here to visit his mother's grave."

"I made him wait that year. I hoped you'd join him then—it's frustrating to have you there, as invisible as selyn but just as potent, enticing him across the border."

"I had two children facing life without their father. I couldn't even think about changing their lives so drastically again, over... someone who abandoned me."

Carla saw Paget's eyes go out of focus, indicating that he was using Sime senses to read her field. "And now?" he asked.

"Tony's every woman's dream on the radio, in recordings, on the stage. He can have any woman he wants."

"Believe me, he only wants you."

"He wants a fantasy," Carla replied, just as Tony reappeared with steaming cups of trin tea.

"Who wants a fantasy?" he asked.

"Zhag thinks you're still in love with me," Carla said before she could stop herself.

"I am," Tony replied, then glanced over at the Sime in mock annoyance. "I suppose you know what great lie detectors channels make. No use trying to hide your feelings."

But Carla's police training fastened on one word. She stared at Paget. "You're a channel?"

"I thought that was in the information you were sent."

Carla shook her head. "How can you possibly be a professional musician as well?"

"I changed over years before Unity. I...used to kill."

That was no surprise. Except for a small minority, all Simes who had changed over before Unity had killed a Gen every month until the treaty had forced them to undergo disjunction.

"Aren't most working channels in Sime territories disjunct?"

Only nonjunct ones—those who had never killed in their lives—were assigned to the Sime Center here.

"Zhag was too old to be trained as a channel when he stopped killing," Tony explained.

Carla sensed there was more, unspoken. She looked Zhag in the eye and asked, "When was the last time you killed?"

"Fifteen years ago," he replied promptly and firmly.

Carla looked to Tony, who nodded. "Not since I met him, Carla, and believe me, I'd know."

"So I'm free to pursue music," said Paget. "And lucky—or maybe it was fate that brought Tonyo and me together."

"I always knew my destiny was in Gulf Territory," said Tony.

"Well," Paget said, draining the last of his tea, "my destiny is lunch and a rest before the concert." He started putting the retainers back on. "Stay here, Tonyo. You two have a lot to talk about. Pol and Belinda can escort me back to the hotel."

"Are you sure?" Carla saw real concern in Tony's expression.

Paget laughed. "Tonyo, I'm as post as you are! And these things—" He winced as he raised one retainer-clad wrist. "Well, they certainly do blur the ambient. All I want to do is go back to the hotel and get out of them again."

"It's all arranged," Carla assured him. "You won't have to wear them again until after the show." One of her tougher jobs had been convincing the mayor that a team of police officers and people from the Sime Center could safely convey their star performers from the hotel to the concert hall without the devices that gave Simes headaches and disorientation—no condition for a performer giving an historic concert.

But one battle she had lost: channels from the Sime Center were not to be allowed to mingle unretainered with the audience.

"Take everybody with you," Tony told Zhag. "I'm just another Gen on this side of the border." At their two skeptical stares, he added, "Besides, I've got a police escort."

"Fine," said Zhag. "I won't expect to see either of you till it's time to go to the concert hall."

When the Sime had left, Carla said, "He seems awfully nice."

"For a Sime?"

"For a famous performer. And he cares about you."

"Yeah—Zhag's my other half, the brother I never had. This

past fifteen years I've fulfilled all my dreams...except one."

It was hard to look away from that angel's face, those deep blue eyes, as he bent closer. Then they were kissing, and it was as if fifteen years melted away.

Remembering where she was, Carla broke the kiss, gently. Tony still held her, pressing their bodies together, whispering, "You're so beautiful."

She pushed him away. "Tony, you've never seen the real me."

"You're wrong. I *always* have." And she recalled that he had always seen her plain features as beautiful.

"You've changed," he added. "You're not afraid of Simes anymore. You can come with me now, Carla."

"What—just like that?"

"Why not? We ought to have a Gen chief of security—this won't be our last concert in Gen Territory. Carla, you're not fooled by the glamor, the fame, the money. An entertainer's never a great catch as a husband—"

"Husband!"

He ran a hand through unruly curls, which fell right back down on his forehead. "You loved me once. I left, and you found someone else. But Matt is gone, and I'm still alive. Your children have their own lives. Come and work with Zhag and me. He likes you."

"And Zhag is part of any life with you, isn't he?"

"I'm not hiding that."

"You would never leave him—go off to live in another territory where he couldn't go?"

His lips thinned. "No. And I didn't do that to you, Carla. You could have come with me. It wouldn't have been any more dangerous for you than it was for me."

She nodded. "I know that now. I didn't know it then."

"You didn't trust me."

"I didn't trust Simes."

"You do now?"

"Some," she said honestly. "I trust Madson Quint, the head channel at the Sime Center. I think...I could trust Zhag Paget."

A smile like sunshine lit Tony's face. "You've got an important job here, but what we're doing is important, too. Territory boundaries won't come down through legislation. The treaty's a huge step, but it's people like Zhag and me who will bring about genuine Unity. Did you know our recordings sell three times as well in Gen Territory as in Sime Territory?"

"That's because there are *ten* times as many *people* in Gen Territory," she reminded him.

"All right," he agreed with a grin. "But if we can really tour, instead of doing just one concert in a border town and being sent right back into Sime Territory, we *will* sell ten times as many here. Gens who've never seen a Sime that wasn't a berserker love Zhag's music. You've heard our recordings?"

"Of course. If I hadn't bought them, the girls would have."

"Well, they're nothing compared to a live concert. The only security Zhag's going to require *after* the concert is to keep people from tearing his clothes off for souvenirs."

And Tony had been right. There were plenty of skeptics in the concert audience, but Sime and Gen together had brought about a Unity that far transcended anything mandated in the Treaty.

But now there had been a Kill—exactly what all Gens feared if they allowed Simes to walk among them.

Paget said he hadn't done it. Tony was certain he hadn't.

But then how to account for one very dead body?

Quint extended his laterals, the smallest tentacles, which lay on either side of his wrists. These were selyn sensing organs, as well as the means to draw life force from a Gen.

Quint entwined his tentacles with Paget's, as if for a channel's transfer of life force. But only their hands, arms, and tentacles touched, as Quint performed a deep reading of the musician's system.

"You're a channel," said Quint to Paget, "but that's on your record. You're post, of course. And...." He frowned. "How did you bury it so deep so fast?"

Curiosity rang so strongly through Carla that Quint glanced over at her. But then his eyes fixed accusingly on Paget's as he announced in Simelan, "You're junct."

But that was one Simelan word every Gen understood. Junct: joined to the Kill. Having killed once, a Sime was instantly addicted to the thrill of killing. Breaking the dependency was said to be the worst suffering humanly possible.

All except a small handful of Simes of Zhag Paget's generation had endured that withdrawal for the sake of Unity, to reunite the two kinds of human beings.

Now Paget was addicted again: junct. Probably, having backslid at the cost of a life, he would never be trusted again, even in Sime Territory.

But Paget said contemptuously in English, "What kind of channel can't tell that you're reading an old scar on my nager? I didn't kill that girl. Zlin it in my systems! I *can't* kill!"

"You are junct," Quint repeated in English.

Paget switched back to Simelan, unaware that Carla understood much better than she spoke that language. "Yes, I'm technically junct," he said in exasperation. "Consider my age, Fool! I was never disjunct."

"Oh, my God," Carla said. "You and Tony lied to me!"

I was considering trusting you two with my entire future. But she didn't say that. Instead, she said, "You've not only killed— you've broken the Unity Treaty."

Quint dismantled his grip, saying, "This man isn't lying. That means he may be insane. Handle him with great caution."

"You may be sure of that!" Carla said coldly, holding her own feelings tightly as she realized that if Quint turned his attention her way he would sense her unprofessional turmoil.

She ordered her officers to take in the suspect—suspects, now, as Tony was an accomplice in helping Paget break the Treaty. Never mind his incidental betrayal of her.

Carla fell back on procedure. "Rafe," she said to Belius, "Logan said he would do two songs and then come off stage. When he does that, arrest him."

"Arrest Tonyo?! No!"

Carla had forgotten the girl in the pink dress. Similla Gordon said, "Lieutenant, I think you'd better hear this witness before you arrest anybody."

The girl, whose name was Charmion Johnson, was obviously very nervous, but she was determined to defend Tony Logan. "Tonyo wasn't even here when it happened!" she insisted.

As Quint automatically placed himself between Paget and the agitated Gen, Charmion shied back from the approach of a Sime. She nearly stumbled over her friend's body, which brought a fresh gush of tears. Taking a shuddering breath, she squared her shoulders and addressed Paget. "Letty wanted to meet you. She loved your music so much. And now she's dead!"

"I'm sorry," said Paget, with what sounded like genuine remorse. "I had no idea anything like this could happen."

"She was supposed to be *safe*!" Charmion protested. "She donated day before yesterday. She was so scared—but she did it for *you*! And now she's dead!"

Carla noticed the First Donation badge on the dead girl's dress. She couldn't have had enough selyn to satisfy any Sime.

"Her fear killed her," Paget replied. "I felt it right through the wall. When I realized no one else was responding...." He shook his head, sorrow in his eyes and voice. "I'm so sorry," he repeated.

A confession in front of witnesses. "All right, Zhag," said Carla, "let's take you in before the audience finds out—"

As Carla held out retainers, Charmion demanded, "Why are you arresting Zhag? He didn't kill Letty."

Both Carla and Quint turned to face the girl. "I think you had better explain," said Carla.

"I wanted to meet Tonyo. Letty wanted to meet Zhag. We thought the light display was our best chance to get backstage. We were trying to be real quiet. Letty got ahead of me—and then there she was!"

"...she?"

"A Sime. A berserker, I guess." A changeover victim without

the sense to go to the Sime Center. Some families still kept their children in such ignorance and fear that they denied the symptoms until it was too late.

Quint said, "I have had channels in this building all day. No changeover victim could have been hiding here."

The girl shrugged. "She was there. Letty screamed—and the Sime grabbed her and—and—killed her! It happened so fast! She dropped Letty and came for me—" Charmion caught her breath and continued. "Zhag was just *there*—like magic, out of nowhere. He grabbed the Sime, wouldn't let her get to me—"

She blinked, and looked at the musician in sudden realization. "You saved my life! She would have killed me, too!"

"How could another Sime get in here?" Carla asked.

"With a ticket," replied Rafe Belius, displaying a stub from the concert. "We found this in the boiler room down the hall. The outer door's locked from the inside, so she's holed up in there. But there are a thousand nooks and crannies."

Zhag said, "I didn't think to warn you. It just *never* occurred to me—"

"*What* didn't occur to you?" Quint asked.

"Fans. They do crazy things at times. You understand, Hajene Quint: a Sime in need, an audience of Gens, my shiltpron, and Tonyo's nageric manipulation...?"

Again Carla was lost in the Sime jargon—but from Quint's reaction she understood a little. "Fanatics," the channel spat. "Thrill-seekers. That's what your so-called 'culture' attracts! I suppose you can't be held responsible for the acts of your followers. But now that you've juncted someone—"

"Hajene Quint," said Belius impatiently, "would you help us find this killer Sime?"

As Quint went off to zlin for the other Sime, Carla turned to Zhag Paget. "I'm sorry," she said. "We thought our security was better. An unretainered Sime should never have gotten in."

He managed a wan smile. "A few determined fans always get past security. But there's never been...a Kill." He turned to Charmion Johnson. "I have to go back on stage. If you feel up to it, come and meet Tonyo."

The girl came forward eagerly. "I'm not afraid of *you*."

The building shook with applause when Zhag Paget returned to the stage. The concert continued for another hour, long enough for the body of Letty Meech to be taken away, and an officer sent to notify her family.

With Quint's help, they found and arrested the killer Sime, an adult Sime woman in a loose, long-sleeved tunic over full-cut trousers. She could have bought her ticket, or ambushed someone on the way to the concert and stolen it. She had obviously relied on the idiotic law that kept the channels retainered to prevent them from zlinning her amid the Gen audience.

Tony and Zhag came offstage to more thunderous applause, grinning, Charmion Johnson walking between them. Madson Quint stopped them. He beckoned Carla to witness as he addressed the girl in the pink dress.

"I need your testimony to support what I zlinned in the Sime who killed your friend. Just exactly *how* did Paget 'grab' that woman?" Quint demanded.

Charmion found the courage to relive the scene of an hour ago. "It was like—like he was gonna kill her. Or she was gonna kill him. I was so scared!"

"It's all right," Carla said soothingly. "Just tell us what you saw and heard."

"The Sime yelled at Zhag. I didn't understand. She was real mad, and she wiped her mouth like he'd made her sick."

"That's it," said Quint. "Zhag Paget, the Tecton charges you with manslaughter and reckless endangerment. You have contributed to the death of a Gen and the juncting of a Sime. Antoine Logan, you are an accessory—you balanced Zhag's fields before I zlinned him, hiding the evidence. Lieutenant Stenner, please take these two into custody until I can arrange transport into Sime Territory for a hearing before the Tecton Council."

Charmion protested, "But Zhag *saved* me! You can't arrest him!"

"Go home," Quint told her, "and count yourself lucky that you were not the one killed."

Charmion tossed her head, started to snap back at him, but changed her mind and instead marched down the corridor toward where the audience could still be heard applauding, hoping to coax the performers back for one last encore.

They were to be disappointed. Carla had to take Tony and Zhag in, as the police station had the only holding cells for Simes. However, she wanted answers before she released them to their fate. Therefore she gathered Tony, Zhag, and Quint in the interrogation room, told both Simes to remove their retainers, and demanded, "What exactly are Logan and Paget charged with—in plain English, not Tecton jargon."

"Zhag gave that woman transfer," Tony said as he and Quint traded glares of anger. "He did it to save Charmion Johnson's life."

"He's junct," Quint repeated. "Fifteen years ago we had to use junct channels because there were not enough nonjunct channels to provide transfer for everyone. Paget would have been drafted anywhere outside Gulf Territory—there they had almost enough channels, and this dangerous practice of matching up the worst juncts with Gens."

Zhag shook his head. "I was far too ill by Unity to become a practicing channel. When I met Tonyo, I was dying."

Carla was becoming exasperated. "You might as well be speaking Simelan! Zhag, what were you dying of?"

"I couldn't kill anymore," the musician explained.

"But no one was killing anymore."

There was sudden silence around the table.

Carla looked from one to another of the three men. "The Unity Treaty says that all Simes in all the signatory Sime Territories will immediately stop killing Gens. Zhag, you told me you haven't killed in fifteen years."

"That's the truth," Zhag replied.

"It's not the whole truth," said Carla.

Tony's response earned him another glare from Quint. "If the *whole* truth becomes known, it could be the end of Unity."

"What whole truth?" Carla asked. "Why do you say Zhag is junct? He doesn't kill."

She was looking at Quint, but it was Zhag who answered. "Because *no* Sime can disjunct more than a few months after changeover."

"But that would mean...Quint? It *is* against Sime Territory law to permit the Kill?"

"Not to...save a life," the channel said reluctantly.

Tony took it up. "It's almost over. In another five years there won't be any more juncts...or Secret Pens."

Quint went white with fury, gripping the edge of the table with his hands, tentacles tightly retracted as if to keep from strangling the Gen. Tony continued, undaunted. "Since Unity, the Sime population has grown only because Sime children of Gens are taken to the channels instead of murdered. The young Simes are all nonjunct or disjunct. But almost all the Simes who were too old to disjunct after Unity are dead, unless they were fortunate enough to find matchmates." He looked disdainfully at Quint. "What the Tecton *ought* to do is teach every Gen to give transfer. We all can, you know, if we're not raised to fear it. Simes would find their matchmates, and everyone would live as nature intended."

"That argument always comes from Natural Donors," said Quint. "You have no idea how many Gens you might inspire to die!"

Carla said, "Stick to the point. Zhag, how can you be junct and not kill? If Tony didn't give you transfer, would you kill someone?"

"No," Zhag replied. "I would die."

"Would he?" Carla asked Quint.

The Tecton channel nodded. "Almost his whole generation is dead. That woman in the holding cell will die—how long depends on her perception of Gens. She accepts the partnership between Logan and Paget, or she wouldn't have come here. The more she sees Gens as people, the less capable she is of killing."

"Isn't that a good thing?" Carla asked.

"Not when it means she'll die in agony," said Tony. "Carla, what the Tecton didn't tell us when they promised to disjunct all the Simes in their Territories was...it's not possible. At least not by the only methods the Tecton will allow."

"You can't understand," said Quint. "Because of you, Zhag Paget doesn't kill—but he is as junct as he ever was."

"That's a technicality," said Tony. "Junct means killer. Zhag doesn't kill. That's the only definition that counts to Gens."

"He's right on that one," said Carla.

Quint shook his head. "There's no use trying to explain—you can't zlin what I'm talking about."

"All right," said Carla, "then explain what Zhag did wrong in saving Charmion Johnson's life."

"He gave junct transfer. The few junct channels still working give transfer only to the few surviving junct Simes."

"Quint," said Carla, as if she were speaking to a not very bright child, "that woman was junct before Zhag gave her transfer. She became junct when she killed Letty Meech."

Tony gave her a big smile of approval.

Quint, though, shook his head. "We can't have renegade channels providing junct transfer!"

"I see," said Carla. "The Tecton will permit a Gen to be killed to save a junct Sime's life. But it's wrong to allow a junct channel to transfer a little selyn to save a Gen's life?"

Tony laughed. "You should be our advocate, Carla."

"You should know better, Logan," said Quint. "You've lived in-Territory long enough to understand how dangerous you are. What you did in that auditorium tonight—"

"I enhanced Zhag's playing, that's all. Did you think I put him in killmode? He faced a terrified Gen in a corridor reeking of the Kill. He didn't touch the Gen, and gave transfer to the Sime. Instead of arresting him, you should give him a medal!"

The media agreed with Tonyo Logan. When they left the interrogation room, the radio was blaring with a Logan/Paget song—one of the rarely-played ones in Simelan. Carla put Tony and Zhag in one of the Sime holding cells; the newly juncted Sime woman was in the other.

The song ended as Carla went to her desk to write up tonight's—no, by now it was last night's—incident. But she paused to listen as the announcer reported, "That was Logan and Paget, of course. Quite the heroes! The mayor and the city council are in emergency meeting with representatives of the Tecton at this very moment, trying to find out why the channels didn't prevent a Kill at tonight's concert, and why it was only the action of Zhag Paget himself that prevented a second.

"Before the meeting the mayor announced that Logan and Paget are to be presented with the keys to the city tomorrow morning, and that they will be invited back to perform at this year's Faith Day celebration."

So—before his meeting with Tecton representatives, the mayor hadn't known that Tony and Zhag had been arrested. Carla knew the mayor. He would *not* be pleased to be given a bunch of Sime technical jargon about Zhag's committing a crime when he had saved a life and the voters thought him a hero.

Of course when it came out that the killer Sime had not been a berserker, but one of Logan and Paget's fans who had sneaked across the border....

Carla got the packet of trin tea from Tony's belongings, and made up some to take in to Tony and Zhag. The radio was playing another of their songs now.

Probably, she thought, that Sime woman would appreciate some trin tea as well—what she had done was probably just dawning on her. So she took a steaming cup over to the other selyn-shielded cell, and opened the small hatch that allowed food and drink to be passed in and out.

Carla's Simelan was good enough to offer a cup of tea—but she was not sure she understood the response, except that it was a rude refusal. She went in to Tony and Zhag. "That's strange. I'm sure she's upset, but why would she call me a wild animal?"

Tony snickered. "I heard that one often enough when I first

went into Sime Territory."

Zhag frowned. "But you don't hear it nowadays. Carla, no one but some lowlife would use that term today—and no fan of ours would refer to a Gen that way. How could she be a Logan/Paget fan without respecting Tonyo?"

"I think I'd better question her," said Carla. "I'll send for a Tecton channel."

"Why, when you've got us?" Tony asked.

Zhag had been able to stop the woman earlier, while Tony... well, she understood that in the years he had spent in Gulf Territory he had learned to manipulate selyn fields, even control Simes' emotions. Between them they could probably prevent the woman from making a break for freedom, and there was little likelihood now of her attempting a Kill. Carla held her gun on the woman until they were safely in the interrogation room, with Belius stationed outside the door, also armed.

Glaring angrily, the woman sat in silence. "Who are you?" Carla asked. Her Simelan was easily up to these basic questions. "Where did you come from? You had no identification, only your concert ticket."

Silence.

Tony said, "You know you're in big trouble. But Zhag and I can help you if—"

"A channel and a Wild Gen!" the woman spat. "You make me sick." She lifted her head proudly. "I am a Free Sime."

Carla looked from Tony to Zhag. "What's a Free Sime?"

Both men shrugged. The Sime woman remained stubbornly silent.

"In Gulf Territory I'm a Free Gen," Tony offered. "It means I have the same rights and responsibilities as a Sime—and pay the same taxes, too."

Zhag chuckled. "I guess that makes me your tax collector." At Carla's questioning look, he explained, "He pays them in selyn. *I* pay in money, which I actually have to earn. There's been some griping, as Gens can produce enough selyn to live well without doing a lick of work." He looked at the Sime woman again. "Is that what this Free Sime business is about—a tax revolt?"

The woman retorted, "My family never objected to pen taxes! We were civilized in Nivet Territory when Gulf was nothing but settled-in Raiders! And then you channels had to start in, taking away the Kill, treating Gens like people. It's sick!"

Carla was quite sure she understood the woman's words. She just didn't understand the sentiment. "What exactly are you saying?" she demanded.

The woman looked her in the eye. "Simes are predators. Gens are prey. Anything that gets between Simes and the Kill is unhealthy. We Free Simes won't accept the Tecton. Sime/Sime transfer is a perversion! So we have been forced to leave our homes and start new communities outside the Territories."

"Is that why you came to disrupt the concert," asked Carla, "because you are opposed to Unity?"

"Yes," the woman replied.

"You are not a citizen of Nivet or Gulf Territories?"

"Not any longer. But I will not tell you where my home is. I don't care how you torture me."

"I'll get it out of her!" said Tony angrily.

Zhag put a hand on his arm. "That's Carla's job. Which she is very good at. Do you realize what she has done, Tonyo?"

What Carla had done was to free Tony and Zhag. Even Quint had to agree that Zhag's providing transfer to this Free Sime was no violation of Territory or Tecton law. The woman had not been enticed to the concert by Logan and Paget's music— any similar event would have done—so the charge of being a dangerous nuisance was dropped as well.

Despite a night without sleep, Carla was buoyed up by her success...but at the same time weighed down by new knowl-edge. Free Simes weren't the half of it. They seemed to be news to the Tecton channels as much as to the Gen government—but now both would be alert for further attempts to sabotage Unity.

No—the difficult knowledge for Carla was that there were still killer Simes in the Sime Territories despite the Unity

Treaty. Not technically junct, like Zhag, but real killers. After the mayor's press conference, she determined to corner Tony for a few final questions.

The groundswell Charmion Johnson had started increased as the press ran with the best story since Unity. Letty Meech's father blamed the city for inadequate security. Still under the spell of the performance, most reporters chose to emphasize the restrictions on channels. Not the concert, but the retainer laws, became the scandal.

Nevertheless, Zhag was back in those restraints for the public ceremony on the steps of City Hall. It was amusing to see the Simephobic mayor cautiously shake hands with him, thank him for saving a life, and invite him to perform at the Faith Day celebration. Charmion Johnson, though, gave Zhag an enthusiastic kiss—and an even more eager one to Tony.

The mayor delivered a prepared statement about the Free Simes, and the fact that the only way to prevent them from disrupting similar events in the future was to allow channels to work security without retainers. The circumstances would be carefully controlled, he promised, and warnings clearly posted.

When the ceremony wound to an end, Carla accompanied Tony and Zhag back to their hotel suite. "We've got two hours," Zhag said, "and I have some new music running through my head."

Carla knew he could zlin that she wanted some private time with Tony. The Sime disappeared into one of the bedrooms, and after a moment, soft strains of shiltpron music drifted out. She was not sure if he was really that eager to play, or if he was reassuring her that he was concentrating on something other than the emotions of the two Gens in the next room.

Tony plopped down on the couch and patted the seat beside him. Carla sat, leaning on him in the old familiar way. "Tony, I have some questions," she said.

His chest vibrated with laughter. "Even I'm too tired to do anything but talk."

"I don't know where to start. For instance, matchmates. Are

you the *only* Gen who can give Zhag transfer?"

"No. He could go for months on transfer from channels or other Donors, but he's at his best with me. And if I left him... even if the Tecton were willing to try to find him another match, it isn't easy."

Carla put the spoken and unspoken thoughts together. "If you were permanently unavailable...?"

"Zhag would probably die."

"Explain that. Why can't he kill? It can't be just having Gen friends—we still get cases right here in which a child changes over and kills a friend or family member."

"Yes, and they come into Sime Territory as emotional wrecks. Disjunction is very hard, but Sime children of Gens have all the incentive in the world. Carla, I've witnessed profound change in the past fifteen years. Parts of Gulf Territory were already Unified before I got there—Norlea was one of them. But Zhag was too old to disjunct when he first went to Norlea."

"He's only a few years older than you are."

"Simes can only disjunct during the year after changeover. Later, they can become semi-junct, killing once or twice a year. When I first went to Gulf Territory it was full of semi-juncts raising their children to be nonjunct. But semi-junctedness is an unstable state. Eventually the Sime sees all Gens as human beings, and aborts out of any kill. Carla...Zhag was already far down that road—but when he accepted a Gen as partner in his life's work, he speeded the process. The channels couldn't force transfer into him, he couldn't kill—if I hadn't been able to give him transfer, he would have died."

"But," said Carla, "other Simes do still kill. You mentioned Secret Pens? In Sime Territory they are still *raising Gens like cattle to be slaughtered?!*"

Tony's face was pale beneath his tan. "Yes," he said flatly. "There are still a few semi-juncts alive. In some Sime Territories the Tecton is so opposed to anyone but channels receiving direct Gen transfer that they won't even try to make matches. To me, that's murder—of the semi-junct Simes who die in agony, and all the Gens they kill before that happens."

Carla stared at him. "This is the world you want me to join you in?"

"Carla, if there were no Secret Pens, there would be far more Free Simes. After only fifteen years, with the exception of the handful of nonjuncts and disjuncts who formed the Tecton, almost every Sime who signed the Unity Treaty is dead. Yes, the Sime governments agreed that all Simes would stop killing. But even in Gulf, juncts far outnumbered nonjuncts and disjuncts.

"But people understood things couldn't go on as they were. With more Simes living longer, and most Simes killing twelve Gens each year, soon the Simes would have killed all the Gens, and then died themselves. The end of humanity."

By this time Carla was shaking. "We had no idea what the Simes were promising, did we? An entire generation in essence agreed to die, for the sake of the future."

"And you wonder why I respect them?" Tony asked.

"It's going to take me time to absorb all this," Carla admitted. "Damn you, Tony Logan—you've turned my life upside down again!"

"We'll set it right," he said tenderly, and kissed her. It was not a passionate kiss, but one of promise. "I'll see you again when we come back for the Faith Day concert. I hope, before then, you'll visit me in Norlea."

"How do you get to be so hopeful, Tony? So trusting?"

But Tony was silent, listening to the music from the next room. It had settled into a melody. Tony sang,

"Come share a dream, my life's dream,
All that was meant one day to be.
Trust in yourself, trust in my dream.
And we'll have no more walls between."

Carla sighed. "If only it were that simple."

"It is," said Tony. "Territory governments complicate it. The Tecton complicates it. But it really is that simple, Carla."

"For dreamers, maybe."

"Well," he replied, "if no one dreamed, nothing would ever

be accomplished, would it? There's my second verse. When you hear this song on the radio, remember, you're its inspiration."

Carla laughed. "When you had so much trouble with literature in school, who'd have guessed you'd end up a poet?"

"Words are good," he replied, "but sometimes actions are better. I'm not so tired after all, are you?" And this time when he kissed her it did stir passion.

And dreams.

ABOUT THE AUTHOR

JEAN LORRAH lives in Kentucky with her dog, Kadi Farris ambrov Keon, and two cats, Earl Gray Dudley and Splotch the Wanderer. The cats are licensed therapy animals who visit schools and nursing homes.

Jean has published more than twenty books through the years, several of them award winners and best-sellers. She teaches the occasional creative writing workshop in person, and with Jacqueline Lichtenberg runs a free workshop online on their domain, www.simegen.com. For information on her latest publications, essays on writing, and anything else currently going on in her life, visit:

www.jeanlorrah.com

ABOUT THE AUTHOR

JACQUELINE LICHTENBERG is a life member of Science Fiction Writers of America. She is the creator of the Sime~Gen Universe with a vibrant fan following (www.simegen.com), primary author of the Bantam paperback, *Star Trek Lives!* (which blew the lid on Star Trek fandom), founder of the Star Trek Welcommittee, creator of the genre term Intimate Adventure, winner of the Galaxy Award for Spirituality in Science Fiction with her second novel, *Unto Zeor, Forever*, and the first Romantic Times Awards for Best Science Fiction Novel with her later book, *Dushau*, now in Kindle. Her fiction has been in audio-dramatization on XM Satellite Radio. She has been the SF/F reviewer for a professional magazine since 1993. She teaches science fiction and fantasy writing online while turning to her first love, screenwriting, focused on selling to the feature film market. She can be found at her website,

www.jacquelinelichtenberg.com

And can be followed on...

twitter.com/jlichtenberg
facebook.com/jacqueline.lichtenberg
friendfeed.com as jlichtenberg